CONTROL

Also by V.C. Kincade

Control
Dominance

Coming Soon

Manipulation (January, 2026)
Revelation (March, 2026)

Control

A Blackburn Erotic Thriller

V.C. Kincade

Northshore Noir Press

This is a work of fiction. All names, characters and incidents are the product of the author's imagination. Any resemblance to real persons, living or dead, is entirely coincidental.

Northshore Noir Press
Toronto, Canada
www.northshorenoir.com

ISBN: 978-1-998648-31-3

eBook ISBN: 978-1-998648-32-0

Contents

Chapter 1

Blackburn stepped from the gas station into an early heat that pressed against her skin like a promise. Light stretched low across the lot, catching oil rainbows on asphalt. Industrial beauty that most would miss. She took in the southeast edge of New Dresden, where warehouses squatted like tombstones, chain-link fencing cutting geometric wounds in the morning, a skyline still dim with sleep.

She rarely made it to this side of the city, but last night's screamer had been worth the drive. Blackburn flexed her hand, feeling the ghost of flesh against her palm, and cleared her throat. An experienced submissive was always a great find; someone who understood the architecture of surrender without requiring instruction.

Movement.

A figure stumbled in from the east. Unsteady, but not drunk. She knew that choreography. His legs buckled with each step, a marionette with severed strings. Blood had dried in a dark line behind one ear, mapping gravity's pull. One eye swelled shut. His shirt hung in tatters like shed skin.

She set her coffee on the curb with care and moved. One eye tracked the street for complications, one locked on him like a targeting system. No cars angled in with predatory intent. No shapes peeled off corners to complicate her morning. The risk felt contained, manageable; the kind she could enjoy.

"Detective Blackburn." The badge caught the morning light as she closed the distance, a small sun she wielded. "Can you hear me?"

His gaze wandered like a lost child before finding her. Shock. She took his forearm, firm but not forceful, the exact pressure that communicated authority without threat. His skin felt cold beneath the grime, vulnerable in ways that stirred something predatory.

"Sit." She guided him to the concrete ledge by the ice machine. The compressor hummed against his back, an industrial lullaby. Cool stone pressed against his shins. His hands trembled once. An involuntary surrender, then he stilled under her attention.

She scanned him in order, the systematic inventory of damage she'd perfected over years. Airway clear. Breathing was steady but shallow. Pulse raced beneath her fingers at his wrist. It was rabbit-quick, prey-fast. Pupils uneven, the left responding as if it was swimming through syrup. Dirt packed beneath his nails and into the creases of his knuckles, clay mixed with something darker that would stain for hours. She knew how earth clung to desperate fingers.

"Stay with me," she said, her voice calibrated to that perfect frequency between command and comfort. "Help is on the way."

She waved to the clerk through glass that distorted his face into something abstract. "Call 911." She went to her car, pulling the first aid kit from behind the seat. Gloves snapped on, a barrier and permission. Gauze crinkled like old promises. The antiseptic cap popped with tiny violence.

She dampened a wipe and cleaned blood from his hairline, each stroke precise and controlled. He flinched but held still. Good boy, she thought but didn't say. She pressed a folded pad above his brow where skin had split like overripe fruit. Steady pressure. "You're doing fine."

The clerk held up his phone, filming instead of calling. Modern instinct to entertain rather than help.

She dialed dispatch, her voice shifting to a professional register. "Detective Morgan Blackburn, Homicide. Badge 259. I need EMS at Fillmore and Sixth. Taylor Gas. Adult male, head trauma, possible assault. Conscious. Respirations stable. Pupils unequal. Bruising around the right orbit. Unknown time down." She noted the soil caked beneath each nail like evidence of resurrection. "Dirt under the fingernails. Request uniform units for scene control, and Major Crimes to attend." She read the exact address from the door sticker and ended the call.

She kept the gauze in place with one hand while the other anchored him upright. Dual purpose, always. "What's your name?"

He worked for the word like excavating something buried. "Evan." It came out rough, scraped raw.

"Last name."

"Hart."

"Date of birth."

Each number he gave was a small victory. She logged it in the notebook from her jacket. Time, vitals as she could assess them, injury notes, a quick sketch of the lot. Memory fades like bruises. Paper endures.

"Any weapons on you, Evan?"

His head moved, conserving energy. "No."

She patted his waistband and pockets. Lint rolled between her fingers. A folded twenty soft with handling. A broken key ring that had once held something important. She lined them beside him on the concrete like evidence. "Allergies."

"Penicillin."

She wrote that too.

Traffic whispered on the damp pavement, the city's morning prayer. A bus wheezed through the intersection, exhaling diesel ghosts. A crow hopped along the lot's edge, black eyes cataloguing everything with avian indifference. The day pressed upward, the air still holding a thread of cool that wouldn't last.

"Thank you," he said. The words frayed at the edges like old fabric.

She nodded. "Save your strength."

He studied her hand on his arm, then the badge again. Both requiring verification in his scrambled reality. She kept her expression steady and readable, the mask she wore for victims. Professional. Present. The performance of empathy she'd perfected.

He started in fragments, each word excavated with effort. "I went to buy pills." His voice carried past the compressor's hum. His fingers picked at a loose thread, nervous energy seeking an outlet. "From a guy I know."

"Where?"

"Under the bridge at Kestrel." He blinked hard against swelling that transformed his face into abstract art. "Then someone was there, and everything went white. I think someone shot me. I don't remember the sound. Just my face. Bright. Hot."

He touched the puffy eye once. Testing reality. Then withdrew. She let silence work its slow magic.

"Woke up underground," he said, and something cold moved through Blackburn's chest. Each word came like he was pulling them from deep water. "Couldn't breathe. Dirt in my mouth. I tried to shout. No air."

"How long?"

His head moved. "I don't know."

"You clawed your way out," she said, recognizing the specific terror in his eyes; the kind that comes from premature burial. She had seen it before.

He nodded and swayed forward like gravity had doubled. She braced him with her shoulder, adjusting the gauze with ease. Blood seeped through. Not heavy, but persistent, like secrets.

"Any names?" she asked. "Supplier. Anyone else."

"Tom. I met him at the Regional ER a couple months back." His voice scraped raw as exposed as a nerve. "Last night was differ…"

"Evan, hey, Evan. Stay with me." She lightly tapped his face and his eyes blinked open. "Last night was different? Evan?"

His head lolled, his mouth opened, and nothing came out.

She wrote it down. Tom. Kestrel bridge. Things different. She underlined *different* twice. He had come from the east, where soil stayed soft, where shovels could bite deep without complaint.

Evan coughed. His eyes tracked to the lot's edge, and fear flickered across his features. Small, animal, honest. His heel tapped concrete once in unconscious rhythm.

"You're safe here," she said with the absolute certainty she wielded like a weapon. "No one gets past me."

He swallowed, throat muscles working hard against invisible obstruction. "I thought I died."

"Not today."

The clerk pushed through the door and hovered nearby like a moth drawn to trauma's flame.

"Stay inside."

The door wheezed shut on pneumatic hinges.

Blackburn shifted her grip and checked his pulse again. Still racing but threadier now, a violin string wound too tight. Faint lines marked his neck in linear patterns, parallel and precise. Pressure marks, but not from hands. Too uniform, too clean.

"Evan, did they bind you?"

"I think so. Tape. Plastic." His eyes fixed beyond the gas pumps on some middle distance only he could see. "A bag. Over my face. Then dirt."

She wrote *Plastic restraints. Bag.* Each detail was another piece of someone else's careful planning.

A siren wailed from the south, growing louder with Doppler certainty. She let the sound work on him, watched his shoulders drop a fraction as help approached.

"Stay with me," she said again, her voice an anchor. "You are still with me."

He nodded. "Yeah."

"What were you buying? Did you take anything besides what you went to buy?"

He shook his head. "Dillie 8s. I didn't get any."

"Did anyone say anything before they shot you?"

"Don't remember." Shame crossed his features like a passing cloud. She left it alone. Everyone had their methods of managing existence.

She scanned the lot with the systematic attention of someone who understood how situations could turn. A cement truck rumbled past, exhaust hanging thick as guilt. A cyclist slowed, took them in with the quick assessment of urban survival, and pedaled on. Nothing immediate threatened the area. She would leave once the uniforms arrived, but she noted his dusty footprints along the curb. If traffic spared them, she would follow that trail back to its source.

He wet cracked lips with effort. "I remember a smell. Sweet. Chemical. Like glue. And metal."

She logged it, building the sensory map of his ordeal. "Any accents. Any words."

"Music," he said, the memory surfacing. "Tinny. From a phone, maybe. A woman singing. Old song. I couldn't place it."

She sketched a square for the ice machine and an arrow showing his approach, the map in her head sharpening with each detail.

"Someone I can call?" she asked. "Family? Friend?"

"My sister." He gave a name and number that she transcribed. She would pass them to Major Crimes, let them handle the notification. This was not her job.

He sagged against her, not fainting but surrendering to gravity's insistence. She adjusted to take more of his weight without comment.

"You're doing fine," she said. "Hold the gauze." She guided his hand up with the same precision she used for everything. "Firm. Not too hard."

He managed it. Dirty fingers, a careful touch. Small tasks always steadied people who needed reality. Purpose cut through shock's fog.

The siren rounded a corner and swelled into certainty. A second engine joined in harmony, the city's emergency chorus. Close now.

"Evan," she said, timing the question for maximum retention. "When you woke up underground, what did you feel? Wood. Plastic. Concrete."

"Plastic," he whispered, the word carrying specific horror. "Thin. It tore when I pushed. Dirt poured in. I swallowed."

She nodded. Plastic sheeting. Noted. Someone's attempt at containment that hadn't accounted for desperation's strength.

"It was dark," he said, lost in the memory now. "Then it wasn't. The top gave way, and there was sky. I crawled. Lights. Train."

Her pen moved across the paper with purpose. The rail spur ran three blocks east. That tracked. Soil tracked. Sound tracked. The account held together with the internal consistency of truth.

A cruiser glided into the lot, lights painting blue ghosts across faded parking stripes. She lifted a hand and directed them to the far side of the pumps, leaving a lane for EMS. Always thinking three moves ahead. The officers read her gesture and complied without question.

She stayed with Evan as the gauze grew warm beneath her palm, morning strengthening around them like a tightening fist. The quiet eased some of his visible tension. Next steps lined up cleanly in her mind.

"Lights," he said, eyes tracking to where New Dresden cut its jagged edge against the brightening sky. "I followed the lights."

Blackburn kept her tone even, professional curiosity masking deeper interest. "Before that. Do you remember who shot you?"

A shiver ran through him despite the warming air. "I don't remember. Maybe they got Tom too." A small nod, processing. "I thought I was dead."

The ambulance rolled in, siren dropping to silence as it stopped with precision. Paramedics moved in with the efficiency that came from repetition. Gauze, oxygen mask, a careful transfer that spoke of experience with broken things.

Blackburn stepped back, ceding territory. She gave them the essentials. The victim is a white male mid-thirties, possible GSW, conscious, fragmented memory, confinement, possible burial site. Each word chosen for maximum information density.

As they secured him to the stretcher, his hand lifted, fingertips brushing her badge. Seeking an anchor in institutional authority.

"We will find out what happened," she said, steadying his forearm with calculated reassurance. "You're safe now."

The doors closed with force. The ambulance pulled away, and she stayed on the curb a moment longer, watching the lights recede into the city's hungry mouth.

She briefed the responding officers with the same economy of language, explaining the scene, outlining next steps while they waited for senior staff who would complicate everything with protocol.

A quick time check. A decision crystallized. She walked east along Lakehurst, following the trail Evan had left in his resurrection. Humanity fell away like shed skin. Warehouses claimed the rest. Industrial tombstones marking the city's transformation. Forklifts beeped in the distance, their warning cries echoing off concrete. Steam curled from vents near the rail spur like the city's dying breath. The river's sour edge rode a shift in the breeze, organic rot mixing with chemical precision.

This part of the city showed its skeleton. Concrete bones, steel sinew, stacked pallets like vertebrae. Plastic snagged on wire fencing, urban prayer flags. New money pressed into old industrial ground with the arrogance of progress. Few people. Fewer witnesses. Perfect for certain kinds of business.

She found the lot by following Evan's path backward, reading the story written in disturbed earth and desperate footprints. Temporary fencing surrounded the space, gate hanging half open, secured with rusted wire that spoke of habitual trespass. Dirt berms and parked equipment formed makeshift walls. A colosseum for private violence. An excavator slept with its bucket caked in clay, a mechanical predator at rest.

A patch to the right broke the grading pattern. Subtle, but wrong to trained eyes.

She closed in, shoes crunching over packed earth. The surface showed recent disturbance, raked by someone who understood concealment but not investigation. Television lessons always lacked. The underlayer still held moisture from last night's work. One edge showed signs of collapse and drag at the margin, as if weight had pressed up from below and shifted sideways in desperate escape. In the loose soil, nail marks caught the light. Thin crescents still packed with grit, each one a testament to the will to survive.

Boot prints crisscrossed the area in a dance of violence. Two tread patterns. One wide with blocky lugs that suggested weight and authority, one narrower with chevron pattern that moved with a more intentional purpose. Both sets stepped in and out with a pivot near the depression. The choreography of burial. A third set broke the rhythm with shallow scrapes. Not a normal gait. Crawl marks or stumbling. Evan's resurrection.

She checked the gate mount. No fence cameras, though the mounting bracket remained. The nearest pole wore an empty mount where one had been, four screw holes describing absence. She logged it along with the utility tag number, building the inventory of what wasn't there.

Heat radiated up from the clay in waves that made the air shimmer. Diesel fumes lingered from idling equipment, industrial perfume. A metallic tang rose where groundwater pooled in low spots, the earth's blood seeping through. A small fly lifted from the disturbed earth and drifted away, sole witness to whatever darkness had unfolded here. A truck rumbled past two blocks over, the city's pulse continuing despite individual traumas.

She called Major Crimes. "Detective Blackburn. I'm at the gas station. When is someone getting here?"

"Sgt. Levy should be on site in five, ma'am."

"You'll need to send CSU," she added before disconnecting, already calculating how much evidence would be lost to their delayed response.

The city kept its rhythm, indifferent and eternal, and Blackburn matched it. She strode back into the gas station with the controlled precision of someone who never rushed. "Officer," she said when the cruiser window rolled down, her tone carrying the weight of authority. "Possible crime scene one block east. Fresh ground disturbance. Multiple shoe impressions."

"What is your name, ma'am?" the driver asked, hand already reaching for the radio.

"Detective Blackburn. Homicide. I am off duty. I'll forward a report to Sgt. Levy. Start a scene log."

"Yes ma'am."

City sounds filtered back in thin layers. The morning returned to its routine. A delivery truck beeped in reverse, warning the world of its intentions. A dog walker approached, saw the tape already being strung, and turned back with the wisdom of the uninvolved. Another cruiser arrived. Not Major Crimes yet, but reinforcement for the perimeter.

Blackburn checked her watch. Time to head to work and leave behind Evan's fever dream, the careful burial, the resurrection through desperate will. She loved New Dresden surprises.

Chapter 2

The door to Carl's office clicked shut behind Brynn Cassidy. The air hung thick with stale sweat and cheap cologne. Something synthetic masking something masculine. Towers of files leaned against walls.

Carl didn't look up from the pages that bled red ink across his desk. "Brynn." Her name landed flat. Statement of fact, not greeting.

"There's a great story there, I swear." Her voice held steady. "A guy is shot and buried alive. It's front page."

Carl looked up. "And you had a chance to interview him?"

Her gaze drifted past him to the map on her own desk, visible through glass partition. Seven crimson Xs marked the surface. Salt and copper bloomed across her tongue. The body's memory of drowning.

"No. The police aren't allowing access. I couldn't get in." Her finger traced the desk edge. She sat.

"Interview the person who found him?" His eyes narrowed at her smile. "Who?"

"None other than Detective Morgan Blackburn." The name sat heavy in the air between them. Blackburn. Always Blackburn. High-profile cases that promised Pulitzer-worthy stories, if only she could break through Blackburn's fortress.

Carl set his pen down. "She's the lead? The guy died?"

"No, she found him, apparently. Just walking down the road." Brynn kept her voice neutral. "What are the chances?"

Carl shook his head. "You will never get a comment from her on a case that isn't hers. You know that."

"Carl, I swear I can—"

"No. This isn't your story. What else have you got?" The chair groaned beneath his weight. Leather and wood in familiar complaint. "What about the orphan story? People love orphans."

She shook her head. His attention settled on her skin. Fever beginning to take hold. "People hate orphans, or they wouldn't be orphans."

Carl rolled his eyes. "People hate all children. But they pretend to love orphans. You know, a feel-good story about success. How they navigate after." His eyes lifted to hers. Pale blue. Calculating. "How they get out of bed. How they look at their own children knowing the systems that almost killed them are still rolling past their windows."

A muscle in her jaw tightened. The only tell she allowed. The rest of her body held perfect stillness. Learned composure that cost everything, gave nothing.

"The systems," she started.

His hand cut through air. Sharp. Dismissive. He leaned forward. His breath reached her first, warm, sour. Morning coffee gone to acid. "Get inside it."

Her pulse knocked once against her ribs. Hard. The leather beneath her thighs had warmed, taking on her body heat. She catalogued these sensations. Clinical detachment. Physiological responses to pressure. To proximity. To the particular violence of wanting to be seen.

His eyes locked on hers. Gray-green, bloodshot at the edges. She didn't look away. Looking away was surrender, and she'd learned long ago that surrender invited worse.

"Shrink the distance," he said, voice dropping to that register that made junior reporters lean in. "That's the job. Shrink the distance between them and the reader. Temporary drama."

"You know it isn't 2025 anymore, right? Drama has to be trauma," she said. Each word precise, controlled. "Schadenfreude sells."

He shook his head, a slow pendulum of sad truths. "Show the loser." The silence stretched between them like a held breath. "The nightmare that won't end." His pen tapped the red-marked pages. Three beats, pause, three beats. "Most reporters don't have nerve."

She watched the pen still. The strap of her bag had carved a furrow into her shoulder, webbing against cotton against skin. These small violences accumulated throughout the day, unnoticed until they weren't.

"Those writers aren't winning," Carl said, and she heard what he didn't say. *You're not winning.* "You want that? Do the work."

His eyes held hers, and she recognized the technique. Silence as a weapon, attention as a blade. "It's emotional. Not rational. You need a person. One person whose pain becomes everyone's pain."

A thud echoed through the office. Sudden, wet. A bird against glass. The impact left a smear of feathers and death. Carl cursed, sharp and reflexive. Brynn didn't flinch. She watched the dark streak on the window, noting how quickly something alive became nothing at all.

"Feed the reader the pain of someone's shame, and they'll devour the story. Hell, they'll share it with everyone they know."

She gave a single, slow nod. "The child who won't look at the camera."

His eyes sharpened, a predator recognizing prey recognizing a predator. He leaned in, voice dropping to that low register that preceded either promotion or termination. "Make them all look."

"Carl." Her voice scraped raw against his name. "I still feel the salt in my throat." The taste of it lingered. The man gone overboard while the cameras rolled.

His expression softened at the edges. Not kindness, but recognition. "You have to unsee the trauma." He slid her draft across the desk, out of reach. "You build a wall. You make the reader feel it through that wall. That's the gift."

His pen stopped its nervous tattoo. Her shoulders remained level, though the effort cost her. Their eyes met across the expanse of scarred wood and accumulated ambition. She didn't reach for the pages. Reaching was another form of surrender.

He leaned in, close enough that she could see the burst capillaries in his sclera, the evidence of his own particular drowning. "Find the ones who've faced the worst. The ones still standing."

Her mind sorted through names and discarded them with mechanical efficiency. Then, a snag. A name that caught like fabric on wire. Willow Adler. Adoptee. Civilian contractor. Police adjacent but not police. Young enough to be sympathetic, technical enough to understand the systems, damaged enough to need the story told.

"Willow Adler," she said, testing it. "I haven't reached out. But she's in my files. I have medical, educational, housing. Child welfare. I have a full record for her."

Carl's interest focused to a sharp point, all his diffuse attention concentrated. "Pursue it." His thumb pressed into the margin of her draft, leaving a faint smudge of ink and intent. "If they grieve, it leads. Always."

She left his office with meaningful steps. The hallway narrowed around her, walls pressing in with the weight of deadlines and expectations. The scent of his cologne clung to her blouse. It was a violation so minor it didn't merit acknowledgment, so persistent it would follow her home.

Back at her desk, the cold resolve in her chest tightened like a leather strap in winter. She thought of her father's office, the empty spaces on the wall where awards should have been. His voice in the quiet moments between disappointments. "Real journalists chase the truth. No matter who it hurts." He'd been wrong about everything except that.

She'd seen the shift in their eyes. Sources, subjects, victims. The moment they understood what she was. Not confessor, not ally. Architect of their public undoing.

Her fingers hovered above the keys, then curled into her palms. The story couldn't just report. It had to eviscerate. It had to make Carl lean back in his chair and whistle, low and appreciative.

Willow Adler. A name becoming a person becoming a story. Brynn pictured the woman's hands on a keyboard. Steady, competent. She wanted to feel the tendons in those hands tighten under scrutiny. To watch her own hands steady in response, drawing strength from another's unraveling.

Carl's words hung in the air like smoke from a fire that had consumed everything worth saving. *Get inside it.*

The memory arrived without invitation, as they always did. The bite of wind that preceded the storm. The deck's sickening lift and drop. The light was strange and green, the color of deep water before it turns black.

The deckhand's boot slipping on wet steel. His arms pinwheeling in that universal semaphore of impending disaster. The silence as he went over. No screams, just the soft splash of a body meeting its opposite.

Rushing to the rail, her legs moving before thought could interfere. Her heart a frantic telegram against her ribs, sending the same message over and over. *Get it in focus.* Seeing him fight the water with the peculiar desperation of someone who'd never considered drowning possible. His eyes wide, fixed on hers across the impossible distance. Then nothing. The ocean swallowed him between one swell and the next, casual as breathing.

She'd screamed then. The raw burn in her throat that lasted for days. The captain's slap against her cheek. Sharp enough to leave a mark, precise enough to bring her back. That sting had lingered longer than grief, had become its own kind of permission.

She blinked. The newsroom reassembled around her. The ambient click of keys like rain on glass, the plasma lights that passed for daylight, the particular silence of people avoiding their own drownings.

That story had won. Not the rescue that never came, but her account of watching it not happen. The prize had felt like another slap, another permission.

She reached for her phone. The plastic case creaked in her grip, a small protest against the pressure of her fingers. Her finger jerked across the screen to the New Dresden Police website, staff directory. A search bar, a trail of intention.

Willow Adler.

A phone number materialized in the results. Her thumb brushed a faint smudge on the screen. The ghost of a cheek's impact, drying to something that would need soap to remove. She left it there, this evidence of work.

She highlighted the number, her finger pausing over the dial button. The moment before connection, when she could still choose to be someone else. Someone who didn't feed on trauma like a specialized parasite. Someone who built walls instead of teaching others how to tear them down.

Then she began. Because beginning was what separated her from the ones who only talked about the work. She pressed the button. The dial tone hummed in her ear like a prayer to an indifferent god.

Willow Adler would answer, or she wouldn't. Either way, the story had started. It had started the moment Carl agreed. It had started the moment the bird hit the glass. It had started years ago, on a deck in a storm, watching a man discover that the ocean doesn't care about your plans.

Chapter 3

Blue light flattened Brynn's pupils. The monitor hummed. Around her, the newsroom's plasma panels stuttered in their failing substrate, but she'd stopped hearing them twenty minutes ago. She'd found the old files.

Column A: names. Column B: dates. Column C: diagnoses. A list, not a conscience.

The server path read ARCHIVE-199X-MERCY-UNSORTED. Last modified: 11/07/2001, by intern-temp03. Thirty years since Carl's crew had pulled medical records from the hospital dumpster behind Mercy General. The court order to destroy them, a PDF dated 1995, sat three folders up, ignored.

Carl had built his reputation on those files. Not on the hospital's failure to shred them properly, though that made page six. On the secrets inside. The mayor's wife's three psych holds. The police chief's son's overdose. Power, properly applied.

The spreadsheet held 1,847 entries. Brynn cross-referenced her list of orphanage alumni against the names. Match on row 1,203: Adler, Willow. Age at first entry: seven.

She clicked through. November 14, 1991: radius fracture, left arm. Set at Mercy ER. February 3, 1992: sepsis secondary to infected puncture wounds, multiple sites. Discharge signed by Dr. Marcus Webb. August 19, 1992: three fractured ribs, contusions to torso. September 4, 1993: second-degree burns, bilateral palms.

Brynn's pulse steadied. This was it.

The phone rang. Once. Twice.

Brynn waited, patient as water finding its way through stone.

Three rings. Then, "H-Hello?"

The voice came through barely above ambient. Brynn kept her own flat. "Ms. Adler? Brynn Cassidy, New Dresden Today. I'm working on a piece about the Christian Children's Home."

Silence. The line's carrier hum filled it.

"I don't talk about that."

"Your medical records show four emergency room visits between 1991 and 1993. When you were under their care." Brynn's pen carved into the notepad. "Radius fracture. Sepsis from what the file calls 'puncture wounds.' Three broken ribs."

Willow's breathing changed pitch. "Those are sealed. How did you—"

"The adoption records show you were placed for two hundred fifty dollars. Standard fee was twenty-five thousand." Brynn let the numbers sit. "Why the discount?"

"I didn't know that."

"Tell me about the puncture wounds. The file says 'multiple sites.' Animal? Human?"

"Please. I can't."

Brynn shifted the handset. The cord coiled tight. "February third, 1992. You were eight. Sepsis means the wounds went untreated for days. Who signed you out of the ER?"

"Stop."

"Dr. Webb's signature appears on three of your discharge forms. Same doctor. Did anyone investigate?"

A sound came through the line. Not quite a sob. Smaller. Brynn's free hand stilled on the desk.

"The burns. August 1992. Both palms. That's not accidental."

"I need to go."

"One more question. Your adoptive parents. Did they know about the medical history when they paid the two-fifty?"

The line went dead.

Brynn set down the handset. Her notepad showed deep grooves where the pen had pressed through three sheets. She did what she needed to. Tomorrow she'd try again. Get the tears Carl wanted.

She saved the spreadsheet to her local drive, then copied it to a thumb drive. The server might get scrubbed if legal caught wind. But she'd have her copy.

The newsroom's coffee had gone to acid hours ago, leaving a film on her teeth. She grabbed her coat. Outside, rain hammered the windows. The city would be a mess by morning. Slick roads, spun-out cars, delayed responses. Good day for news.

Her desk phone rang. Internal extension.

"Brynn."

"My office." Carl's voice, then disconnect.

She found him standing at his window, watching the sleet streak the glass. His reflection showed nothing.

"You pulled the Mercy files."

Not a question. She waited.

"IT logs every access. Legal will know by morning."

"I saved copies."

He turned. Under the overhead plasmas, his skin looked gray. "The orphanage story. You found something."

"One of the kids. Four ER visits in three years, and the same doctor cleared her. Fractures, burns, sepsis. Adopted for pocket change."

"Name?"

"Willow Adler. Works for the city now."

Carl's expression didn't change. "Did she talk?"

"Not yet."

"Make her." He moved back to his desk, pulled out a manila folder. "If legal comes asking, you found them looking for some archived material. Keep physical copies."

Brynn took the folder. Inside were photocopies of medical records. Willow Adler's name at the top of each page. A thirty-year-old abuse scandal would shift the headlines.

"Get me tears," Carl said. "On camera if possible. In print if not."

She left his office with the folder. At her desk, she compared the photocopies to the digital files. Identical except for one detail. The physical copies had a sticky note on the first page. Carl's handwriting said it all. "Prize winning."

He'd sat on this. Waiting.

Brynn picked up her phone and started to dial Willow's number again. Stopped. Tomorrow would be better. Let her stew overnight. Let the fear build.

It was a perfect day for making someone cry.

Chapter 4

Blackburn hunched over her desk, eyes scanning digital case files in quick, exact passes. Plasma light threw flat shadows along her cheekbones. Her fingers flew, each keystroke a clean strike as she updated reports. The clack of keys carried in the quiet, a metronome to her pace.

The desk phone split the room with its ring. Caller ID said it was Freddie from IT. Her brow creased. They didn't call unless there was a problem. She saved her work with a sharp click and lifted the receiver.

"Detective Blackburn," she said, voice crisp, professional.

Freddie's low, hesitant murmur bled through. "I thought you should know that Willow is in her office, crying."

Her gaze thinned. She set the pen she'd been using parallel to the mouse pad, a beat of control. "And how is that my concern, Freddie?" Patience shaved to a fine edge.

"As her boss, I just thought you should be aware," he said, concern edging his words. "She's really upset."

"Fine. I'll be down in a minute." She hung up, the handset settling with a soft slap.

The irritation sat under her skin. Freddie liked to insert himself, hovering for gossip under the guise of help. She could see him waiting with his phone, angling for a shot he could float around the building.

She glanced toward the bullpen. Her detectives were buried in their monitors and cross-talk. Good. She lifted her phone, flipped to the front-facing camera, and studied the image. Blonde hair, eyes that lived cold when no one was watching. She smoothed a stray strand behind her ear. Then she softened her gaze, eased her mouth into concern. A mask. It fit without effort.

Phone off. Her eyes landed on the blue and black pot on her desk. She rotated it a degree, catching the seam where light skimmed color. Her fingertip traced one repaired fracture. Strength in the ruin.

Now the line under her touch stung. Some breaks didn't knit cleanly. Some scars stayed raw no matter how you gilded the split. Some pots should be shattered and thrown away.

She exhaled, pushed back from the desk, and took the tissue box. The stairwell down to IT held the recycled chill of the building's gut. On the descent, the tangle of their history crowded her steps. Two years, dense and bright. Then the new HR memo a month ago and the tidy language that cut. No relationships permitted within the same division between supervisors and reports. Willow posted to Homicide on paper, assigned to Blackburn's crew. Off limits. Clean in policy, messy everywhere else.

The hallway outside technical support smelled like stale coffee and the vinegar tang of last night's cleaner. Freddie stood in the corridor with a camera lifted to his chest. She extended a finger. A small shake.

He dropped his gaze, scuttling to a side desk with a guilty shuffle. She didn't need a witness. She was here as a colleague. That was the story. But the thought of Willow crying tightened something absolute.

She pushed Willow's door open. Humming server racks bled a constant note through the wall. Screen glow trimmed the cramped room in cold light. Willow folded in on herself in the chair, knees hugged tight, sobs catching against the recycled air. Blackburn paused, eyes flicking over the scene. She did not do tears. Performing empathy for a stranger was work. For Willow, it cut closer.

She stepped in. The door clicked shut. The air felt stale with salt and breath. Blackburn crossed to her quietly. She slid a tissue free, set a hand on Willow's shoulder.

"Shh," she murmured steadily. "It's okay. Just breathe."

The sobbing softened under her touch, but Willow still trembled. Then Willow lunged, arms cinching Blackburn's waist, dragging her in. The grip was sudden, clumsy. Blackburn went rigid on reflex, then allowed the pull, spine loosening by degrees.

Willow clung. Blackburn's hand lifted, thumb smoothing the damp skin along Willow's cheek, slow small circles. Muscle memory. For a breath, she let the habit carry her.

Then the calculation slid back into place. Lines. Roles. She eased Willow's arms down, fingers firm, stepping back to carve space.

"What happened?" she asked, voice even and contained. Inside, the gears did not stop.

Willow sniffled, swiping at her eyes with the back of her hand. "New Dresden Today reporter, Brynn Cassidy," she got out between hiccups. "She called me out of the blue, asking about my childhood at the orphanage. All those horrible memories came flooding back, and I just couldn't handle it."

The words tumbled out, ragged with anger and hurt. "She said she was writing a story about the orphanage. But she already knew so much about me, about the orphanage, about my adoption. My hospital records! She'd done all this research without ever talking to me. It feels like a violation. She was so mean to me!"

Blackburn's focus tightened. Her face went neutral, eyes hardening by a degree. Cold moved up her arms in a small, rippling climb. If Brynn Cassidy had lines into Willow's files, what else had she pulled? The possibilities mapped fast. That could not happen. Not to Willow. Not to her. She angled the tissue box into Willow's hands so she'd stop streaking her glasses with her sleeve.

Her palm stayed on Willow's shoulder, a steadying pressure. With the other hand, she reached the desk phone and hit the #2 speed dial without looking. The line rang twice.

"Jimmy's Chinese. Can I take your order?"

A quiet snort. She cut the call, expression flattening at her own lapse. Wrong device. Willow's phone, Willow's speed dial. Annoyance flickered. She buried it. She keyed Chief Hayes's number from memory, each digit pressed with precise intent.

While it rang, her fingers drew a slow line down Willow's back. Not comfort. Regulation. Her plan was already taking shape. There would be a consequence, and it would land where she pointed it.

After four rings, Chief Hayes answered, voice gruff. "Chief Hayes speaking."

Blackburn kept her tone controlled, edged with purpose. "Sir, we have a situation with Brynn Cassidy from New Dresden Today."

A brief pause. "Detective Blackburn? Why are you calling from Willow's phone?"

She glanced at Willow, wet lashes clumped, glasses fogged at the edges. "Freddie from IT alerted me that Willow was upset. Brynn Cassidy contacted her."

Hayes's exhale came as a rough sound. "Staff, especially civilians, should never engage with the press. That's standard procedure."

"That's not the issue here, sir," she said, frustration tucked behind clean diction. She drew a breath, kept it clipped. "Ms. Cassidy was asking personal questions about Willow's childhood for an exposé. This cannot be tolerated."

The shift in Hayes's tone was small but real, exasperation giving way to a tighter concern. "Let me speak with Willow," he demanded.

Blackburn extended the handset. Willow's tear-streaked face blanked at the sight of it, confusion hardening into panic. Red-rimmed eyes flicked from the phone to Blackburn. Her hands rose, hovered, then dropped, trembling.

"Willow? Are you there? Can you hear me?" Hayes pushed, impatience edging higher.

Silence swelled, broken only by Willow's ragged breathing and the low whirr from the wall beyond. Blackburn watched the struggle play out, face smooth, eyes intent. She let the quiet work.

"Willow? Damn it, someone answer me! Blackburn? Are you still there?" Hayes's volume climbed.

She held the phone out at arm's length and met Willow's gaze, a steady, anchoring lock. Willow stared back, eyes wide and unfocused.

"Blackburn! I need a response!" Hayes's voice hit the small room hard and loud.

She lifted the receiver to her mouth when the tension peaked. "Sir, can you hear me? This reporter called one of our staff at work to ask personal questions. This tells me she is stalking Willow, if nothing else. You need to call the New Dresden Today publisher and stop Ms. Cassidy. Whatever the article is, it cannot include Willow."

"Look, I can't control—"

"It's a lawsuit waiting to happen. Retirement level payout."

Silence on the line, heavy enough to feel. Math being done. Optics, liability, exposure. Then Hayes spoke. "I'll call the publisher right away."

"Thank you, sir," she said. The word left her on an even breath, shoulders easing by a notch.

"Keep me updated if anything else comes up," he said, and the line went dead.

She set the phone down and turned back to Willow. She let her expression soften, let her voice drop. "It's going to be okay," she said. "I've taken care of it."

Willow's sobs gentled to small shivers. Her breathing evened. She looked up through wet lashes, gratitude open and naked. "Thank you," she whispered, voice trembling. "I love you. I need you. You protected me, and I need you."

Something pricked under Blackburn's ribs. A flicker. "You know we can't be together anymore. The relationship has to be over."

Fresh tears glazed Willow's eyes. "My Lioness," she pleaded, a hush of a voice. "I need you to take care of me."

Blackburn's hand moved without thought, thumb stroking the curve of Willow's cheek. "My little Fawn," she said, her voice thick with emotion. "I wish I could. You poor thing."

Willow's lower lip trembled. "I can't do this without you," she said, gaze fixed on Blackburn's face.

"I know," Blackburn sighed. The pull was familiar and strong. Her mind ran the angles. Then, after a beat, "Maybe, maybe I can transfer you to Schmidt."

"No! I—"

"Administratively only. He can sign your vacation requests. You will still work with me."

Willow's face brightened at the word. Hope blew through her like air. She leaned forward a fraction, hunger in her eyes.

Willow had been the only one who could match her intensity without breaking. Others gave her more, submitted deeper. But none of them could hold her gaze the way Willow did when she said no. The thought of reclaiming that honesty set her nerves alight.

She pressed a quick peck to Willow's cheek and straightened. "I need to get back to my office," she said, the authority sliding back into place. "We'll talk more later."

Out in the corridor, the hum of equipment pressed up from the basement, cool air seeping from vents, the after-scent of cleaner faint on her skin. By the time she hit the stairs, her calm settled into something harder. Brynn Cassidy. The intrusive reach of that call. Her hands curled, nails biting her palms as she pictured routes to shut it down. In the climb back to her floor, the options arranged themselves. By the time she reached her office door, Blackburn was consumed with plotting her revenge.

Chapter 5

Brynn leaned back in her chair, letting a small, satisfied curl touch her mouth as she twined a strand of long brown hair around her finger. The receiver was warm against her ear. Toner hung in the air, sharp, and the old police scanner crackled. She nodded as she listened and let her pen move fast across the legal pad.

"Yes, thank you so much for your time, Jauylen," she said, her voice sweet and sincere. "Your story is what we need to—"

The desk jumped. Carl's fist hit the edge hard enough to flex the cheap particleboard. Her pen clattered and rolled. His face had gone a blotchy red.

"I'll have to call you back," she muttered hastily into the phone before hanging up. "Carl, what's—"

"What the hell do you think you're doing?" Carl demanded, his voice booming. "I just got off the phone with Llano, who just spoke to the chief of police. He says you're stalking his staff!"

Her jaw parted. Heat climbed her throat. "Stalking? That's ridiculous! I was just doing my job. If they weep, it's deep."

Carl's eyes widened. Coffee and mint were on his breath. "I never told you to stalk and scare women! Christ, Brynn, what were you thinking?"

"I wasn't stalking or scaring anyone!" Brynn shot back, pulse ticking in her neck. "I was conducting interviews, gathering information. That's what investigative journalism is all about! You told—"

"Investigative journalism?" Carl scoffed. "You call harassing traumatized orphans 'investigative journalism'?"

Volume rose with the plasma hum. Heads tilted above cubicle walls, then ducked. Brynn kept her shoulders squared and her hands flat on the desk.

"You told me to get the voices of the victims, Carl!" she shouted, eyes lit hard with purpose. "That's what I've been doing. Good journalism is never easy, you know that!"

Carl's gestures went broad, fingers splayed, a vein tightening at his temple. "For Christ's sake, Brynn! I never told you to cold call anyone!" His breath got hotter as he got closer. "The medical records?" he hissed. "Do you have any idea what kind of damage you've done?"

She didn't yield a step. The legal pad edges bit her palms. "Jauylen was fine talking to me. She was eager to share her story, to have her voice heard!"

Carl threw his hands up in exasperation. The office went still. "I don't give a damn about Jauylen! She's not with the New Dresden police. She's not the one who got the chief of police to call Llano who then called me! Do you realize your recklessness almost cost New Dresden Today our good relationship with the force?"

The room tightened. The scanner hissed. A chair wheel squeaked and stopped. Someone pretended to shuffle copy. Brynn clocked who was watching and who would carry this down the hall.

"This story is bigger than just one crybaby, Carl," Brynn argued, her voice trembling with passion. "It's about reporting on decades of abuse and corruption. We have a responsibility to these victims!"

Carl leaned in. "Our responsibility is to report the news ethically and maintain our relationships with our sources. Your cowboy tactics have put all of that at risk. You've gone too far this time," Carl growled, running a hand through his thinning hair.

The floor seemed to drop a fraction under her feet. Air thinned, bile nudged the back of her tongue. "Ethics? You? That's rich."

"What the fuck did you just say to me?"

Brynn stepped back from his animal breath.

"The piece is canceled. End of discussion."

"Canceled? But Carl, this story could be huge! It could earn me inter—It could earn us international attention!"

"Nice try." Carl's laugh was bitter. "You'd better start acting like a professional journalist if you want to have a career at all. One more stunt like this, and you're fired. Got it?"

Brynn fell silent.

Carl stormed into his office, slamming the door behind him. The hollow thud traveled through the glass. The muted shouting that followed blurred into scanner static and the bark of a copier. Keyboards resumed. Brynn watched the office door and let the shape of the threat settle, cold and exact.

She glowered and sat, staring at her computer as if it had done something wrong.

The sun had dropped behind the New Dresden skyline, throwing long, blade-like shadows over the street. Bus brakes sighed, a delivery truck idled somewhere, hot exhaust curling up from the grill. Brynn pushed through the revolving doors with her laptop bag dragging her shoulder down. The day had carved a dull ache behind her eyes, and the skin at the corners pinched. She'd stayed at her desk, combing notes, refusing to leave with nothing. Yet here she was.

Outside, the air cut clean against her face, cooler than the newsroom's stale heat. She filled her lungs and let it out slowly, trying to rinse Carl's ultimatum from her head. Her fingers went into her bag, fishing for keys. Metal edges clicked against charger cords as she walked, already orienting toward hot water and a glass of wine.

She turned the corner and scanned the curb where she'd left the beat-up car. Empty asphalt. A greasy scuff marked where tires had been. A curled receipt stuck to the gutter grate. She looked up and down the row, replaying the morning. Same tree, same dented signpost. No car.

The sign finally registered. Thin municipal red on white: No Parking 4PM-6PM. Her eyes dropped to her watch. 6:05PM. She'd walked past that sign a hundred times after six and had never been towed. She pressed her palm to her forehead, a short, sharp tap.

"You've got to be kidding me," she muttered, her voice carrying in the nearly empty street. She turned in a slow circle, as if the car might slide into frame if she changed angles. The street offered nothing but the after-smell of hot brakes and a faint scrape where a dolly had bitten the curb. Her car was gone.

Her shoulders sank. The day, already heavy, shifted another notch. She reached for her phone on reflex, then froze, the realization coming with a little jolt. It was still on her desk, plugged in and charging.

She stayed there a moment longer, shoes nudging grit. The city moved on without looking at her, taxis threading through yellow lights, voices leaking from an open bar door. She scuffed at the curb and headed back to the office.

Chapter 6

Heat radiated off the concrete plaza outside police headquarters, the sun's glare ricocheting off nearby glass towers. The light felt white and hard. Blackburn stood in the precinct's shadow, a cool strip of shade against her back, eyes on the press pack boiling in front of her. Sweat stood on her upper lip. She didn't move.

Brynn Cassidy, sharp in a red blouse, threaded the knots of tripods and bodies. Purpose in the shoulders. Precise hands. Blackburn tracked her without blinking, taking in the calibrations, the small corrections.

"Joseph, pan from the skyline down to me," Brynn said, voice clear, clean. "We need to set the scene before we dive in."

Joseph, big and careful, rolled his wrists to level the camera. Smooth. Efficient. He framed her just as he had ten thousand times.

Blackburn watched Brynn test her mic, fingers checking the cord, the clip. Quick. Accurate. Beneath it, the tells. Color climbed at the throat, breath a notch faster. Brynn's touch settled on the microphone head and stayed a second longer than necessary.

"Now, the B-roll," Brynn said, tipping her chin at the city. "Show them the good, the bad, the ugly. The Autonomous Project is supposed to change everything, right? Let's show them where we're starting."

Joseph swung the lens. New Dresden unfurled for him. Gleaming tech headquarters stabbing the blue, logos polished to a shine. Below them, neon that never slept flickered even in full sun. "Girls! Girls! Girls!" burned a lurid pink. A pawnshop's "Cash 4 Gold" pulsed sickly green.

A Raider Straight Line slid past, paintwork clean, windows dark against the grit. It skimmed around a food delivery robot skittering along a cracked bike path. Teenagers huddled under an awning, passing a pipe, eyes tracking everything and nothing.

People drifted through the frame like afterimages. A woman in a crisp suit walked past a man curled into himself in a doorway. She kept her eyes forward, blind by choice. Two worlds side by side, never touching.

Blackburn let her mouth tilt as Brynn watched Joseph's footage. The small furrow at Brynn's brow. The way her teeth worried at her lower lip. Always working. Always reading the edges. It hit like liquor.

Blackburn stayed off to the side, formal blues neat, collar biting her neck. Sunlight took her hair and threw it back at the crowd. She scanned the bodies, the gear, the faces without hurry. Conversations paused when she straightened. Lenses shifted in her direction even before she stepped up. She knew what they called her. Brilliant. Problematic. A star you had to handle with gloves. They let her get away with things because her record said she could.

The camera swung back to the makeshift stage. Blackburn lifted her chin. In a minute, she would step into frame. Become part of Brynn's cut. A familiar thrill slid down her spine and settled low. Controlled.

The game was about to begin.

Reporters bumped and shuffled, elbows in ribs, foam windscreens bobbing in the heat shimmer. The partnership with the Stan Raider Group had pulled everyone with a press pass into the heat. They wanted to be first. They wanted blood.

Stan Raider stood off to the side, wiry and restless, eyes that hopped like code scanning for syntax. His fingers twitched at his side. On paper, he belonged here. In person, he looked like he'd rather be back inside a clean room.

Blackburn gave him a curt nod and moved her attention back to the only thing that mattered. Brynn looked up. Their eyes held. Blackburn let a slow smile climb, lazy and precise, as if she'd tasted something and decided to take it. She didn't blink.

Color rose along Brynn's throat. She didn't drop her gaze.

Blackburn cut the look and flicked her hand at Chief Hayes. Time to move the pieces.

Chief Hayes stepped up and cleared his throat into air thick with chatter and generator hum. The sound went nowhere. He opened his mouth, shut it, opened it again. The moment started to turn on him.

A compact, heavy shape slipped from behind him. Willow. She moved quickly when she cared, her focus a straight line. She pressed at his shoulder with no ceremony, leaned in. Her rounded fingers, rough at the tips, tested each connection at the mic. No wasted motion.

Against the crisp reporters and crisp blues, Willow's rumpled clothes and greasy hair were a smudge. She didn't care. Her eyes were on the tangle. Nothing else existed.

Her tongue edged out of the corner of her mouth as she worked. Automatic. Private. For a breath, she vanished into the tight universe of circuits and slack.

Then she twisted her wrist, found the angle, and pulled a shriek out of the speaker. The feedback hit like a blade. Conversations snapped off. Faces tightened. Hands jumped to ears. The air tasted of copper and ozone.

Willow let a small smile ghost her mouth and took a step back. She clocked Brynn, and retreated behind Hayes. Her eyes met Blackburn's in the gap. Heat. Regret. Hunger. Gone.

Chief Hayes took his moment back. He cleared his throat again and let it land. "Ladies and gentlemen, thank you for joining us today. We have an important announcement regarding the future of law enforcement in New Dresden."

The press settled, phones lifted, bodies tipping forward. Blackburn kept Brynn in her peripheral, the line held tight. All the players on the board. All the exits noted.

"It is my pleasure to introduce Mr. Stan Raider, CEO of the Stan Raider Group. Mr. Raider and his team have been working tirelessly on a project that promises to revolutionize law enforcement in our city." Hayes gestured a little too big, then stepped aside. "Mr. Raider, if you would."

Stan edged to the mic, wiry frame coiled, glasses nudged higher in a tic. He started thin, then found his voice as he hit code he knew.

"The Autonomous Project," Stan began, his voice gaining strength, "is not just another technological advancement. It's a paradigm shift in how we approach crime prevention." His hands drew diagrams in the air no one else could see.

"This initiative promises to leverage an advanced AI system for the police that integrates with our popular Raider Straight Line autonomous and driver-assist cars. The system will provide real-time data analysis to predict crime hotspots, allowing police vehicles to preemptively patrol high-risk areas. This would highlight the dual purpose of the technology enhancing public safety while also improving policing efficiency."

Stan's voice quickened, excited by the fruition of his 10-year project.

"We've harnessed the power of artificial intelligence and machine learning algorithms to process vast amounts of data from crime events across the country. Written police reports, audio from 911 calls, even security camera footage. All of it feeds into our system." Stan's eyes gleamed with excitement, his earlier nervousness forgotten.

"Our AI can direct police on the ground, in their cars, to trouble before the trouble happens. Imagine our sleek Straight Lines detouring around slow traffic thanks to AI, arriving sooner thanks to AI, at the spot where AI says trouble is brewing." He continued, eyes lit, voice taut. "It's about understanding patterns, predicting behaviors. Our AI doesn't just see individual crimes, it sees the interconnected web of factors that lead to criminal activity. Socioeconomic conditions, weather patterns, social media trends. These play a role in shaping the landscape of crime. And this system will get police there first."

Stan paused and let the silence do its work. Reporters crowded closer, feet edging over taped lines, arms outstretched. Blackburn let the cadence wash the crowd forward. She felt the hot metal of the barricade near her thigh and the tacky give of a cable under her shoe.

"Police will arrive sooner, catch criminals faster. Hopefully, even prevent the crimes from happening in the first place," Stan said, voice dipping toward reverent. "A system that can deploy police resources proactively, preventing crimes before they happen. That's the promise of the Autonomous Project."

Noise exploded. Hands shot up, mics thrust forward, bodies angling for a clean line of sight. Heat and breath surged.

"Mr. Raider!" A balding man with metal-rimmed glasses called out. "How do you address concerns about invasion of privacy? Aren't you essentially spying on every citizen?"

Stan's jaw tightened. He kept his tone flat. "We're not spying on anyone. The system processes publicly available data and information already in police databases. We're connecting the dots more efficiently."

A young woman with a pixie cut cut in. "But what about data security? How can you guarantee this information won't fall into the wrong hands?"

"Excellent question," Stan said, steadier now. "We've implemented state-of-the-art encryption and multi-layered security protocols. Our systems are regularly audited by independent cybersecurity firms. The data is as safe as it can be. But again, it's already out there, public."

A tall man with a cigarette tucked behind his ear lifted his arm. "Just how much data are we talking about here? Can you give us a sense of scale?"

Stan brightened. "We're processing petabytes of data daily. To put that in perspective, if each piece of data were a grain of sand, we'd be analyzing entire beaches every single day."

A low ripple of appreciation moved through the pack. Then Brynn's voice cut cleanly through it. "Mr. Raider, isn't this just 1984 and Big Brother all over again? How is this any different from the dystopian surveillance state Orwell warned us about?"

Stan shook his head hard and leaned toward the challenge. "Nineteen Eighty-Four explored the dangers of totalitarianism, highlighting how those in power can manipulate truth and language to control the masses. It's hardly comparable to our efforts at stopping murder. I assure you, I am not manipulating anything." He'd been waiting for that one.

His gaze skittered, then fixed. He pulled air in, steadied.

"Look," he said, pitching his voice to earnest, "Orwell's vision was about a totalitarian state using technology to oppress its citizens. That's not what we're doing here. Our goal is to protect people, not control them."

He stopped, gathered, cameras pushing in, the sun hot on his scalp.

His hands drew an invisible weather map. "Think of it like a weather forecast. We're not controlling the weather. We're just trying to predict where the storm might hit so we can be prepared. That's what this system does with crime."

Blackburn held herself still, face arranged, eyes bright. Weather is chaotic but honest. By contrast, people lie to themselves and everyone else, and no algorithm can catch the truth.

"Furthermore," Stan said, stronger now, "in Orwell's world, there was no transparency, no accountability. We're standing here today, openly discussing this technology. We welcome scrutiny and oversight. This isn't about creating a surveillance state, it's about using data responsibly to make our communities safer."

Brynn's brow tightened as she wrote, pen scratching, jaw set. Joseph adjusted his camera gear, catching every spike of Stan's hands as they chopped the air.

"The Autonomous Project is about prevention, not punishment," Stan emphasized, voice rising. "We're not arresting people for 'thoughtcrimes' or future actions. We're helping police allocate resources more effectively, to be in the right place at the right time."

"You'll send police to an area where a crime has not happened, but where you think there are people hanging around who, in fact, are likely to commit a crime? Using your own data analysis?" Brynn asked. "How is that not Orwellian?"

Stan Raider's face tightened and twisted. He snapped. He turned his back on the mics and walked away from the podium without another word. The press line froze for a beat, stunned, then buzzed louder. Space opened where he'd been. Questions died, undelivered.

Blackburn watched the exit route he chose. She nudged Hayes with her elbow, a small, precise prod. Her gaze flicked to the empty podium, back to him. Take it.

He shrugged. A small lift. He wasn't going to step into it.

She let out a breath, not quite a sigh, and stepped up. The noise fell as she set her hands on the edge of the podium. Presence did work.

"Thank you all for coming today," she said, voice carrying clean across concrete and cord coils. "We appreciate your interest in this groundbreaking initiative."

They leaned in. Hunger still on their faces. Phones up. Mics up. Waiting. She made the choice.

"I understand you may have more questions," Blackburn said, tone trimmed to authoritative and open. "Chief Hayes and I will be available for individual inquiries. Please feel free to approach us with any specific questions you may have. For more about the technicalities of the project, you can follow up with The Stan Raider Group."

They pivoted, equipment snapping into travel positions. They started angling toward the hole Raider had left, bodies already moving to catch him at the curb. The current shifted the way she wanted.

No one wanted to talk to the cops. They all wanted the strange tech guru who was bringing Orwell to life.

Chapter 7

The formal press conference broke apart and the plaza turned into a tangle of cables, hot lights, and overlapping voices. Brynn wasted no time. She gathered her microphone and notepad, eyes fixed on Blackburn as if everything else were a blur of tripods and elbows. She threaded through the knot of cameras with impatient steps.

Blackburn clocked Willow at the periphery, where the shadow of the riser cut a thin line against the sun-glare off the tripods. Willow stood off to the side, tracking Brynn's approach. Jealousy tightening the corners, a small narrowing of the eyes that no one else would read for what it was. Blackburn knew the tell. She liked the way Willow's attention anchored on her and refused to budge.

As Brynn reached Blackburn, her face flushed with excitement and the thrill of the chase, Blackburn saw Willow's fingers twitch at her sides. Willow had been on the receiving end of that attention, that focus. She knew what it did to people. Blackburn shifted half a step to angle her shoulder toward the cameras, the sweat-slick mic foam smell riding on the heat. She felt Willow's gaze like a wire, taut.

The hum of conversations swelled and broke around them, reporters clustering near the officials for scraps. Police radios crackled. Someone's mic squealed and then went dead. None of it mattered.

Blackburn kept her attention on the reporter closing in and on the woman at the edge whose world, when fixed on Blackburn, let the rest fall away.

"Exciting day, isn't it?" Blackburn said. Smooth, easy. Letting the line sit just long enough to become an invitation.

Brynn looked up, startled. She pulled herself together, hearing it was meant for her. The color that had risen in her cheeks during the earlier volley with Stan Raider returned for something else entirely. "Detective Blackburn," she greeted, respectful, curious. "I didn't expect to see you out here with the rest of us today. You're usually working."

Blackburn watched the micro-shifts. The pen in Brynn's fingers stilled for half a beat. The chin lifted a fraction. The crowd noise thinned between them. She let her smile change by degrees, not a show but a calibration, closing distance without moving. She leaned in just enough that Brynn had to follow to hear over the ambient roar.

Blackburn shrugged, her smile widening. The movement was fluid, almost feline in its grace. "This is work. Even I have to make an appearance sometimes, especially for something as significant as this. The partnership with the Stan Raider Group could be a game-changer." Her eyes stayed on Brynn's face, drinking every micro-expression, every subtle shift. Calculation without hurry.

Brynn nodded, interest bright in the quick flicker of her eyes. "Yes, it's a big story. But, if you don't mind me saying, you seem particularly invested. Do you have a special interest in this partnership?" Her instincts kicked past nerves and went straight to the question.

Blackburn let her posture go still. A deliberate reset. She held Brynn's gaze and cooled her own. She didn't need to raise her voice.

"Excuse me?" Blackburn's voice was low. "Did you just imply that I have some sort of...improper interest in this partnership between the Stan Raider Group and New Dresden police?" She carried the words without hurry, letting each land.

Good. Confusion crossed Brynn's face in a quick flash, followed by a small recoil. Blackburn watched it hit. She could feel the weight of her own silence and let it do the work that explanations never could.

"I, I didn't mean to imply anything improper, Detective," Brynn stammered, her earlier poise crumbling under Blackburn's icy glare. "I was asking about your professional interest in the project."

Blackburn stretched the pause, counting it out. Then she let warmth return the way light returns after a cloud moves. The speed of it always unsettled them.

"Of course," Blackburn said, the invite back in place. "I apologize for my reaction. It's just that this project means a great deal to me, professionally speaking. Perhaps I'm a bit sensitive about it."

Brynn visibly relaxed. The shoulders dropped a notch. Relief softened her mouth. Blackburn didn't look away. Vulnerability, offered in a measured dose, always made them step closer.

"You know," Blackburn continued, voice lowered so Brynn had to lean in again, "I admire your dedication to uncovering the truth. It's rare to find someone so passionate about their work."

The compliment hit with the accuracy she intended. Brynn's cheeks warmed, her eyes brightened. Pride, and something that wasn't just professional.

Blackburn watched the reporter's defenses lower, piece by piece. The pen moved again, a small nervous ricochet. This part was always simple. The puzzle wasn't whether Brynn would move closer, it was how quickly. The thrill of the chase, the lure of being singled out, the path to exclusive access. It rarely failed.

"I heard you got yourself into a jam with the chief. But I'm sure you didn't mean any harm, hmm?"

"No, of course not."

"No, you just misspoke. Put the job before the heart. I get it. Sometimes I have to treat innocent people with toughness, just to get the information I need. It's just that I am trying to solve a murder, not earn revenue for a newspaper."

Blackburn watched the line slide into place. She didn't have to raise policy or cite the MOU in front of the cameras to make the point. The mention of the chief was enough to remind Brynn where gatekeeping lived. The apology on offer could just as easily become a closed door.

She let herself enjoy the small tilt of power as Brynn's weight shifted toward her. No rush. The best traps closed slowly, edges tightening so cleanly that escape didn't register as a possibility. She adjusted the spacing again, a half step that put her in Brynn's space without crowding it. The words, the silence, the small smile. That was the work.

Even Willow, still watching from afar, hunched closer, her interest piqued by the unexpected turn of events. Blackburn felt Willow move, a shadow cutting in to block a local blogger trying to sidle into the shot. Willow's service always found the seam before anyone asked.

Blackburn edged closer to Brynn, her voice dropping to a hushed tone. "I always like to be where the action is. Do you like action?" she asked, tone smooth and inviting.

Brynn blinked, caught by the pivot. That magnetism people named and didn't understand did the rest, bringing her in while keeping her on guard. The reputation did its own work in the background.

"Action is key to a reporter's job," Brynn said.

"Exactly. It's just that we don't manufacture the action the way you do. We don't have to."

"I don't man—" Brynn stopped when she caught the eye of Willow. Her guilt silenced her.

Blackburn tracked it. The quick hit of shame, the glance ricocheting from Willow to Blackburn and back. Admiration, shame, intimidation layered across Brynn's face in a flicker she couldn't fully hide. Reliable tells.

Blackburn's eyes, now warm once more, drank in every nuance of Brynn's expression. Her lips curved into a small, knowing smile, as if she could read every thought passing through the reporter's mind. She loved the woman's shame.

"I'm interested in your last murder case. I always keep a close eye on your cases," Brynn replied, managing a confident smile. "Maybe we can have a more in-depth conversation later? An exclusive?"

Blackburn's smile grew, the edge brightening in her eyes. "Maybe we can. But be careful what you wish for, Ms. Cassidy. You never know where a story might lead." The uptick in Brynn's pulse read across her throat. Anticipation and caution, braided.

Before Brynn could respond, David Quan from KLL News stepped up to Blackburn for questions, and the moment was lost in a flurry of activity. Willow slid closer without being called, positioning herself just out of frame, keeping a camera operator from drifting too tight. As the camera rolled and the microphone captured every word between David and Blackburn, Brynn lingered just beyond the lens, pulled tight to the edge. The line between them held, humming.

David's voice boomed, his coiffed hair gleaming under the sun. "Detective Blackburn, can you tell us why you are involved in this public relations show?"

Blackburn shifted without effort into the official register and gave him the version fit for air, the procedural spine visible enough to signal competence. She didn't lose sight of Brynn.

"The Autonomous Project could revolutionize our approach to crime prevention," Blackburn explained, her voice carrying a hint of excitement that seemed genuine. "Imagine stopping a murder. Show up before an abused partner is killed. Save a life. Just by putting officers in places where they are needed. We hope all crime will go down. But I am here to represent the possibility of saving lives."

Heat came off the camera battery. The wind pushed at the edge of the mic flag. Blackburn kept her stance steady and let the words work. At the edge of the shot, Brynn watched, reading the performance for angles that weren't only about tech. She would keep tugging on the thread that wasn't on the podium.

In the background, Willow observed the scene with unease. Blackburn saw it in the way Willow's shoulders went tight and then settled, in the way she repositioned to block a second approach from the blogger. Willow knew Brynn was being drawn in. Part of her wanted to pull away. Part of her wanted to see what Blackburn would do to the adversary. She knew something would happen.

The scrum thickened as the interview continued, bodies pressing in for soundbites, elbows lifting, phones extended. Blackburn held her ground, answered cleanly, let the institutional language do its work. And still, despite the chaos, that unseen line kept Brynn tethered just off-camera. It was just the beginning of the web.

Chapter 8

Heat rolled off the TV lamps and stuck under Blackburn's collar. Sun glare came hard off the glass, throwing long shadows across cables and tripods as reporters and camera operators scurried, adjusting microphones and checking camera angles. In the center of it, Brynn Cassidy smoothed her loud red shirt, eyes bright with anticipation. She'd just snatched Blackburn away from KLL News.

The familiar jingle of New Dresden Today bled thinly from Brynn's earpiece, and Donald Baker's distinguished voice boomed through the mix.

"Good afternoon, New Dresden. Today, we bring you an exclusive report on a groundbreaking initiative set to revolutionize crime prevention in our city. The Stan Raider Group is partnering with our police department to launch The Autonomous Project, an AI-powered predictive policing system. Our on-site correspondent, Brynn Cassidy, has the details."

The red tally light snapped on and Brynn's face lifted to meet it. She stood in front of police headquarters, framed exactly where Joseph wanted her. Modern glass and steel rose behind her, cut by classic stone accents. A large banner bearing the Stan Raider Group logo fluttered, its sleek design a stark contrast to the weathered facade of the police station. Blackburn clocked the angle Joseph had chosen and the wind catching the banner at the edge of the frame.

Brynn's voice was clear and authoritative as she began her report. "Thank you, Donald. I'm standing here at the heart of New Dresden's law enforcement center, where today marks a pivotal moment in our city's fight against crime. The Stan Raider Group, a leader in AI technology, is rolling out its latest innovation, 'The Autonomous Project.' This initiative promises to leverage AI-powered predictive policing to anticipate and prevent criminal activities before they occur."

As she continued, the camera panned and Blackburn felt the lens swing past her cheek. Chief Hayes stood beside her, short, stocky, balding under the lights. Next to him, Blackburn's height, lithe lines, and almost perfect blonde hair read clean in glass reflections.

"Chief Hayes, what can you tell us about the new project?"

"Today, we stand on the threshold of a new era in law enforcement. The partnership with Stan Raider Group is not just a step forward, it's a commitment to making our community safer through innovative technology. Together, we are dedicated to elevating our policing practices to meet the challenges of the modern age."

"Thank you. Detective Blackburn, you are the lead detective with New Dresden's police Homicide Division. What do you think of the Autonomous Project?"

"This Autonomous Project is a game-changer for our force. With cutting-edge AI and autonomous vehicles at our disposal, we can be proactive rather than reactive in preventing crime. It's time we leverage technology to protect our streets, ensuring that we stay one step ahead of those who threaten our safety."

In the background, Willow watched the proceedings. Her fingers twitched, itching to be back at her keyboard rather than in front of the cameras. She held herself still, eyes on Blackburn, ready.

As the segment drew to a close, Brynn's final questions were asked, each laden with implications. "This all sounds impressive. Detective Blackburn, what's your take on this new technology?"

"Well, Ms. Cassidy, I understand the pain of murder. I have complete confidence in this project. The team at Stan Raider Group are experts, and their technology has the potential to save lives and make our city safer. I'm excited to see how it will enhance our capabilities in solving and preventing crimes. I'll be most impressed if we see a dramatic cut in the city's homicide rates."

"Last year's clearance rate for homicides in New Dresden was 54%. Do you think AI will help your division?" Brynn asked as she then thrust the microphone into Blackburn's face.

Blackburn's smile tightened. A slight narrowing of her eyes registered as the jab landed. She straightened until her spine felt like a rod, fingers tapping once against her side, then still.

When she answered, her voice stayed smooth, a cool edge under the polish. She held Brynn's gaze without blinking, a stillness that made the air go thin.

"I personally have a clearance rate of 100%, so I don't need this AI. Of course, as the lead detective, I am happy to use any tool to help us bring up the overall clearance numbers. Or, as with the Autonomous Project, prevent homicides in the first place."

"Thank you, Detective Blackburn. I look forward to the day when every detective has the same clearance rate as you. This is certainly a significant step forward for our city. Detective Blackburn, any final thoughts on what this means for the future of crime fighting in New Dresden?"

Blackburn, distracted and now impatient with the young woman, said, "Just that I'm hopeful. Our priority is the safety of our citizens, and any tool that helps us achieve that goal is worth exploring. We're ready to embrace this technology and see its impact firsthand."

Brynn turned back to Joseph and his camera. "Thank you, Chief Hayes and Detective Blackburn. As we can see, New Dresden is on the verge of a technological transformation in law enforcement. The Autonomous Project promises to predict crime and to redefine how we think about safety and prevention. Reporting live from the police headquarters, this is Brynn Cassidy for New Dresden Today. Back to you, Donald."

Joseph's viewfinder went dark.

"We're clear," he said, lowering the electronic eye. Brynn gave him a high-five and smiled.

Chapter 9

The sun dipped low, stretching shadows across the sidewalk as Brynn Cassidy and Chief Hayes left the press conference behind. Cables snaked across the lot, generators coughed, and the hum of traffic pressed against the fence. They veered toward the coffee truck at the edge of the police lot, its oxidized panels and dented bumper set against the clean glass of headquarters. A line curled out from the window, uniforms shifting in place, boots scuffing at the oil-dark asphalt.

Chief Hayes joined the queue, his voice gruff but intentional. "Nothing personal in that phone call."

"No, of course not, chief. I think it was just a misunderstanding," Brynn said as she shrugged. "Happens to everyone."

"Yes, I hear you on that one," Chief Hayes replied as the line moved and he shuffled forward. The conversation held in formal cadence, smiles pinned in place. Chief Hayes continued, "The Stan Raider Group partnership is a big step. Their resources will be a game-changer."

Willow approached, shoulders hunched, eyes darting behind thick glasses. She hesitated at the back of the line, eager to blend into the background.

"Willow, join us," Chief Hayes called, his tone commanding yet friendly.

She shook her head, inching away. Not wanting to be near Brynn. Blackburn cut through the knot of bodies and slid into place, already facing Officer Zimmerman a few spots back.

"Mind if we cut in?" Blackburn asked, voice even, unarguable. She lifted two fingers to Willow without looking.

Zimmerman swallowed hard, eyes flickering away. "Not at all, Detective."

Blackburn turned, her gaze landing on Brynn. The tilt of her head was permission and demand. "Your question?"

Brynn's stomach fluttered. "We were discussing the new tech project." Chief Hayes cleared his throat.

Willow stood still, fingers twitching, the scar on her hand throbbing. She longed to be back at her desk, but remained rooted.

Blackburn nodded, her expression thoughtful. "It's about trust and collaboration. Their tech could revolutionize our work, but we can't let it overshadow our protocols."

Brynn held her phone up, recording. Blackburn's voice rose just enough to carry. "Not sure it's ethical to record this, Ms. Cassidy. People here might not want their conversations recorded."

Brynn met Blackburn's gaze, switching off her recorder. "And your ethical considerations, Detective? Privacy concerns?"

Blackburn let the silence work, then allowed a small smile. "The struggle between progress and privacy. We're gaining tools, not losing trust. Transparency is key, right, chief?"

Chief Hayes nodded, brow furrowed. "Absolutely. We're involving community representatives, lawyers, consultants, ensuring no rights are infringed."

They reached the window of the coffee truck. The grinder shrieked, steam hissed, and coffee oil hung thick in the heat. Blackburn stepped forward first.

"I'll have an Americano, black," she said, her voice smooth and confident. She turned to the others, a slight smirk playing on her lips. "What about you all? It's on me today. You too, Zimmerman. What's your order?"

Chief Hayes ordered a regular black coffee, his voice appreciative. Brynn hesitated before requesting a vanilla latte, while Willow mumbled her order for a simple black decaf coffee, her eyes fixed on the ground. Zimmerman wanted a black coffee.

"Americano, two black coffees, vanilla latte," the coffee guy chimed back as he prepared the orders.

"And a black decaf," Blackburn said. She'd heard Willow. It was her job to hear her.

"Yes, ma'am."

As Blackburn pulled out her wallet, she turned to Brynn with a spark in her eye. "Now, don't go thinking this is a bribe or anything," she quipped, her tone playful but with an underlying edge. "I wouldn't want to compromise your journalistic integrity."

Brynn laughed nervously, her cheeks flushing slightly. "Of course not, Detective. I wouldn't dream of it."

They moved to stand under the awning. The canvas snapped in the breeze, a repetitive tick over the compressor's rattle. Waiting held the space.

As the barista called out their orders, Blackburn and Willow's eyes met for a brief moment. Blackburn moved forward to collect her coffee, consciously pressing herself against Willow as she reached past her.

In a swift, almost imperceptible motion, Blackburn's lips brushed against the tip of Willow's ear. The kiss was fleeting, ghostly. Heat rose through her wrist into the cup, a calculated spike in pulse. A tremor ran down Willow's body, her shoulders tensing as a subtle shiver rippled through her spine. It was against policy and right in front of the chief. Blackburn pulled away just as quickly, coffee in hand, her face a mask of innocence as if nothing had happened.

Willow stood frozen, her chest tight. Her fingers trembled as she reached for her own cup.

Zimmerman, Chief Hayes and Brynn, oblivious to the charged moment that had just passed, collected their drinks without comment. The group, sans Zimmerman, now armed with their caffeine fixes, made their way towards a nearby tree, seeking refuge from the afternoon sun.

As they walked, Blackburn took the lead, her stride confident and purposeful. Willow lagged behind, her steps hesitant, her mind clearly elsewhere. Chief Hayes and Brynn fell in between, engaged in a quiet conversation about the upcoming changes to the department.

The shade of the tree offered a welcome respite from the heat, the leaves rustling overhead. They formed a loose circle, sipping their coffees and exchanging glances. Willow stood behind Blackburn. Her wall.

Blackburn leaned against the rough bark of a tree, cradling her Americano, her eyes studying Chief Hayes. "We need to be prepared for every scenario. The media, the public, they're going to scrutinize every move we make with this new partnership. We can't afford any missteps."

Chief Hayes sighed, weariness in his voice. "I know, Blackburn. This is a chance to make real progress, but it's also a minefield. We'll need to navigate carefully."

Blackburn turned her full attention to Brynn. "I'm a people person, you know? Computers and algorithms aren't my thing, but I know how to get results with just my skill. That's why I have a 100% clearance rate. But if AI is the magic everyone says it is, then the detectives should take full advantage of these tools. It's like having an edge, an advantage that will bring them up to my level. We all want success, right? The chief trusts me to lead, and so do the families of murder victims. That's who count," Blackburn said as she held her coffee cup up to her mouth. Only after she spoke did she drink.

Brynn nodded, noting the tension between Blackburn and Willow. There was a story here. She could sense the undercurrents of concern, the cautious optimism laced with the fear of potential backlash.

"I'll be following this closely," she said. "The public has a right to know how this partnership will affect them. And I'm sure they'll be interested in the department's approach to these ethical concerns."

Blackburn's gaze locked onto Brynn, her smile unwavering but her eyes hardening like steel. "We welcome the scrutiny as long as it's fair and balanced. We have nothing to hide, after all. And when we record someone without telling them, we have a court order to do it."

Chief Hayes cleared his throat, his voice steady but cautious. "Yes, well, the technology promises a lot, and while there are always challenges with new implementations, we're hopeful it will make a significant difference."

Brynn tilted her head, her eyes lifting to meet Blackburn's. "Your confidence is quite impressive. It must be a lot of responsibility being the face of such a high-profile initiative."

Blackburn leaned in, her voice dropping to a conspiratorial whisper. "Well, you know, I've always had a knack for being in the spotlight. It's not just about solving crimes, it's about leading, inspiring. When people see me on TV, they feel safer, more assured. That's a power in itself. And trust me, it takes a special kind of person to handle that pressure. Not everyone can do what I do."

Chief Hayes nodded, a hint of amusement in his eyes. "Detective Blackburn does have a unique ability to connect with the public and the team. Her presence is a big part of why we're confident in this project."

Brynn's gaze roamed over Blackburn's face, her voice probing. "It sounds like you both are playing crucial roles in making this work. I'm looking forward to seeing how it unfolds."

Blackburn flashed a charismatic smile, her eyes gleaming with confidence. "Stick around, Ms. Cassidy. You're going to see some real changes. And who knows, maybe one day you'll be reporting on how we turned New Dresden into the safest city in the country. And when that happens, remember who told you first."

Brynn smiled. "I certainly will. Detective Blackburn, will you be at tomorrow's fundraising dinner for Charles Roche?"

Blackburn tapped her coffee cup with her fingers, her voice cool. "Well, it's not for him, is it? He's dead. But yes, the family asked me to attend, a thank you for solving his murder. An example of how New Dresden police connect with the community."

"I'm covering the red carpet. I'll see you there," Brynn said with a shy smile.

A brief silence hung in the air, charged with unspoken words. The conversation turned casual, with comments on the beautiful weather and the influx of tourists.

They finished their drinks, and as Blackburn stood and stared, Brynn saw a woman who thrived in the chaos, a detective who would stop at nothing to achieve her goals, regardless of the consequences.

As the trio tossed their coffee cups into the truck's recycling can, Willow still sipping her coffee, and walked back across the parking lot to the waiting media members, the atmosphere grew more charged with anticipation. The streets bustled with afternoon traffic, but the focus was squarely on the group, especially on Blackburn and Chief Hayes.

Brynn, trailing behind, paused by her truck. She watched as the two senior officers were surrounded by a crowd of reporters and photographers who had been waiting outside headquarters. Willow stood back, ready to answer the technical questions that no one had. The press conference earlier had whetted their appetites, and now they were eager for more quotes and sound bites, not computer jargon and mumbo-jumbo. Brynn had stolen these two from the pack, and now the pack was hungry.

Blackburn faced the cameras with her usual poise and charisma, her confident smile commanding the attention of the press. Chief Hayes stood beside her, his demeanor more reserved but steady. The press shouted questions, their voices a tangle of competing pitches, each reporter straining for a clean pull.

As the questions flew, Blackburn handled them with ease, offering just enough information to satisfy without revealing too much. Her words were measured, her tone authoritative, commanding the attention of the press. Chief Hayes chimed in occasionally, reinforcing the department's commitment to transparency and public safety.

Brynn, still by her truck, took a moment to observe the scene. The contrast between Blackburn's composed front and the chaos of the press was stark. It was a reminder of the delicate balance of power and perception that Blackburn navigated so effortlessly.

"You ready, Joseph?" Brynn asked her videographer.

Joseph turned to Brynn, his brow furrowed with concern. "You haven't noticed? We've got a problem," he said, his voice serious. "Someone slashed all four tires on the TV van. We're waiting for a tow truck."

Brynn's eyes widened, shock registering on her face. "What? Are you serious?" She rushed over to the van, crouching down to inspect each tire. The rubber was split, each tire flat and useless. "Who would do this?" she asked, her voice shaking with disbelief.

Joseph shook his head, his expression grim. "I don't know. I grabbed a taco. Came back to this. I didn't see anyone near the van."

Frustration building, Brynn marched back to where Chief Hayes and Blackburn were speaking with reporters. She interrupted their conversation, her voice urgent. "Excuse me, but we have a situation. Someone slashed all four tires on our van."

Willow, who had been standing quietly behind Chief Hayes, leaned out slightly. She glanced towards the van, then back at Brynn. "Actually," she said, her voice soft, "the spare tire on the back door is slashed too."

Brynn's face flushed with anger. "This is outrageous! I demand a police investigation immediately!"

Blackburn let out a laugh, her eyes glinting with amusement. "Now now, Ms. Cassidy. You'll have to file a complaint just like everyone else. We can't show favoritism to the press, can we?"

"But there must be surveillance footage!" Brynn protested, her voice rising.

Blackburn shrugged, a sly smile playing on her lips. "Sometimes the cameras go out, but usually they work. The way to have it checked is to file a formal complaint. Why don't you go inside and speak to the desk sergeant?"

Brynn's frustration was palpable. "Why can't you or Chief Hayes take the complaint right now?"

Chief Hayes chuckled while Blackburn's smile grew wider. "There are protocols and procedures in place," Chief Hayes explained, his tone patronizing. "We won't be breaking those for anyone."

Defeated, Brynn called Joseph over. Together, they walked into the building to speak with the desk sergeant. As they left, Blackburn turned to Willow. "We should get back to work," she said casually.

Chief Hayes nodded. "I'll stay and answer a few more questions from the reporters."

As Blackburn and Willow made their way towards the main door, Willow leaned in close. "Did you do that?" she asked quietly, nodding towards the van.

"You know me so well," Blackburn grinned.

"But why?" Willow pressed.

Blackburn's eyes hardened. "Because Ms. Cassidy should never have called you." Willow's heart flooded with love.

They walked past Joseph and Brynn, who were engaged in an animated conversation with the desk sergeant. Without a backward glance, Blackburn and Willow passed through the locked doors and into the restricted area, leaving the chaos Blackburn had created behind them.

Chapter 10

Blackburn sat at her desk as late afternoon sun sliced through the blinds and threw jagged shadows across her office. She scrolled through her inbox with a hunter's focus. The Autonomous Project pressed at the edges of her mind, a promise of power and control she was determined to master.

Email after email yielded nothing. No substance. Nothing to sink her teeth into. A muscle twitched beneath the flawless skin of her jaw. She was Blackburn. Head of Homicide. The woman who commanded respect and fear in equal measure. How dare they keep her in the dark.

She clicked open a new message and addressed it to Willow. Her fingers twitched with impatience.

"I need the policies and procedures manuals for the Autonomous Project. Now."

She sent it and leaned back, a small smirk curving her mouth. Willow would comply. She always did. There was history here, a purposeful tangle of power and submission Blackburn had cultivated with care. She shut her eyes and let herself remember Willow trembling under her touch, begging for more, whimpering in exquisite agony.

The ping of an incoming email snapped her eyes open again. Willow's reply came fast, as expected, but it wasn't enough.

"I'm obtaining them now. I'll forward them by the end of the day."

Blackburn's eyes narrowed. Her lips curled in a thin snarl. End of the day. Not good enough. She needed the information now, every nuance and loophole in her hand. She craved control, and knowledge was the key to maintaining it.

She flicked her gaze to the wall clock. Its steady ticking mocked the minutes slipping away. "End of the day" stretched into an eternity. Every second left her in the dark about the Autonomous Project. Another chip in her facade of control.

She rose in one fluid motion, restless energy tightening her body. She paced the length of her office and let her mind settle on Willow. The shy IT specialist contrasted Blackburn's own commanding presence. Yet the web of desire and power between them was one Blackburn had woven with meticulous care.

She saw it easily. Willow hunched over a screen, fingers riding the mouse, collating the data. Scrambling to fulfill Blackburn's demand. The image coaxed a small, satisfied smile. Even from a distance, she held sway. Strings pulled with manipulation refined to an art.

It did not satisfy. Not today. The small, quiet manipulations felt hollow. The Autonomous Project loomed too large. The implications too vast for small victories to count.

Her heels clicked the polished floor, each step clean and sharp through the silence. Heat and anger simmered beneath her composed surface. LED lights flickered. Angles of her jaw and cheek-bones cut, shadow split across her face.

She took the stairs and entered the basement. The air cooled abruptly and carried the hum of machines. The shift from the bright chaos above to this gloom was abrupt. Light evaporated into shadows. Order thinned into disarray. Dust and ozone thickened the musty odor. A scent of decay masked by technology.

She moved down the narrow corridor, eyes fixed on the door at the end. Willow's lair. She pushed it open. The door groaned, a reluctant welcome.

Inside, the room cramped around them, drowning in electronics. Towers hummed. Screens spilled endless data. Cables writhed like serpents across the floor. The space vibrated with unsettled energy. Shelves sagged under hardware and half-understood tech.

Willow sat in the clutter, her face washed in the glow of the monitors. She looked up. Eyes widened. The atmosphere thickened. Electric. Primal.

Blackburn's mouth curved into a sly grin as she took in the chaos. Here, in Willow's domain, the power shifted and settled toward her. She stepped fully in. Her presence crowded the room. Corners seemed to bend to her will. She was not here to comfort or calm Willow. Not this time.

"Willow," she purred, voice charged. "We need to chat about priorities."

"Uh, I. I, uh," Willow stammered, voice a whisper. "I wasn't expecting you. If I'd known, I would have cleared a seat."

Blackburn's smile was both inviting and cold, a seduction edged with calculation. "I prefer things a little cramped."

The innuendo hung and heated the air. Willow's cheeks flushed crimson. She twisted in her chair, acutely aware of Blackburn's looming presence. A predator circling close.

"Now," Blackburn said, voice quiet and iron, "show me that documentation I asked for. I trust there's been progress."

Willow nodded and pulled files up on one screen, fingers nimble and precise. "Yes, I've accessed some preliminary documents. They're extensive, but I can summarize."

Blackburn moved behind her. She set her hands on the backrest. The leather creaked under her grip. Willow imagined those hands pressing down on her shoulders. A weight that both excited and terrified.

"Show me," Blackburn commanded, her voice silk and shadows, sending a delicious shiver down Willow's spine.

Willow scrolled. Blackburn leaned closer, enclosing the space around Willow. The faint trace of her perfume, subtle and intoxicating, muddled Willow's focus. Documentation slipped from her mind, displaced by proximity.

Blackburn's gaze devoured the screen. The Autonomous Project's policies flickered. Plans crystalized. Potential weaknesses took shape.

Willow's breath went shallow and quick. Blackburn's warmth pressed in. The small office constricted. Tension spiraled and held between them.

Willow's eyes softened when Blackburn slid her hands from the backrest to her shoulders. Desire tangled with fear. The fierce grip. The rough heat of her touch. The sweet, suffocating scent, overwhelming Willow's senses.

A protest rose and dissolved. No words. Willow's eyes snapped to the documents. The cursor flickered like a frantic heartbeat. Blackburn's hands caressed and held. Willow's mind fought the heat rising inside her, battling the instinct to resist.

Blackburn leaned to Willow's ear. Lips brushed it. The sultry whisper curled like smoke and sent chills down Willow's spine. "I've been thinking of you," she purred, an amused smile twisting her lips.

Blackburn's hands slid off Willow's shoulders and down her sides, the intimacy sending shockwaves through Willow's body. Her breath hitched. Guilt and pleasure collided. Her fingers hesitated over the keyboard.

The screen flickered. Data swarmed and frayed as Willow's focus fractured. She felt ensnared. A fly circling a web spun with authority and desire, each thread pulling her deeper into a tangled embrace.

Resistance and want warred beneath her skin. Yet escape stayed elusive. The dim room and the heat of her arousal held her in a tight purgatory.

Blackburn's eyes blazed. She gathered a fistful of Willow's hair, not to yank, but to hold her head perfectly still. With her other hand, she pressed her palm over Willow's mouth, silencing her. The pressure was firm, absolute.

"Shhh," Blackburn breathed into her ear, her voice a low vibration. "You don't get to make a sound until I say you can. This focus is mine. Your air is mine. Every breath you take is because I allow it."

Willow's world narrowed to the scent of Blackburn's skin, the steady pressure over her mouth, and the thrilling, helpless stillness enforced upon her.

Blackburn drank the electric thrill as she watched her lover in that vulnerable angle. She sensed Willow's arousal, felt the pulse of it under her hand. In her mind's eye, she saw delicate skin flush. Breath quickened. Surrender forming as Willow obeyed each silent command.

She pressed harder, enough to underscore her dominance, and took pleasure in Willow's gradual descent into submission. The room pulsed. Exquisite tension. Pleasure and pain in a narrow, intimate symphony.

Blackburn's spine tingled at Willow's moans and desperate pleas. The sound turned raw. The air grew heavy with the scent of sweat and musk. Forbidden desires added another layer to the dim-lit atmosphere.

A muffled sound, a desperate, pleading *mmph* vibrated against Blackburn's palm. Willow's body hummed with tension, a live wire begging to be grounded. She didn't need words to ask. The arch of her spine, the frantic beat of her pulse under Blackburn's hand, the way she pressed back toward Blackburn. It was all a silent, screaming plea for more.

Blackburn savored the control, reading every twitch and tremor like a language only they shared. She pressed her palm harder, stealing another fraction of breath, another degree of sound. She drew out the suspense, watching the sheen of sweat bloom on Willow's skin, watching her eyes squeeze shut then flutter open, glazed with surrender.

A raw, choked cry, barely audible, escaped around the edges of Blackburn's hand. It was all the answer she needed. Blackburn leaned in, her lips brushing against Willow's sweat-damp cheek, her hot breath a promise and a threat against her skin.

"Was that a 'yes'?" she whispered, the vibration humming straight into Willow. Her hand slid from Willow's mouth, but the dominance did not break. Her fingers trailed down, a searing path over the frantic pulse in her neck, coming to rest at her collarbone, digging in with a possessiveness that made Willow shudder. "Or are you asking me to stop?"

The question was a formality. They both knew the answer. There was no choice here. There was only Blackburn's will.

Blackburn held her there for one endless, breathless second more, savoring the absolute silence, the total submission. Then, she released her grasp.

The sudden freedom was a shock. Willow gasped, a ragged, raw intake of air that burned her lungs. Her head spun, her body swaying forward before she caught herself on the desk. The world rushed back in a dizzying wave of sound and sensation, every nerve ending screaming, hyper-aware of the woman behind her who had given her breath back as casually as she had taken it.

Blackburn watched her, a predator satisfied with the hunt. She didn't move to steady her. She simply let the aftermath ripple through Willow, letting her feel the full, disorienting weight of her release.

Then, as if the interlude had never happened, the heat climbed. Blackburn's hand slipped over Willow's shirt. A groan escaped her as she grazed Willow's nipple and felt it stiffen under her touch. Her breath hitched as she moved lower and unzipped Willow's pants. The friction of the zipper sent a sharp shock through her.

"Now what, Lioness?" Willow whispered. Her voice cracked. Her body went taut with anticipation. Blackburn traced her hand up Willow's belly. Her touch sent shivers along Willow's skin. Willow's lips trembled as she felt her own wetness.

Blackburn's hands roamed, eager and hungry. Every touch, every slow, conscious pass sent a bolt through Willow. Her body ached to be held, to be consumed by Blackburn's possession. Willow's breathy moans filled the room as Blackburn's fingers teased her nipples.

In a swift motion, Blackburn spun Willow around in her chair. Willow's hips lifted on instinct. Blackburn's hands went to Willow's jeans and pulled them down, catching at her ankles. Bound. Exposed. Vulnerable. Eager.

Blackburn thrust her hand between Willow's legs and felt the wetness. Proof of desire. She entered her, her finger moving inside Willow with purpose. She leaned in close, aligning her body in front of hers. One hand between Willow's legs, the other hard at her shoulder. Owning. Possessing. Her eyes locked on Willow's, refusing to let her look away.

Willow's hips rocked, urgent, pushing back. The ferocity startled them both. Rapid breaths and slick heat fueled the pace. Blackburn's strength, driven by arousal, moved within Willow, each thrust striking the spot that had Willow bucking.

Their bodies found a rhythm and bore down. Eyes chained together. Teetering on the edge of release. Tension coiled deep. Willow's stomach clenched. Her voice turned hoarse when she pleaded. "May I?"

Blackburn pressed her forehead to Willow's. Sweat mixed. She held Willow still as she answered. "You may not, little Fawn. You're mine, so prove it."

Willow obeyed and bit back the cry. Her body pulsed with the force of her desire. Blackburn kept her poised on the precipice, drawing it out and out, until she relented and surrendered to her animalistic hunger.

"You've been waiting for me to come back, haven't you? Anticipating this moment. Tell me, how much do you want it?"

"God, yes, Lioness. So much. I've missed this... your control. Please." Willow groaned and arched. Her teeth ground as she fought to hold back, to prolong it, to succumb only when Blackburn allowed. She craved Blackburn's control. The surrender only she could elicit.

Willow's world narrowed to the relentless pulse of Blackburn's finger. Each stroke landed and brushed the sensitive sweet spot. Every touch edged her closer. Tension coiled like a live wire ready to spark.

"You're not allowed to come until I say so. Hold back, or else."

"Yes, Lioness." She fought the urge to let go. Blackburn's commanding tone and Willow's spiraling arousal made the fight thin. "H-holding."

"The more you squirm, the more I know you like it. Don't hold your reactions back. I want to feel you. Come now."

With a final, desperate, muffled moan, Willow's body surrendered. Pleasure surged in relentless waves and took her whole.

"Yes, please," Willow gasped, her body convulsing beneath Blackburn's touch as she peaked.

Feeling the force of Willow's climax, Blackburn eased her rhythm and let her drift in the haze. Then, swift and almost cruel, she withdrew and left Willow breathless.

The absence jarred her. Emptiness opened and made her feel exposed, vulnerable. With a quick motion, Blackburn wiped the evidence of Willow's orgasm onto her t-shirt. A bold memento of their transgression. The token of sexual prowess made Willow gasp, a visceral jolt back into the room.

Blackburn's voice was a low whisper, her breath tickling Willow's ear. "Still with me, little Fawn?"

The question was tender, yet it carried the weight of a command, a demand for confirmation. She pressed a soft kiss beneath Willow's ear, the touch sending a fresh shiver down her spine.

"I'm here," Willow breathed, the words barely audible. "I'm yours."

A wicked smile played on Blackburn's lips. "That you are."

Blackburn lifted Willow's hand to her mouth. Her gaze held an unspoken promise. She kissed the small scar. The kiss was delicate and sent an electric shock through Willow. That scar held memories. A physical symbol of their past intensity, and the dangers beneath their passion.

Willow's breath hitched as Blackburn's tongue traced the scar. Dark eyes held Willow's gaze. Blackburn savored the taste of their encounter, her scent, and the salt of sweat on Willow's skin.

"Don't forget who owns you," Blackburn murmured, her lips close, her voice low. She pulled back, straightened her clothes, and let her collected demeanor slide back into place like a switch flipping.

Her hand closed on the cool brass doorknob. A final pause. Her gaze swept over Willow. An unsatisfying mess of unraveled composure. For a single, unguarded breath, something perilously close to tenderness threatened the ice in her veins. Then it was gone, locked away. Detachment returned, a familiar and more useful armor.

"Documentation. Now." Her tone was a lash of cold air, designed to make Willow shiver with the fresh memory of her power.

The door clicked shut behind her, a sound that contained the entire encounter. The hallway was silent, sterile, a different world.

In the women's washroom, she scrubbed her hands until the scent of sex and sweat was erased by the astringent bite of institutional soap. She dried her skin with a rough paper towel, methodically and precisely.

Stepping back into the hallway, she pulled out her phone. The stairwell door swung shut behind her, cutting off all echoes. He answered on the second ring.

"Schmidt. It's Blackburn," she said, her voice purposeful. "I need to park a technical asset on your roster. Administrative fiction only. She remains under my direction. She's one of my best, so don't let HR tie it up in red tape."

"Always the charmer," Schmidt said. "You found the walking dead guy, right? Evan Hart?"

Blackburn's eyes narrowed. "Yes. Levy from Major Crimes has my report."

"Not anymore. Died. Now he's mine. And now he's yours," Schmidt said.

Blackburn stopped, shoulder to the cold wall. "Why do you want to give up a high-profile case? You're up to something."

Schmidt snorted. "Of course I am. First, your name is already all over the damned thing. Second, we just found another head."

Blackburn gave a thin laugh. "That's four now."

"Yeah. My whole team is swamped, and we're bringing in some federal help. You solve it. Give me the evidence, warrants, everything. It stays on my stats," Schmidt said. "Administrative fiction."

Blackburn smiled, minimal. She liked the way he thought. "Deal. Send me your files."

"Good working with you, Blackburn," he said before hanging up.

Chapter 11

Willow had sent the technical documentation as promised. Blackburn pored over it for hours that evening, absorbing every detail about the autonomous patrol units' capabilities and limitations. This afternoon, it was time for Blackburn to shine. She had agreed to be photographed with the new autonomous cars, a publicity stunt featuring the seasoned homicide detective and the sleek silver vehicles poised to transform the New Dresden police department.

They crossed the asphalt toward Blackburn's car. Late sun pulled their shadows long across the lot, the heat lifting off tar and paint. The click of Blackburn's heels cut through the quiet. Willow kept close, her steps quick, trying not to stumble.

"We're going to the Stan Raider Group's headquarters," Blackburn stated, her voice low, a command wrapped in casual indifference. "Give me directions."

Willow's face tightened, breath catching. "I don't know the route."

Blackburn let a thin smile rise. "Then you better conjure it up. No maps or GPS. Once you are inside the car, it's just your brain."

Willow's fingers moved fast over her phone, urgency tightening her shoulders as she pulled the path together.

Blackburn opened her door, slid into the driver's seat, and let the cabin's hush close around her. She shut the door with a clean, final thud. Bio-lock. Starter. The engine woke with a restrained thrum. Willow eased in, careful, seatbelt clicked. Blackburn leaned over, close enough for fabric to brush skin.

"I have always liked these," Blackburn murmured, fingers grazing Willow's breast with a teasing familiarity. Willow's gaze checked the lot. "Okay, Willow, where to?"

"Baker Street. You'll want to turn right out of the lot." Her heart raced, exporting every nerve ending straight to her throat.

They pulled out. Blackburn threaded them into traffic, the sedan settling into the flow. Willow stared at the side glass, her reflection trying on a smile that would not hold. "Head northwest on Baker toward Shining Lake Boulevard West, half a mile," she instructed, voice doused in forced calm.

"Which way is northeast?" A flicker of amusement touched Black-burn's eyes. Her hands stayed steady, grip strong and ready.

"Right! Right onto Baker!"

Blackburn nodded and took the turn. The brick fronts along Baker sat worn and steady, windows throwing back the light. The street worked through its late-afternoon rhythm, horns, foot traffic, the usual compression of a city changing shifts.

"Half a mile," Willow breathed out, tension palpable.

Blackburn let the wheel rest in her hands. The car ran smoothly. She kept space ahead of them, watched the mirrors, listened to the engine's clean note. The air between them held the charge from the touch, contained, live.

At the end of Baker, Willow cleared her throat. "Turn right onto Shining Lake Boulevard West at the end of Baker," she commanded, her voice gaining a solid edge. "Here. Turn right onto Shining Lake Boulevard West for seven-tenths of a mile."

Blackburn pivoted the wheel and slid them onto the wider artery. Glass towers on either side spat back the sun, a hard scatter that made her squint and hold her line.

"Use the right lane to veer slightly right toward York Street in three hundred feet," Willow pressed on, the narrowing road tightening her chest.

"Three hundred feet? That's hardly any time to switch lanes in this traffic," Blackburn snapped, her fingers tapping on the steering wheel.

"Just do it," Willow insisted, impatience slicing through her tone.

Blackburn braked hard and clean, the car planted, stopping the lane. Willow jolted forward, the belt locked her back. A horn hit behind them, long and useless.

"What's wrong?" she asked.

Blackburn turned, calm and cutting. "I don't like your tone."

Color pushed up Willow's neck. "I'm sorry," she murmured, looking away.

"That's one punishment owed," Blackburn stated, a mix of authority and playful menace lacing her words. She released the brake and took them forward again. The engine note rose. Willow's stomach flipped. Want and dread, both awake now.

They left the wider strip for smaller storefronts. Signs blinked to life. Dusk settled, not soft, not kind. Steam and gasoline hung in the air.

"Turn right at the first cross street onto York Street," Willow's voice quivered. Then she stiffened. "No! Wait, the second cross street—look! Signs for York Street North to Franklin Avenue. It's one and a half miles ahead."

Blackburn cut her a look and lifted two fingers without a word. Noted. The car took the turn on cue and found the quieter run of York. Buildings dropped in height. Trees pushed over the sidewalks.

"This place is a damn maze," Blackburn complained. "How do you keep track of it all?"

"I know it matters to you," Willow replied, determinedly staring ahead, fingers twisting together in her lap. "It's like decoding. I get that chaotic tangle, then the patterns emerge."

They rolled onto Franklin Avenue, and the city loosened. Lots widened. Houses stood back from the curb, edges crisp, driveways spared. The quiet here felt installed, mechanical. A delivery bot hummed along the walk, its sensors blinking.

"Turn left onto Richmond Road West and drive for two miles," Willow instructed, her voice smooth but threaded with urgency.

Richmond Road West stretched straight. Oaks arched above and sifted the light across their dash. Blackburn kept speed and lane, eyes up, jaw set.

Breaking the quiet, Willow's voice slipped into the air again. "Turn right onto 46th Street and continue for 350 feet."

Blackburn took the right. Her movements were minimal, stripped of anything extra. The neighborhood tightened, small homes pressed together, driveways stacked. It felt watched.

Willow shifted in her seat, her pulse quickening as she prepared for the next command. A foreign feeling.

"Turn left onto Church Street West and go for a mile," Willow directed, scanning the whispers of the town as they rolled past. The houses here wore age like a shroud, their peeling paint and sagging porches telling tales of abandonment and forgotten promises. A place seemingly suspended between past and present, neglected by time's relentless march.

Blackburn drove the straight length, fences creaking, wind pushing loose boards. The street wanted to lean on the car. She did not let it.

"Continue on White Cat Road," Willow continued, her tone softening as she pointed ahead. "Then drive to Pine Street—just around 590 feet. Turn right onto Pine. The next street is Indian Road, you'll want to take that right."

Blackburn breathed in deeply. "Willow, isn't there a more direct route?"

"I only had time to find this one," she said. They followed her winding directives, the scenery melting into a blur of indistinct homes. Each faded structure wept memories of neglect, overgrown lawns spilling out like unkempt dreams.

"There it is, up on the left," Willow whispered, her voice heavy with the journey's toll.

The Stan Raider Group office broke the line of houses, glass and steel lifted above the block. The SRG logo pulsed in blue against the dim, clean and sure, out of step with the rust near it.

Blackburn's black sedan glided into the parking lot, a vast expanse where over a hundred silver Raider Straight Line cars gleamed under the dimming light. The polished bodies twinkled in dusk hues, creating an almost ethereal landscape of technology. She idled past the rows, coolant scent and new polymer off-gas hanging faintly, then stopped at the building entrance, near the gathered crowd.

As she stepped out, her grace contrasted with Willow's sloppy emergence from the passenger side, her footsteps scuffing as she followed. The moment they arrived, Stan Raider broke through the throng, a smile spreading across his face as his eager entourage, and a handful of camera-wielding photographers, flanked him.

"Detective Blackburn! So glad you could make it!" Stan exclaimed, his voice rich with genuine enthusiasm, as he extended a hand.

One photographer in the crowd, lanky with crooked glasses, chimed in, "Thank God she's good-looking!" His name tag read "Jonas."

At the compliment, Blackburn's lips curled into a smirk, satisfaction flickering in her eyes. "Well, I do try," she purred, the sweet poison of her false modesty wrapping around her words.

"Fantastic! We're featuring you with the cars." Jonas gushed, urgency spilling from his lips. "These shots will be everywhere. Digital, print, the shareholder's reports, you name it! This is going to be huge!" He waved his arms animatedly, beckoning the group of lackeys toward a cluster of parked Raider Straight Lines that stood ready like soldiers awaiting orders.

"It makes sense they'd want the best face, and the best mind, on their project. If these cars can keep up with me, they'll be unstoppable."

As they walked, Jonas summoned a young man burdened with a clipboard. "Just need your signature here, Detective," he said, excitement quaking in his voice. "And you?"

Willow stopped short, her eyes flickering to Blackburn. "Wh-wh-"

"She's my tech geek. She won't be in the photos," Blackburn said, grabbing the clipboard, her eyes flicking over the document with an easy casualness before signing it with a flair, the smile broadening on her face as she relished the spotlight and what it promised.

The golden hour cast an otherworldly glow over the parking lot, illuminating the scene as the photo shoot kicked off. The autonomous cars were arranged in a perfect semi-circle, their sleek forms reflecting the controlled lighting that lent an almost living quality to the machines. Willow compulsively ran her fingers along the sleek lines of every car they passed.

At the center of the semi-circle stood Blackburn, a beacon of human grace amidst the technological marvels. Her tailored black suit clung to her athletic form, radiating authority. Sunlight caught the meticulous work of her hair, enhancing the angles of her face. Sculpted perfection.

Jonas flitted around her, his camera capturing every nuance of her poise, excitement sparking in his voice. "Perfect, Detective! Now, look just past the camera—yes, that's it!"

Blackburn's relentless drive shone through as she focused her eyes just beyond the lens. With each snap, she embodied a fascinating duality: captivating beauty and stealthy strength. The stark contrast of her living presence against the sleek, cold vehicles hinted at an electrifying tension.

In some frames, the polished concrete beneath her reflected the cars, merging their identities into something cohesive. The atmosphere hummed with an empowering synergy, where beauty seamlessly intertwined with innovation. Lackeys oohed and ahhed as Jonas snapped and praised.

In the other photos, Blackburn stood against the backdrop of sleek, high-tech vehicles, the sun catching on the polished metal and throwing light across her features. She leaned against one of the cars, her stance relaxed but purposeful, as if both she and the machine shared an unspoken power. Long shadows stretched behind her, the scene taking on a moody, cinematic edge. The cars gleamed in the fading light, their chrome surfaces reflecting her figure. The interplay between her poised presence and the machine's quiet strength captured their authority.

Then, like a switch, Blackburn's expression faltered. Her intense gaze flicked toward Willow, who stood at the fringes, observing. Lust flashed in her eyes, a magnetic pull that parted her lips ever so slightly.

Jonas captured the brewing heat shining toward his lens. "Oh, that's fantastic!" he exclaimed, fingers racing over the shutter button. "Such intensity, such passion! You're a natural, Detective!"

Amused by his misguided enthusiasm, Blackburn allowed a small, knowing smile to dance across her lips while her eyes remained locked on Willow. The images captured that spark of desire layered with control, a complex energy that Jonas, buoyed by his own excitement, naively attributed entirely to his skill behind the camera.

As the photo shoot drew to a close, Jonas stood idle, satisfaction radiating from him like the fading sunlight. "That was incredible, Detective Blackburn," he beamed, the camera resting loosely around his neck. "I'll have the copies sent to you and Stan by tomorrow morning. You'll love them!"

Blackburn smiled, a gracious curve tinged with a shadowy undertone. "Thank you, Jonas. It was a pleasure," her words sliding out like smooth silk.

Just as the group dispersed, Blackburn pivoted, locking her gaze on Stan with a relaxed yet commanding presence. "Before we leave, mind if I take a closer look at the cars? I want to wander through the lot, get a feel for them."

Stan's face lit up, genuine delight breaking through. "Of course, Detective! Take all the time you need. It's an honor you're interested in our technology." He gestured widely toward the impressive rows of vehicles. "Please, explore to your heart's content."

With nods of farewell, Stan, Jonas, and the remaining team retreated into the building, leaving Blackburn and Willow alone in the sprawling lot. The sun dipped, long shadows stretching across the asphalt while the sleek cars basked in a dying glow.

Blackburn turned to Willow, mischief dancing in her eyes. "Stay close to me," she murmured, her tone low, simmering with command. Willow nodded, a shiver tickling her skin.

Chapter 12

Rows of cars held their line, paint catching the last light, reflecting two figures threading through the lot. The surfaces threw back Blackburn and Willow in thin, warped duplicates as they moved between bumpers and fenders.

Evening slid over the Stan Raider Group lot. Blackburn kept pace, chin tipped up to the camera domes along the building. She watched lens arcs, clocked timing by the red status blink, picked out the dead wedges where a body could vanish from view. She mapped approach, retreat, and the thirty-second window before the next sweep.

Satisfied, she turned to Willow. Authority and intent set in her eyes. "You're going to receive two commands to atone for your earlier mistakes, Fawn," she whispered, taking in the flinch and the flash of shock that moved through Willow's face.

Willow's breath caught. Her head dropped. Clean compliance. Blackburn noted the quiet grip and raised a finger.

Her phone rang. Blackburn took a deep breath, and pulled it from her pocket. Unknown number. She held it out. "Answer it."

Willow took it, fingers unsteady, then steadied. "Detective Blackburn's line," she said, professional in a beat.

"Atlanta Police Department. Can I speak with Detective Blackburn, please?"

Willow looked at Blackburn, and handed it over.

Blackburn's tone went flat and controlled. "Blackburn."

"Detective, this is Lieutenant Nate Harris from Atlanta PD, Homicide," the voice tight and low urgency, lacing his words. "We have your suspect in custody. Ira Malone. He was arrested earlier today. Your department was notified, but we haven't received an extradition packet."

Blackburn's spine set. Hand on warm metal. She let the facts arrange themselves. Hemingway had not sent the paperwork. This should not be her problem. Malone was Dawson's case. "Thank you for the update, Lieutenant Harris. I'll reach out to the prosecutor and get the paperwork moving." She cut the call.

Focus tightened in her face. Willow moved beside her and waited. "Everything okay?"

"No." Blackburn pulled in a breath and sorted next steps. "I need to contact the prosecutor's office. There's a problem." She looked over once, irritation showing and gone. "And I need to get you home."

Blackburn caught her and closed the gap. She kissed hard, a short, hot press, breath mixing. Her fingers hooked into Willow's hair and pulled for seal. She broke it clean, then put her mouth to Willow's ear. "You're lucky. Let's go."

She moved them through the metal bodies, Willow at her back. Reflections broke and reformed along the doors they passed, distorted echoes sliding by.

They reached Blackburn's black sedan. She opened the door and motioned Willow in.

The sun sank and left a hard band of purple-blue at the horizon. Blackburn took to the streets of New Dresden. GPS on, turns tight, speed measured, neon warming along the avenues. Signs flickered on and threw color across wet concrete. The engine hummed a steady base and held the silence between them. Willow's fingers twitched against her leg. Blackburn kept eyes ahead and hands steady on the wheel. Control sat in the space like static.

Willow shifted, mouth still marked by the kiss. She glanced over, light picking the angles in Blackburn's profile. "Good shoot today," she said, rough-voiced.

Blackburn didn't look away from the traffic. "Yeah, let's hope it impresses Chief Hayes," she said, flicking a wrist, tone even, the hunger audible for anyone trained to hear it.

A sleek blue self-driving cab moved alongside. Blackburn looked in. A driver sat slumped forward, passenger sprawled in back, both out. She tapped the horn. Nothing. She paced the cab, rolled down a window, and laid on the horn. The blast cut the street.

She braked, took a hard right, and reset the route. Willow grabbed the seat edge, startled at the fast course change.

They ran the dark streets. The tension climbed with the speed. Willow watched Blackburn's profile for anything readable and got stone.

"What can I do to help?" Willow asked, fighting the hum of the engine to be heard.

"I don't have all the information yet. There's nothing you can do right now."

"I could head into work if it would help—"

"No." It snapped out and cut the offer. "You need to go home."

Silence fell again. It ticked.

Blackburn put a hand on Willow's knee without warning. The contact broke the hold of the silence and pulled a small start from Willow. Blackburn kept her eyes ahead, let her mouth tilt. "You did well yesterday," she said, low. "I've missed that. The way you surrender control, the way you trust me implicitly."

Heat moved in Willow's face. A small smile. Devotion, simple and visible.

Blackburn reached across and slid across Willow's cheek, fingers skimming skin. "I'm looking forward to exploring that dynamic again," she said, the words deliberate. "About how good we were together, and how much better we could be now."

Willow leaned into the touch, breath catching. "I want that too," she said, voice trembling. "I've missed you, missed us, more than I can put into words."

Possession flared clean. Blackburn let it show in her eyes. "We're already making up for lost time," she said. Something fierce sparked in Blackburn's eyes.

She dropped her voice. A question sharpened into a test. "How long had it been?"

Willow's pulse picked up. "Forty-two days," she said, nearly under her breath, eyes down, the gap obvious.

Blackburn's hand tightened on her knee. A check, a message. "Forty-two days without me. How did you take care of yourself?" It came out like a confessional prompt. Willow swallowed.

Blackburn knew her heart. Willow had lived in pain until meeting Blackburn. Lonely nights, isolation, loathing. Her life was thick, scar on scar. Unloved and unlovable until a beautiful blonde angel pulled her from the abyss, taught her how to live, how to feel pleasure, how to love. Adore. Idolize. Hurting herself had been immediately forbidden.

A beat. Then the small nod. Throat tight. Eyes sliding away from the truth she couldn't say.

"Show me." Blackburn kept her voice low.

Shame shone in Willow's eyes, but refusal was not an option. She lifted her shirt, pulled back her bra, and exposed fresh scars. Three small parallel cuts, red and tender, set across her breast.

Blackburn felt heat go cold. Her hand dug into Willow's knee. "You know those are mine," she said, voice a growl. "Even when I'm not with you, your body is mine to claim. You've damaged what belongs to me."

Willow flinched. Excitement and fear sparked together. The pleasure of being owned threaded through it. She nodded once and took the logic.

"You remember every word of our contract?" Blackburn pulled her hand back. "You deserve to be punished for that." The edge of her voice vibrated.

Willow drew in a breath. "I agree."

A red light caught them. The moment hung on the stop. Blackburn looked at Willow and didn't look away. "Will it happen again?" Her intensity didn't drop. "Will. It. Happen. Again?"

Willow shook her head hard. Eyes begging. "No, never. I promise."

Green. Blackburn rolled them forward. Willow's heart knocked around her ribs. Her palms sweated. A flood of anxiety and want and love hit hard at once. She kept watching the set of Blackburn's mouth, the pulse at her throat, unable to look away.

Cars. Construction. Delivery bots. People. All in the way. Every breath Blackburn took was a choice to hold steady.

Willow shifted, bit at her lower lip, twisted her fingers in her lap, keeping herself from reaching.

The ride stretched, a clean, intentional strain. Every light another test. Willow wanted the end, the verdict, the release. She also fed on the build, letting the pressure stack in the sealed space, their small world holding it and holding it, promising a breaking point that would come when she was told.

As they pulled into Willow's apartment complex, Blackburn braked hard and set the gear in park. She turned, gaze steady and assessing.

"For damaging my property, for those three cuts, you will get three rocks from the parking lot," Blackburn decreed, her voice a compelling command. "And you will put them in your underwear. As punishment."

Willow went still. The quiet inside the car pressed against her until language slipped away. The order was absurd and exact. Her body leaned toward obedience before her mind caught up.

Blackburn watched her without blinking. "You'll keep them there until you've ordered a butter chicken dinner for me at the office," she said, even, controlled. "Then, and only then, are you free for the night." Soft delivery, but no give.

Willow's brows drew in, lips parting. Nothing came. She blinked fast, sorting the instruction, the terms, the limit. Blackburn didn't look away. That settled it. Willow nodded once, shoulders lowering.

"Get out and gather the rocks. Then come around to my window." Blackburn kept it crisp.

Willow's hand paused on the door handle. One breath. She opened it. Cool night air slid in across her skin. She stepped onto the gravel, each shift underfoot too loud. She crouched, fingers trembling as she scanned and picked three stones from the mix. As round and smooth as she could find in a second. Still, their edges pressed into her palm when she stood, a small churn of discomfort in her gut. She inhaled, set her jaw, and walked to the driver's side.

Blackburn had the window already down, elbow on the frame, eyes on Willow's approach. She didn't speak until Willow stopped beside the door. "Do it," she breathed.

Willow brushed off grit and, after a pause, slid the stones into her pants. The sudden cold shocked her skin. An intrusion. Also steadying.

Blackburn's mouth lifted, pleased at the compliance and the wince. "Now," she demanded, "kiss me."

Willow shifted, the rocks catching and pinching as she leaned in. Their mouths met, heat against constraint. The stones made sure she felt every movement. Desire threaded through the discomfort, pleasure edged by pain.

They broke. Blackburn's voice went ordinary, as if they'd discussed scheduling. "Goodbye," she said.

* * *

Willow stepped back. Blackburn's car eased away, leaving her in the lot with the weight tucked out of sight. She could have use her phone right now to order. But didn't.

The walk to her building was a series of checks and corrections. Each step rolled the stones against her most sensitive skin, sharp one second, blunt the next. Heat rose in her face. Embarrassment at the setup. Arousal still humming from the kiss. Blackburn's taste stayed with her, an anchor and an irritant.

The elevator doors slid open and she went in, the cabin bright and clean. In the mirror, the glass gave her back what it always did. Doughy curves, plain features. Not the woman Blackburn summoned out of her with a look. Yet Blackburn's gaze had registered something else. Appetite. Recognition.

The elevator chimed for the fourth floor. Willow moved out, gait tight, balancing pressure and a strange pleasure. Her keys rattled at the lock. The stones bit at each twist. The door opened into low light and quiet. She shut it behind her and leaned hard on the solid wood. It hurt.

Shoes off with a grimace, she headed for the bathroom. The tile leached cold into her soles. She went straight to the sink.

Her hands shook as she undressed enough to let the rocks fall. They hit the floor with a hard clatter. She crouched, gathered them fast, breath short. At the basin, she ran the tap hot and pumped antibacterial soap, scrubbing until foam covered her fingers. Rinse. Turn. Rinse again. She kept at it until they were clean to the eye and slick in her hands.

She glanced up mid-task. The mirror showed wide pupils behind her glasses, a precise mix of want and confusion. How much she felt for Blackburn sat in the set of her mouth, the tension at her temples. Exposed.

She took a towel and dried each stone with care. Every pat exact. The rough against plush registered in her fingertips. A sound left her throat before she could stop it. Raw. She pictured the stones resting at her throat like a hidden charm that tied her to her lover. She scrubbed herself quickly and functionally. Not the priority.

After putting on a fresh pair of underwear, Willow placed the rocks back inside. Cold again. Damp against skin. A gentle jab with each step. Better now that they were clean.

Blackburn's hold on her was total, a pull Willow did not contest. Logic had no weight here. Her Lioness's presence flipped her systems at once, power coursing through her even as she gave it up. A pattern she craved.

Food felt ridiculous with everything churning in her body. It was also the condition. She had a task. She took her phone with unsteady hands and tapped the number for her usual Indian place.

The ring sounded in her ear. Her mind slid toward Blackburn again, to what the rocks in her underwear would do to her eyes when she heard. Would Blackburn take it as proof, as provocation?

The line clicked, and a bright voice cut in. "Hello, Singh's Kitchen!"

"Hi, um, I need to place an order for delivery," Willow said, throat tight.

"Sure thing. What can I get for you?"

"Butter chicken, extra spicy, and a side of garlic naan." Willow's voice leveled, a small current of certainty returning. "And make sure it's really spicy this time," she added, a sly edge creeping in.

"You got it! Anything else?"

Willow paused, gathered herself. She hoped the spice wasn't too bold.

"No, that's everything. Thanks." She rattled off the address of the New Dresden police headquarters and her credit card details.

"Enjoy your meal," the voice chirped. "It'll be there in half an hour."

The call ended with a click. Willow exhaled and let the completed task settle over her, warm and heavy.

Chapter 13

Blackburn sat at her desk, the precinct's background noise sliding to a distant hum as her focus narrowed to a razor's edge. Phone pressed to her ear, she drummed impatient fingers against the wood, each tap counting seconds she had no intention of wasting. Anger simmered under her skin at the inexcusable delay. When she'd arrived at the office, she knew she had just missed her men. She wondered if Atlanta had called the office, and Dawson knew he'd better get out before she got there.

"Azhya Hemingway."

"Detective Blackburn. Homicide. Why hasn't the extradition request for Ira Malone been sent to Atlanta?" Her words cut clean through the line, cold and unforgiving. On the other end was the prosecutor.

"Let me get to my study."

Paper rustled as Azhya rifled through files, her sigh crackling across the connection. "Detective Blackburn. The holdup's on Mitch Dawson's end. He hasn't provided the proper paperwork."

Blackburn's jaw tightened. Her free hand curled, knuckles whitening. Colleagues' incompetence never ceased to offend. "Dawson was supposed to have that paperwork to you," she growled, eyes ticking to the clock, every second a personal affront.

"I know, Detective. I've been chasing him, but you know how he is. Always looking for the easy way out." Azhya's tone walked the line between placating and exasperated.

"What's outstanding?" Clipped, patience thinning.

"Primarily the cell phone information. The definitive link to Malone. Without that, we can't justify the request. He had it for the warrant, so it's just a matter of forwarding it along." Azhya kept things concise, eager to end the call. She wanted to get back to dinner and a life.

"Thank you." Blackburn ended it. The line went dead a heartbeat later.

Silence pressed in as she sat motionless. Dawson's negligence wasn't just cutting corners; it was dereliction masquerading as laziness. Rage pushed her up and into the bullpen, straight to Dawson's desk.

She went through the disarray, grateful for his disregard of clean desk protocol. The clutter, his slack approach, set her teeth on edge, but it meant the paperwork might still be buried here. "Where are you hiding it?" she hissed, barely above a breath, shuttling folders and loose sheets into his unlocked drawer, agitation rising.

Her hands moved fast over the detritus, hunting any trace of a link. A phone contract, a receipt, a screenshot with Malone's face. Nothing. The definitive tie between the suspect and the cell remained out of reach.

Lips pressed thin, she swept the desk again. A muscle jumped in her cheek. Scattered papers, misplaced files, timestamps that told on him. Was he truly this careless, or did his incompetence tilt toward intent? She was a magnet for jealousy, and jealousy begat desperation, which begat lies. The thought of conscious obstruction slid cold down her spine.

Sitting amid his mess, she felt control pull against her grip. The case, her team, her reputation, all teetered on the razor's edge of ruin because of one man's actions. Or inaction.

A commotion in the hallway pulled her from the paper drift. A delivery guy strode in, her butter chicken, her guilty pleasure, balanced in his hands. The rich aroma moved through the room, a brief reprieve from tension that never really left.

"Detective Blackburn?" He grinned, holding out the steaming container.

"Yeah, that's me." She forced a smile, took the food, tipped the kid, and returned to her desk. The scent loosened her shoulders by degrees. She ran options, weighing outcomes with the same cool math she used everywhere else. One thing was certain, Dawson would pay.

She set the butter chicken down and paused. Willow, rocks, rough edges against soft flesh flickered across her mind.

With that, she dug in. "Oh, this is spicy. This is going to give me heartburn." Blackburn sighed and tossed her bamboo fork into the food, and the container into the garbage.

* * *

In the dim Irish pub, the air smelled of stale beer and fry oil. Four men huddled at a weathered table, condensation tracking down half-empty pints. Dawson, cheeks flushed, let a belch rattle the glasses. Sinclair, unwilling to be outdone, answered with his own, the sound of his name lost in the guttural release. Laughter popped and bounced off dark wood.

Cooper's nose wrinkled, lips curling. "Christ, do you have to be so fucking crass?"

Dawson swiped at watering eyes, a smirk riding his mouth. "Aww, what's the matter? Jealous you can't burp worth a damn?"

Reeves's shoulders shook, his head dipping. "He's not wrong, you know."

Their laughter thinned as Reeves's phone buzzed against the table, the screen's pale light cutting his face. He glanced down, then pushed back his chair, legs scraping the sticky floor. "Duty calls, gentlemen."

Dawson's grin went sly, words slurring at the edges. "The ol' ball and chain beckons, eh?"

Reeves's jaw set, eyes hardening to flint. "At least I'm not some little miserable divorced fuck."

The easy camaraderie evaporated as quickly as spilled beer on hot concrete.

Cooper cleared his throat, hunting an exit. "You good to drive, man?"

Reeves shook his head, gaze still pinned to Dawson. "Nah, my self-driving ride will be here in a few."

Cooper perked, sensing relief. "Any chance I could snag a lift? Got a date just a mile away."

Reeves shrugged, anger bleeding out. "Yeah, alright."

They threaded through the crowd, the door thudding shut behind them. Dawson and Sinclair remained, argument settling over them like a suffocating blanket, the room's energy flattening to match the beer.

Dawson lifted a finger to the bartender. "Another round, bro." He turned to Sinclair, alcohol softening the lines of his face. "Fucking Reeves and his cabs. I'm looking forward to them. Those new autonomous rides the department's rolling out."

Sinclair snorted, mouth twisting. "Why? Too lazy to drive your own damn self around?"

Dawson leaned back. His chair creaked under him. "Nah, man. It's about working smarter, not harder."

Sinclair's eyebrows shot up, a chuckle breaking free. "Shit, that sounds like something straight outta Blackburn's mouth."

At her name, Dawson's eyes darkened. His upper lip twitched as he spat out the next words, dots of spit speckling the table. "Fuck that bitch. Always riding my ass, like she's got nothing better to do."

Sinclair's eyes lit with something wicked. His tongue flicked across his lips. "I'd like to ride her ass." He thrust his tongue out in a crude pantomime.

Dawson grimaced, nose wrinkling. "Christ, you're a fucking pig."

Sinclair laughed, the sound harsh in the tight space. "Like you wouldn't jump at the chance."

Dawson shook his head, fingers tightening around his empty glass. "Not even with a borrowed dick."

The bartender arrived with two frosty mugs. He set them down with a thunk, foam sloshing. Dawson and Sinclair reached for their drinks. "Cheers," they said together.

Dawson drank long, the cold working against the heat of his temper. He set the mug down hard and wiped his mouth with the back of his hand. "All I'm saying is, those self-driving cars are gonna make our lives a hell of a lot easier. No more worrying about DUIs. And when it drives me to the scene of some fucking murder, it can handle the goddamned traffic."

Sinclair shrugged, interest already thinning. "Whatever you say, man. I still think it's just an excuse for lazy fucks like you to avoid doing any real work."

Dawson's jaw flexed, the retort right there. He swallowed it. No point arguing when Sinclair went all piss and vinegar and looked for a fight.

He lifted his beer again. Amber sloshed against his teeth, a few drops escaped and ran down his chin. He dropped the glass onto the table, the clunk cutting through the room. "She's fucking insufferable," he said, venom in it. "Strutting around like she owns the goddamn place, rubbing her perfect solve rate in everyone's face. Like we're all just there to bask in her brilliance."

Sinclair leaned back. The chair complained. A smirk returned as he raised his drink, then paused. "You can't deny it's impressive, though. A record like that? Unheard of."

Dawson sneered, lip curling. "It's all a fucking act. No one's that flawless. She's just putting on a show, making sure everyone knows she's the only one who can do the job. Doesn't leave any room for the rest of us to breathe."

Sinclair's eyes glinted in the low light. "Confidence is sexy. It's why she's so damn good. No second-guessing, always one step ahead. That's hot in a leader."

Dawson scoffed, his breath beer-sour. "You're thinking with your dick. She's a manipulative, power-hungry bitch who cares more about her image than the cases or the people around her."

Sinclair's gaze went distant, almost dreamy. "There's something about the way she works. The precision, the focus. It's more than just a pretty face. She's got something you can't fake."

Dawson leaned in, voice dropping. "It's all a fucking lie. She's got you wrapped around her finger, just like everyone else. Makes you feel special, like you're lucky to be in the same room with her."

Sinclair grinned, challenge bright in his eyes. "Maybe I like being in her orbit. Feels pretty damn good when she's looking your way."

Dawson sat back, his face hardening. "Keep dreaming. She'll chew you up and spit you out, just like all the rest. Just you wait."

Sinclair's laughter rang out, harsh and grating. "Spit, swallow. I don't give a fuck. I'm gonna enjoy every minute of it."

* * *

The rocks against her flesh felt strange and solid. Willow's breath hitched as she shifted, rough edges pressing. A shiver ran her spine, goosebumps lifted across her arms.

Blackburn's food would have arrived by now. A spicy kiss. She decided to run a bath, heat to answer the nipping between her legs. She would keep the rocks in place with her hands, for now.

In the bathroom, candles threw shadows across tile. Water whispered, promising warmth to soothe the ache. Willow sank into the tub, hands cradling her secret. Submerged, body blurred, stones held fast. Eyes closed, she conjured phantom fingers in place of her own. Blackburn's touch, calculated and unyielding.

Bathwater wrapped Willow as rough edges teased, a sharp counter to liquid heat. The smallest shift sent shivers racing.

She imagined fingers playing over the stones. She marveled at Blackburn's effortless control of her. The bath's warmth amplified the rush coursing through her as she thought of Blackburn. She swallowed hard, fighting the constant urge to check her phone. One wrong move could unravel everything. Blackburn could vanish, a whisper in the night, as she had before. The thought cinched around Willow's chest, a band of anxiety squeezing the air thin.

In that suspended moment, Willow made a silent vow. She would savor every shared breath, every brush of skin against skin. She would embrace the labyrinthine depths of their connection, cherish each twist and turn. She would cling to Blackburn's affection like a lifeline cast into a churning sea. Above all, she would never let go.

The rocks became an idol, a secret talisman binding them soul-to-soul.

Lost in reverie, time slid past. Candles flickered, shadows writhing on the walls. Cooling water whispered against her skin, a soft pull back to the room. With a shuddering sigh, Willow rose from the tub's embrace and left the stones gleaming on its edge.

She toweled off with reverent touches, then slipped into worn pajamas.

In the bedroom's hush, she arranged the rocks on her nightstand. She paused, drinking in their plain weight, their quiet power to steady a spinning world.

Willow blinked, the clock's tick loud in her ears. She glanced at the time, a jolt running through as she realized how long she'd drifted. She moved to the balcony, seeking the cool of the dark. The apartment's heat clung to her skin, a veil she wanted off.

Elbows on the railing, she tilted her face to the sky. Stars winked back, distant and unknowable. She searched their cold light for answers, for reassurance that Blackburn's presence in her life was an immutable truth.

In the bedroom's shadowed calm, Willow moved. The closet door whispered open, letting out secrets. Her hand found a shoebox on the highest shelf, unassuming and full. This container held a treasure trove of tempestuous memories she shared with Blackburn.

Perched on the bed's edge, Willow lifted the lid with careful fingers. Inside, a black leather collar gleamed. The first talisman Blackburn had pressed against her throat. A totem of their power exchange, a sacred relic that still lit an inferno at her core. Willow stroked the supple leather, surrendering to sense-memories from that unforgettable night.

Beside the collar, faded photographs lay, relics of brighter days. Each image held passion, pain, moments alive with warmth. A small gallery of love.

Scattered among the photos, handwritten notes whispered for Willow to decipher. Inside jokes, sweet murmurs, explicit guidelines for their passionate rendezvous on the pages, steeped in their shared history.

With care, Willow placed the three stones into the shoebox. Their rigidity stood stark against the collar's softness and the photographs' delicate feel. She closed the lid and returned the box to its sanctuary in the closet.

Darkness gathered as Willow switched off the light and crawled into bed. A romance movie flickered, glow washing over her, easing the day's intensity. She let herself sink into the familiar comfort of the story on the screen, a small escape from the relentless ache in her chest.

Night settled over the apartment. The sky stretched calm beyond the windows. Willow's mind wandered over the day's events, each charged moment returning.

As the movie built to a crescendo, her eyelids grew heavy. The rhythm pulled her under.

Her eyes closed. Her mind went quiet.

In dreams, Willow stood before a majestic throne, the three stones glittering atop it like captured stars. They pulsed with an ancient, primal power, beckoning her closer. When her fingers brushed their surface, energy surged through her, igniting every nerve with a clean blaze. In that moment, she knew she could command the respect she craved in the world of technology, even as she surrendered to the demands of her lover. The dream shifted, the stones melting into shimmering lines of code that poured from the monitor in a blinding cascade, engulfing her in their radiance.

Chapter 14

Early morning rain traced diagonal lines down the window of Blackburn's office, distorting the gray morning light. She spread the Evan Hart case files across her desk, each document and photograph arranged with precise intention, edges catching against her fingertips as she squared them to the blotter.

The victim's sister's statement drew her attention first. "Evan wasn't into drugs," she had insisted. "He never touched the stuff." Major Crimes hadn't gotten to interview Evan himself. He had died without regaining consciousness. But dead men left evidence, and evidence spoke.

Blackburn lifted one of the crime scene photographs, studying the cast impressions of boot prints left at the burial site. Wide, blocky lugs formed a distinctive tread pattern, while a second set of shoes with chevrons cut sharp angles through the plaster, the solvent-ink smell of the print faint and chemical. Someone had taken care with these casts, each ridge and groove captured with scientific precision. She made a mental note to thank the CSU team for their thoroughness, and to spend that praise on a priority tread match.

The plastic bag came next. Translucent red, biodegradable, 26 by 33 inches. Torn apart where Evan had clawed at his face. She set the photo aside, reaching for Dr. Burani's autopsy report, paper rasping her thumb. The clinical language did nothing to soften the brutality it described. Gunshot wound to the head. Traumatic brain injury. A constellation of bruises, abrasions, and lacerations mapped the violence inflicted on Evan Hart's body. Three fingernails torn away. Digging himself out, most likely. Dirt in his lungs.

Not the gunshot. Not the beating. Insulin. Blackburn's eyes narrowed as she re-read the toxicology findings. Cause of death was insulin overdose, the doctor's neat handwriting noting the unusual circumstance, death had come so quickly after the attempt on his life that she'd conducted an especially thorough autopsy. The blood work told its own story. Elevated insulin levels paired with correspondingly low C-peptide. Someone had administered the insulin directly. This wasn't natural causes.

Blackburn pushed back from her desk, letting her mind work through the connections, the clean click of a mechanism falling into place. Evan had been trying to buy hydromorphone. Dilaudid, specifically the 8mg pills. Those weren't street drugs, they came from hospitals, usually stolen and resold. The same hospital where, Evan said, he'd met Tom.

The rain intensified, drumming against the glass as Blackburn pieced it together, syncing her breathing to its metronome as the field narrowed. A dealer working the ER, picking out patients in pain, offering relief at a price. Someone who knew the hospital's rhythms, who would not draw attention in the chaos. Someone named Tom. Maybe an employee, maybe a regular visitor. Maybe a shark.

New Dresden Regional Hospital's emergency room needed a visit. She gathered her notes, sliding them into her satchel, the strap biting into her shoulder in a way she allowed. The case was taking shape in her mind. Did the killer make a second attempt, or was it unrelated? Either the same hand circling back or a second predator. One simplified the target list.

The rain had soaked through her jacket by the time she reached her car, but Blackburn barely noticed. Her focus had narrowed to the investigation's next steps, to the questions that needed asking, to the leverage to be applied.

The emergency room doors parted with a soft hydraulic sigh, releasing a wave of antiseptic air that carried the underlying scents of fear and pain. The sting hit the back of her throat. Blackburn let it tighten her focus. She scanned the waiting area, categorizing each person present with brisk economy. No obvious dealers, but that meant nothing. The best predators knew how to blend in with their prey.

Ten people occupied the hard plastic chairs. An elderly couple leaning into each other for support, two middle-aged men nursing visible injuries, a family of three with a child who couldn't stay still, and several younger people trying to contain their discomfort. All of them projected legitimate need. The tight faces of genuine pain, the restless movements of genuine anxiety. None displayed the predatory awareness of someone working the room. No head-on stare, no angle on a purse, no appetite that clocked her badge and recalculated.

The security guard's desk stood empty, but Blackburn spotted him making his rounds. Older man, weathered face, alert eyes that tracked her approach. His name badge read "Beek," but she didn't bother using it. A name was a lever. She would pull it when it bought something.

"Detective Blackburn," she said, presenting her badge. "I need to speak with the medical staff about their time during Evan Hart's final hours."

He studied her credentials longer than necessary, professional caution warring with bureaucratic procedure. She let the pause work, said nothing, watched him decide. "You'll want the nurses' station," he said finally, gesturing down the hallway. "Second intersection, can't miss it."

The corridor stretched before her, hard white LEDs casting everything in stark relief. The hum needled at the base of her skull. Every surface gleamed with aggressive cleanliness, but Blackburn knew better than most how much darkness could hide behind institutional shine. She kept her pace unhurried. She owned the space as she moved through it.

The nurses' station rose like a fortress, screens glowing with patient data while staff moved through their duties. A clerk turned a monitor a fraction away when she drew near. Another avoided her eye and over-explained to no one. Blackburn approached the counter, badge already in hand, and set her forearm on the edge. The station adjusted around her.

"I need to speak with someone about Evan Hart," she said, keeping her voice pitched for authority without aggression. "Nothing covered by privacy, of course. Just routine 'did you see anything' types of questions."

"That would be me." The voice came from behind her, accented and precise. Blackburn turned to find herself facing a woman in her mid-fifties, plastic-rimmed glasses perched on a narrow nose. "Dr. Krejcikova. I was on duty that night."

The doctor's movements were restrained, his hands speaking in small, precise gestures as he led Blackburn to a quieter spot near the wall. The antiseptic bite hung higher here, threaded with coffee gone stale. "Evan appeared to be recovering well," he said, each word carefully chosen. "The sudden heart attack was... unexpected."

"How long did it take you to respond to the Code Blue?" Blackburn watched the doctor's face, noting the slight tightening around his eyes.

"I was with another patient. Perhaps... three minutes? Four? Marie Austin, our nurse manager, she called for a Code Blue." Dr. Krejcikova's accent thickened slightly, betraying tension. "By the time I arrived, it was clear we were losing him."

Blackburn made a note, her pen scratching quietly against her notebook. Three to four. In an arrest report, that was a window. In a hospital, it was a liability. "Who else was working that shift?"

The doctor's eyes unfocused slightly as he recalled. "Marie Austin, as I mentioned. Thomas Greene. Lidia Muhammad. Benjamin

Shaw." Each name came with a slight pause, as if being checked against memory. She noted each name. She circled Thomas.

"I'd like to speak with Marie Austin."

"She's in a meeting," a nurse offered, not looking up from her computer screen. "Budget review with administration."

Blackburn's jaw tightened imperceptibly. A meeting. She let the word sit. Policy could cut through that in seconds if she chose. "Thomas Greene, then."

Dr. Krejcikova nodded to a younger nurse, who picked up a phone and paged Greene. The waiting settled around them, heavy with unspoken questions. Blackburn used the time to observe the staff's movements, their interactions, the subtle hierarchies at play. A tech slowed when he spotted her and then sped up, overcorrecting. Someone killed the volume of a TV without being asked. Somewhere in this carefully ordered system, someone had seen something. Someone knew something.

The LED lights hummed overhead, their clean brightness doing nothing to dispel Blackburn's thoughts. The sound threaded under the ring of phones and the intermittent alarms, a steady needle against her nerves. She'd seen too many cases where institutional efficiency became the perfect cover for calculated violence. The hospital's rhythms continued around her. Call buttons chiming, phones ringing, the constant flow of patients and staff, all while she waited for Thomas Greene to appear. She held her ground and made the waiting belong to them.

Thomas Greene arrived at the nurses' station with the movements Blackburn expected of anyone who lived on a schedule carved into fifteen-minute blocks. Lean, keyed-up, tuned to other people's weather. Useful.

"Detective Blackburn," she said, offering her hand. He matched her pressure exactly, reflective instinct already on display. "Do you go by Thomas or Thom?"

"Thomas," he said, quick and clipped. "Never Thom." His shoulders tightened around the word as if bracing.

"We need somewhere quiet," she said, voice low and even. "Private."

"The break room," he offered, already in motion. "It's empty most of the day."

They'd barely cleared the station before she clocked it. A laundry hamper by the room door, the hand-scrawled sign taped to the plastic lid. *Soiled gowns only.* The translucent red bag hanging half full under it looked to be the same make and color as the one that Evan had clawed at. Her pulse lifted. She let her breath slow a shade, just enough. Thomas glanced back and smiled. She consciously matched the rhythm of his breathing. Short. Sharp.

She had to control it.

The break room held the residue of long nights. A coffee machine sighing, a microwave clock blinking 12:00 like a small failure, a wall of dented lockers with taped-on names and residue from names before. The air smelled faintly of disinfectant over reheated pasta. A corkboard announced a potluck no one would attend.

Thomas hovered by a two-top and waited. Blackburn sat first.

"I know you can't give me any medical information. I won't ask. Walk me through your shift the night Evan Hart died," she said, keeping her tone level, the cadence steady enough to set a metronome. His shoulders softened half a notch.

"Routine," he said. "I checked on him during my rounds. Everything seemed fine." His eyes flicked to the door and back. Tell noted.

While he talked, she glanced down. His shoes were clean, hospital-issued with a chevron tread. Wrong geometry, wrong depth. They didn't match any of the prints lifted from the crime scene. One thing off the list.

"Okay," she said. After years of saying that word, is slid easily off her tongue. It controlled breath. It calmed heartbeats. "Okay."

She crossed her right leg over her left, hands loose on the table, breath rhythmic. He copied her posture beat for beat without knowing he had, fingers lacing the way hers did, ankle settling into a careful angle. Good boy.

The door opened. A doctor stepped in, gave them a casual nod. "Hey, Thom." The name hit a nerve. Thomas's jaw clicked tight, but he said nothing. The doctor spun his locker open, swapped his rubber-soled hospital clogs for street shoes, shrugged out of his white coat, then left with a soft thud of the door.

"You're certain everything was fine?" Blackburn asked, not changing her volume, not changing her pace. "No concerns noted. Nothing unusual."

"None," he said. His fingers tightened against each other before he made himself uncurl them. "I did my checks and moved on."

She let a small silence land. Then, "Thank you, Thomas."

They stood. In the corridor, LED light flattened everything to one plane. Marie Austin appeared at the far end as if summoned by the word. Steel-gray hair pulled back, eyes that took inventory in a blink. Authority gathered tight around her like a well-worn coat.

"Detective," Marie said, stopping in front of them. Professional, clipped.

Thomas seized the exit she offered. "I should get back to my rounds." He looked at Blackburn without meeting her eyes, and relief moved him faster than his feet. She nodded him on.

"Ms. Austin," Blackburn said. "If you have a moment."

Marie gestured back toward the door they had just cleared. "In there is fine."

They returned to the break room. The air felt fresh on reentry, smaller. Blackburn took Thomas's vacated chair. She didn't bother with mirroring now. Marie Austin would not bend to someone else's pattern. Blackburn adjusted to that truth with the same care she used for everything else that mattered.

The break room's light was unforgiving, all glare and angles, the kind that stripped color from skin and patience from anyone stuck beneath it. Blackburn let it do its work. She watched Marie across the small table, studying the planes of her face for anything that didn't belong. Fear, deflection, the hairline fracture in a composed expression. Marie met the look with calm, the nurse manager's authority sitting on her like a clean, pressed coat. This one would require careful handling.

"As nurse manager, you oversee the medication inventory," Blackburn said. She kept her tone loose and faintly bored, as if this were a box to tick on a long list.

"Yes." Clipped and even. "Every shift, every dispensation, every return. But I thought you were here about Evan Hart."

"I am. These are just routine questions. Staffing. Medication. Just crossing Ts. Any problems with your tracking system?" Blackburn's eyes slid to Marie's hands on the tabletop. Steady, almost still. Almost. The right index finger tapped once against the pad of her thumb and stopped.

"No." The answer arrived, too sure. "Our protocols are thorough."

Blackburn eased back in her chair, shoulders softening. She let a thread of concern into her voice, the small concession that signals cooperation rather than threat. "This isn't about paperwork. I'm not here to make waves. I'm not even the lead detective. The last thing I want is to take this to your CEO or see anyone lose a job over something we could just as easily handle with a conversation."

A change, slight and immediate. A loosening around the eyes, a shift at the jaw. Marie exhaled. "There have been discrepancies," she said, choosing the word with care. "With the dihydromorphinone and oxycodone. We're investigating internally."

"Missing pills?" Blackburn kept it gentle.

"Yes." A seam opened in the professional veneer. "Eight-milligram tablets specifically. We've adjusted our security procedures, but..." She let the rest stay implied.

Blackburn nodded once. "Who worked directly with Evan that night?"

The names came without hesitation. "Thomas did a saline line flush. Benjamin did another later. Georgina checked his vitals."

"Two line flushes in one shift?" Blackburn let the question hang as if she were talking to herself.

"We might do twenty or more with some patients," Marie said, a defensive note entering the control again. "It's standard."

Blackburn wrote, the scratch of her pen the only sound for a moment. She closed her notebook with care. "You've been helpful."

Marie stood, reclaiming the coat of authority she'd shrugged free of a minute before. "Oh, that's it? Will you need anything else?"

"Not right now." Blackburn rose. "No. Just routine questions."

The corridors outside felt altered as she moved through them, no longer neutral hallways but channels carrying something darker beneath the bright work of care. The emergency doors parted on their motor's patient sigh, releasing her into a gray afternoon where the rain had thinned to a mist.

Her car waited under a sheen of beads. She slid behind the wheel and didn't turn the key. She sat with the quiet tick of rain on glass and let the pieces fall into place.

Dihydromorphinone gone. Eight-milligram tabs. Two separate hands on Evan Hart's IV in the same shift. A man who had tried to buy hospital-grade narcotics, found instead by insulin. Thomas, who swore he was never "Thom," the kind of correction a man makes when he wants to be known exactly, shoes that didn't match the prints but a nervous energy that spoke to something deeper. Patterns. Names. The beginning of a map.

Blackburn started the engine. The purr barely rose above the gentle hiss of weather. She had the thread now.

She eased out of the lot. The wipers kept steady time. Behind her, New Dresden Regional resumed its endless rhythm. Healing and harm, life and death, and whatever shadows ride between. There were more questions to put to the same faces, more threads to pull until the weave came apart. For now, there was enough to begin unwinding the knot that had cinched shut around Evan Hart.

Chapter 15

Blackburn carved through the paperwork, each page turning with the whisper of a blade. Her jaw carved angles in the morning light streaming through venetian blinds, shadows striping her face in bars of concentration. The buff folder lay open before her, Brynn's data request, and her fingers drummed a funeral march against mahogany, hunting for the flaw that would let her bury it.

Yesterday felt like theater now. She had dressed down Dawson about the Malone extradition, her voice sharp enough to draw blood. Teased Reeves when he stumbled from his autonomous cab like a man afraid of his own shadow. Ignored Sinclair because his desperation for her attention tasted like copper pennies on her tongue.

Today brought Cooper to her door.

A tentative knock fractured her focus. He filled the frame, all shoulders and careful politeness, a blue binder tucked against his ribs like armor, coffee balanced in his other hand like an offering to an unpredictable god. Clean-shaven jaw, eyes that asked permission for breath itself.

She didn't lift her gaze, only tilted her head a fraction. "What?" The word hung in the air between them, neutral as a scalpel.

"Boss, I need about half an hour. It's CCTR-02399. Almost three months old now." His voice roughened. "It's giving me nightmares."

That brought her eyes up. Full attention, sharp as a spotlight. The buff folder whispered aside.

He entered her gravity, sinking into the chair opposite. Relief loosened his shoulders. "Thanks for your time, ma'am." He extended the coffee like a peace treaty. "Tall, skinny latte, single pump of caramel, just as you like."

The cup warmed her palms through its cardboard sleeve. She drank, let the heat anchor her pulse, let caramel cut through espresso bitterness like mercy through judgment. Her eyes closed for a heartbeat, the closest she came to vulnerability. The cup settled against her desk with barely a sound.

"Tell me about the case."

Cooper leaned forward, conspiracy made flesh. "Young woman, nude, strangled in an alley behind the restaurants parallel to Guildwood, between Whitecap and Pharmacy. Known spot where prostitutes take clients."

She rotated the binder toward herself, pages falling open to reveal what someone's daughter had become. The alley materialized in her memory. Delivery routes carved through urban decay, shadowed doorways that had witnessed her own desperate encounters years ago when loneliness wore her down to bone. A ghost of a smile touched her lips, died there.

"Female victim, 18-25, Caucasian, short blonde hair." Cooper's hand raked through his own hair, a nervous tell she filed away. "No clothes, no ID, no tattoos, no jewelry. Nothing to identify her."

She turned to the autopsy photos. Clinical lines documenting the end of someone who had once learned to walk, to speak her first word. The bureaucracy of death reduced to measurements and angles.

Cooper's voice stayed steady while she read, but she heard the tremor underneath. Jane Doe. No prints in any system. Time of death between 7 and 10 AM on May 3, discovered by a delivery driver who would carry this image to his grave. One witness reported a loud motorcycle. Probably meaningless.

Bruising circled the throat like a terrible necklace. Manual strangulation. No defensive wounds. She'd trusted her killer or been taken by surprise. Tox screen clean as morning rain. No drugs to soften the terror of those final moments.

No clothing, no personal effects, nothing in nearby dumpsters. The killer had been methodical, careful. Signs of recent sexual activity. A thread to pull, if she could find where it led.

"What's giving you nightmares?"

"Boss, she had dirt inside her."

"Dirt?" Her brow furrowed. "She ate dirt?"

He shook his head, color draining from his face. "No, ma'am. She was packed with dirt. Every orifice."

She let the report settle against the desk, laced her fingers like a prayer she'd never say. The air in the room grew heavy.

"What?" The word came out flat, dangerous.

Cooper rolled his shoulders as if he could shake off the images. "Packed full of it. Mouth, vagina, anus." His voice cracked like ice under pressure. "I mean, who does this? What kind of man does this?"

Her lips pressed into a line thin as wire. She studied the ceiling tiles for one beat, two, letting the horror settle into the place where she kept all the other horrors.

"Any similar cases?"

"No. A couple of older cases across the country, but in each of those, the killer's still behind bars, ma'am. There was a lot. The photos are in Section 32." He tapped the binder like it might bite.

She drank again, let heat and caffeine fortify her against what she was about to see. Section 32 opened like a wound. The photographs locked her attention with magnetic horror.

"And you haven't identified her?"

His shoulders sagged under invisible weight, voice roughening like sandpaper on raw wood. "We released a sketch shortly after she was found. Good media coverage, but not a single call."

"Remind me of the exact location."

"The alley between Whitecap and Pharmacy."

She nodded. The corridor behind kitchen kingdoms. Loading doors like mouths in brick walls, dumpsters squatting like metal toads, light struggling through even at noon. Wide enough for trucks, the asphalt pitted and scarred, puddles reflecting nothing but sky. Doorways carved deep enough for secrets. Useful and filthy, like so many things in this city.

Cooper watched her think, recognizing the machinery of her mind engaging. "What are you thinking?"

She ignored the question. "Was there any evidence found at the scene? Anything at all?"

"Everything we found—water bottles, condoms, cigarette butts—all too old and weathered to be connected. He took her clothing and everything else to stop us from easily identifying her."

She turned to her computer, brought up a map. The screen glowed like an oracle. "Find me all of the dirt photos."

He flipped pages while she summoned aerials, the city spreading below them like a circuit board of human desire and failure.

She studied three close photographs. Dry, reddish-brown earth the color of dried blood. Brown and green leaves holding color beneath decay's advance. Pine needles scattered like tiny spears. Small twigs. Serrated leaves sharp enough to cut skin.

From her peripheral vision, she felt Sinclair's attention like heat from a furnace. His eyes tracked the motion of her brushing hair from her shoulder, his hand freezing over his keyboard as if her gesture had stopped time itself. She frowned and flicked her gaze toward him. A dismissal sharp as a blade. He looked down, resumed typing with the mechanical rhythm of a man trying to convince himself he hadn't been caught staring.

Cooper rounded her desk, leaning into her space. "What am I looking at?" His voice dropped low, curious as a confessional.

"Point out where the dirt and leaves came from."

He took the mouse, swept across the digital landscape. Zoomed in, panned out, searched with the desperation of a man looking for salvation. After a minute that stretched like an hour, he surrendered the mouse and shook his head. "I don't see anywhere."

"Wait." Understanding dawned in his voice like sunrise. "Does that mean she was killed somewhere else?"

She nodded once, decisive as a judge's gavel. "Since there's no dirt like that in the area, she was killed elsewhere and dumped there. The motorcycle sound is irrelevant. No one transported a body on a motorcycle."

Cooper huffed, swallowed coffee like it was medicine. "Now we have to find a crime scene that could be almost anywhere."

"She was found within hours of her death." Each word precise as a surgeon's cut. "The scene has to be within driving distance of that location."

"True, but it's still too large an area to search effectively."

She kept her eyes on the photographs, seeing not just evidence but possibility. Her drawer whispered open, revealing arrow-shaped sticky notes like tiny weapons. A yellow arrow peeled away with the sound of skin separating. She placed its point against a brown leaf in the first photograph.

Cooper watched her hands move with the fascination of a man witnessing magic. Another arrow to a green leaf. A third to a pine needle. A fourth to a serrated leaf. The next to twigs. The final three to the reddish-brown earth in each photograph, marking territory like a general planning a campaign.

His chair creaked as he leaned forward, eyes moving between her hands and the images like he was reading scripture. He stayed quiet, understanding that revelation required patience.

She turned the binder back to him, the look she gave him equal parts reward and challenge. "You can identify the crime scene location once you identify each of these leaves and the dirt."

He frowned, confusion creasing his forehead. "How am I supposed to do that? They could be from anywhere."

She laughed once, a sound sharp enough to cut glass. "They could be from anywhere except that alley." The mockery in it was gentle, almost fond. She leaned forward without rising, held his eyes like she was holding his future. "Contact the city arborist, or forester, or park ranger, or whoever the city has who knows about plants. Ask them to identify these. Once they tell you what these leaves are, and maybe where that type of dirt comes from, you can ask where all of it can be found together."

Understanding exploded across his features like fireworks. "Oh!" He straightened as if electricity had coursed through his spine. "Since all of this was found inside her, she must have been killed in a place where all these plants grow close together."

She nodded once, tapped her temple with one finger. "Good man. That's right. Good thinking."

He lit up like Christmas morning. Back straight, binder clutched in hands that trembled with excitement. He practically levitated as he stood. "Hey guys! Check this out!"

She shook her head, amusement softening the edges of her mouth for just a moment. Then the buff folder whispered back toward her across the desk. Her face hardened like concrete setting as she opened it and returned to Brynn's request, other people's ambitions settling on her shoulders like snow that would never melt.

Chapter 16

Day bled into night, the precinct slipping from bustle to something that held its breath and waited. Blackburn sat at her desk while the lamp carved a circle of white heat across scattered papers, case files catching light like broken glass. The building had shed its daytime skin. LEDs cut to bone, exit signs bleeding their dull red into corners, the rest surrendering to shadow. Cleaner carts hummed their mechanical prayers in distant corridors while the old frame settled into its bones with the tired sigh of something that had seen too much.

Well past midnight now. Her eyes moved across print like fingers reading braille, pupils contracting against the lamp's relentless glare.

She dragged fingers through blonde hair that had lost its morning perfection, strands roughened by hours of unconscious tugging when the cases wouldn't yield their secrets. The coffee mug beside her elbow sat empty, its ceramic walls stained with the archaeology of a long day. Rings of brown sediment marking each desperate refill. She pushed it aside without looking, her attention claimed by the Stan Raider Group's partnership documents that had arrived like a virus in her inbox, multiplying into protocols and procedures that demanded her complete anatomical knowledge.

She blinked until the blur sharpened into focus. Rolled shoulders that carried knots of tension like rosary beads, each one marking another hour spent hunched over evidence that refused to confess. The wall clock's plastic tick found the base of her skull and took up residence there, a metronome counting down to something she couldn't name. Her gaze stayed surgical, cutting through margins and subtext with the precision of someone who understood that details were where cases lived or died.

When something snagged her attention, the pen descended like a raptor, red ink flowing in tight script that transformed margins into battlefields of annotation. She didn't need to announce her thoroughness; the evidence mountain beside her elbow testified with obsession made manifest.

Blackburn found there was so much more to the project than the public would ever be told.

Air conditioning breathed its steady arctic exhale across the back of her neck, lifting the fine hairs there in a shiver she refused to acknowledge. The bullpen had been abandoned to darkness, desks standing like tombstones in the blue glow of emergency lighting. The faint cocktail of toner dust and burnt coffee hung in the air, threaded with bleach trails from the cleaning crew's passage.

For her, the work never ceased its demands. Reputation wasn't built on promises but on the evidence board that told its unforgiving story. Her name sitting alone at the top of the clearance column like a sniper's position. Every closed case, every arrest that held water in court, wasn't virtue but proof that she could do what others couldn't: transform chaos into conviction.

The cleaning crew drifted past like ghosts, their voices barely registering as human speech. One paused in the doorway, caught between admiration and concern for the woman who worked while the city slept. She existed in a sphere of concentration so complete that his presence failed to penetrate its borders.

Her attention snapped to the Malone file like a compass finding true north. She lifted the receiver, pressed #8 for Dawson's cell, and listened to rings that struck her nervous system like hammer blows. Each hollow pause between rings gave space for heat to bloom across her scalp, anger building with mathematical precision.

Voicemail. "You've reached Detective Dawson. Leave a message." The beep arrived like a period at the end of a sentence she'd rather not finish.

"Dawson." Her voice carried the temperature of a morgue drawer sliding open. "You're holding two pieces of paper that stand between us and losing Malone permanently. The phone records and the 77C extradition packet need to be filed with the clerk before 0900, or our probable cause evaporates like morning dew. This isn't a request for a favor. It's basic competence. Do your job."

The receiver met its cradle with more force than necessary, plastic striking plastic with the finality of a gavel.

She moved to Sinclair's folder, thick as a metropolitan phone book and stamped with his name like a brand of ownership. Her nail traced its corner once before opening it, paper whispering against paper with the dry intimacy of skin touching skin.

Her reflection caught in the monitor's black screen. Lipstick still perfect despite the hour, nail polish unblemished, every detail of her appearance maintained like armor. Let them mistake polish for softness. The reversal was sweeter when she dismantled cases that had defeated every other detective in the precinct, watching their assumptions shatter like safety glass.

Tonight carried the weight of all the other nights, unsolved cases pressing against her consciousness like physical objects. Brynn's earlier request for information threaded through her thoughts. Another reminder that the team's collective clearance rate needed elevation to match her personal standard. The department board showed the gap in stark numerical terms, her row isolated in its perfection while others struggled in mediocrity's comfortable middle ground.

She consumed Sinclair's pages with the hunger of someone who understood that inconsistencies were breadcrumbs leading to the truth. Her pen circled contradictions, underlined missed connections, filled margins with questions written in block letters that could cut glass. The bullpen's emptiness helped. Silence allowed patterns to surface like oil rising through still water.

She leaned back until vertebrae popped in sequence, a small symphony of relief. They looked to her for answers, this collection of detectives who carried badges but lacked her particular gift for seeing what others missed. Each closed case wasn't just a win, but a standard enforced, a line drawn through someone's worst day with the authority of absolute competence.

Her hand sought the coffee mug in an automatic gesture, found nothing but a ceramic memory of warmth. She set it aside with the mild irritation of someone whose body had betrayed her concentration.

Blackburn closed Sinclair's file and carried it to his desk, the thud of its landing echoing through the empty space like a judge's gavel. She moved to Dawson's workspace, a disaster of competing priorities and abandoned intentions. His file emerged from the chaos like an artifact from an archaeological dig.

Back in her chair, she opened his narrative to pages dense with his particular brand of linear thinking. The red pen's cap came away between her teeth, metal and solvent creating a sharp taste that focused her attention like smelling salts. Her eyes began their surgical work, flicking, underlining, questioning, marking corners with the precision of someone performing microsurgery.

Every red mark was evidence of standards maintained in the face of entropy. White pages, red ink; a color contrast that steadied her pulse and reminded her that some things in this world could still be made clean and correct.

She wrote in the margin and could hear Dawson's future objections echoing off the precinct wall, wounded indignation wrapped in masculine ego. She'd watched him flush that particular shade of defensive red before. Bruised pride wasn't her concern. The record mattered. Perfection wasn't affectation but necessity, a shield against the random violence that sought to slip through bureaucratic cracks, a lever that moved mountains of evidence into positions where justice could find its footing.

Her pen moved while her mind drifted to the people who existed in case files as "surviving family members." Mothers whose sons wouldn't call, partners who slept alone, children who would grow up carrying the weight of unanswered questions. She had to be perfect because imperfection had names and addresses. Someone else always paid the price when she failed to be absolutely right.

The door opened with the soft complaint of hinges that had witnessed too many late-night conversations. Chief Hayes filled the frame, concern carved into the geography of his weathered face.

"Detective Blackburn." His voice carried the careful neutrality of someone approaching a wild animal. "It's late. Early. Time loses meaning after midnight. You should go home. This can wait for morning."

She didn't lift her gaze from the page. The pen continued its dissection of Dawson's work, circling a date that didn't align with the timeline. "Can't. There's something here. We missed it, and I need to find it before it finds us."

He moved closer, floorboards announcing his approach with small protests. "You've been at this for hours. Your team's work is solid. You're pushing yourself past the point of effectiveness."

She looked up then, meeting his eyes with the direct gaze of someone who had never learned to blink first. "If there's even the possibility we overlooked something, I have to find it. I can't let this go."

His face softened under the force of her stare. He understood what drove her and what it cost. A blessing and a curse wrapped in the same relentless package. It kept bodies from stacking up, but the price was written in the shadows under her eyes.

She leaned into the paragraph before her, studying words as if they might surrender their secrets under sufficient pressure. He watched her brow furrow over a misplaced comma, knew the reputation that preceded her through courthouse corridors and precinct break rooms.

"Besides," she said, her pen circling a spelling error with the precision of a surgeon marking an incision, "you're here too, chief."

His gaze swept across her desk. Margins threaded with notes in her distinctive hand, sticky flags arranged in a color-coded system that would confuse anyone else but guided her through complexity like a roadmap. Thoroughness, commitment, yes. But also something darker. Obsession. Conviction. The inability to accept that some things couldn't be perfected through sheer force of will.

"Morgan." The use of her first name was planned, a key tested against armor she'd spent years forging. "I understand your dedication. But you can't solve every case in one night. The team needs you fresh and alert, not running on fumes and stubbornness."

Her pen stopped its relentless movement. She looked at him with frustration that she allowed him to see because vulnerability, carefully deployed, was another kind of weapon. Her shoulders dropped a fraction, posture loosening just enough to suggest fatigue rather than calculation. The shadows under her eyes deepened, and when she looked up, the crack in her composure was exactly the shape he expected to see, the one that made protective men want to smooth her hair and tell her everything would be fine.

"I know, chief." Her voice carried just the right note of exhaustion wrapped around unshakeable determination. "But every time I close my eyes, I see their faces. The victims, their families. They're counting on us. On me. I can't let them down."

He placed a hand on her shoulder, found muscle tension that felt like cables under stress. His touch was meant as comfort, but she felt the heat it left behind when he lifted his palm. Another piece of information filed away for future use.

"You haven't let anyone down, Morgan. Your work sets the standard here. But even standards need maintenance, and that means rest."

"Good night, sir."

"Good night." He sighed with the weight of someone who recognized a battle he couldn't win.

A ping sliced through the silence. Her monitor glowed with the time. Quarter to three. A new message from Azhya Hemingway. She clicked, and the mouse felt dense as mercury in her grip. The email arrived clean and sharp as a blade between ribs. Dawson hadn't filed. Ira Malone's extradition paperwork remained missing. Release risk: high.

Her lip curled into something that would have made wolves step back.

She typed her response with fingers that moved like they were loading ammunition. *Thanks for the heads up. Maybe we should both clock out and get some shut-eye.* The taste in her mouth was copper and disappointment. Sleep wasn't negotiable, not with a reporter keeping score and a team dissolving under pressure.

Send. The message disappeared into the digital ether with a sound like wind through dry leaves. She leaned back, chair leather creaking its familiar protest. Her eyes closed for a heartbeat, darkness cutting the monitor's harsh glow and leaving geometric afterimages floating behind her lids.

Relief lasted exactly as long as a single breath. Faces assembled in the darkness, victims whose names were carved into toe tags, survivors whose lives had been cut in half by violence they never saw coming. She opened her eyes and let the ghosts evaporate into the lamp's unforgiving circle.

Dawson's file lay open, her red annotations scattered across it like drops of blood at a crime scene. Anger moved through her system, clean and hot as whiskey. He was careless with other people's lives, and carelessness in their line of work had a body count.

She lifted her phone, thumb hovering over the screen. A text message formed in her mind. Sharp, demanding, designed to cut through whatever excuse he'd offer in the morning. But the clock's digital face reminded her that some battles were better fought in daylight.

Resentment hung in the air like smoke from a fire she couldn't see. She breathed it in and transformed it into fuel. Perfection wasn't a slogan printed on motivational posters. It was structural, load-bearing, the foundation that kept everything else from collapsing into chaos. One misspelled word, one misplaced comma, one detail overlooked, and a case could crumble like a house built on sand.

Time moved with mechanical precision, each tick of the clock pressing against her nervous system like a fingertip testing a bruise. Exhaustion pulled at her shoulders with gravitational force, but she turned another page, chased another thread, locked another piece into the puzzle that would eventually resolve into truth.

The price of failure wasn't theoretical. It walked on two legs and carried guns and knew how to disappear when paperwork went missing.

Her body finally claimed its due. She moved to the worn leather couch in her office, case files still burning bright behind her closed eyes as sleep dragged her down into darkness where the faces waited, patient as saints, demanding justice she might never be perfect enough to deliver.

Chapter 17

Thin bands of dawn cut the blinds and nudged her out of fractured sleep. Blackburn's eyes opened to the room's stale mix. It was bleach, gun oil, old toner, burned coffee, and the dust of case files. She groaned as she pushed upright, her body balking after a night on the office couch. She arched, testing range. Her spine cracked once. Muscles lit with that slow, punishing burn.

She scrubbed at her eyes and headed for the basement locker room. Concrete underfoot. Metal lockers cool against her shoulder as she slipped past. The air was colder down here, a prickle along her skin. She folded her work clothes with the reflex of someone who orders mess by hand, creases pressed in with a thumb. The fabric's wrinkles stared back, the city's demand stamped into cloth. Running gear next. Soft, breathable, no weight. She laced her shoes by feel, eyes on nothing, fingers threading and cinching until the knot sat flat. Each pull set her mind. Fog lifted. Focus slotted in.

She slipped outside and started the ritual jog through New Dresden. The first steps shook out the stiffness. Her mouth twitched at the habit. This morning routine existed to break her habit of falling asleep at the office. The couch marks pressed into her cheek had their own argument.

She pushed forward. Breath steady. Inhale cool and astringent. Exhale controlled. The city stirred, half awake. The first commuters moved with heads down and single purpose, collars up, eyes on the clock. Her feet landed in a cadence that matched her mood, a firm, controlled thrum that carried urgency without waste.

Steam lifted from the manhole covers in clean white ribbons. Up ahead, a delivery truck eased into Sally's Flower Market, the reverse beeps bouncing off brick as workers heaved out buckets of roses and chrysanthemums, the flower-wet chill riding the air. She skimmed past the fan of shattered glass outside Marcel's Jazz Club without looking, then the crooked newspaper stand where the owner already stacked front pages announcing last night's drug bust in blunt type.

Her phone pressed against her hip. She slid it out mid-stride, checked. No new calls. No messages. She hit redial on Dawson. Ring after ring until the voicemail took it.

"Dawson, it's Blackburn," she snapped, breath fogging the air. "Still no response from you? If you've forgotten how to hit 'send,' I'll come over there and do it for you. Get those files to Hemingway now." She cut the call and slipped the phone away, pace unchanged, a time stamp filing itself in her head.

The 6:15 AM bus ground to a stop at Norver and Main, brakes sighing. She ran past, the smell of yeast and warm crust spilling from Giuseppe's Bakery and colliding with diesel. She leaned into the run, pulse loud in her ears, as if daring the city to keep up with her.

Her rhythm matched the distant clatter of the elevated train, steel on steel, both of them racing the approaching day. Behind her, sunlight threaded between tower faces, turning glass to blade-sharp reflections. Ahead, the old quarter held its narrow shade, old brick and tight alleys keeping their secrets for one more block.

Images from Dawson's case file cut in and out like a damaged reel. Colin Hargrove, point-blank against a wall of silence. No casings. Witness statements turned to static. The rain-dark bush with a weathered cellphone nestled at its base, a line that ran to Ira Malone. Thin, frayed, still the only line they had. Footfalls answered back. Thud. Close. Thud. Something's missing. Thud. Can't let this go cold.

She pushed harder. Legs burned. Dawson's sloppiness flashed again, his notes jammed into the wrong folder, coffee rings bleeding through key lines, the autopsy report torn at the corner, text missing. Amateur errors that got cases tossed. Her stomach tightened. Acid rose. It wasn't the run. It was the gap between what he promised and what existed.

The horizon turned pearl gray. Her mind slid to the Roche gala. The invitation waited in her desk drawer, cream cardstock with gold leaf that caught at the light. Charles would have appreciated the extravagance. He always said presentation was everything.

She cut into the station, legs rubbery for a beat before they steadied. Sweat tracked down her temple. Her chest lifted and fell as she drew air back under discipline. The burn in her thighs read as proof of capacity, not cost. As her breathing leveled, the case fragments that had jostled during the run locked into their places. Each mile had set a peg. She moved to the showers. The steady drip in the tiled room cooled the heat off her skin. She stripped out of sweat-damp clothes, each piece dropped straight into the hamper. Shed the run. Keep the focus.

Blackburn stepped under the spray. Water hit her shoulders, pressure steady and controlled. She adjusted the temperature with a precise twist, heat calibrated to her preference. Steam rose. The tiles warmed under her feet. She worked shampoo through her hair with methodical strokes, fingertips mapping her scalp in soft patterns.

The water pulsed against muscle knots from the couch, from the run, from the accumulated tension of Dawson's incompetence. She rolled her shoulders under the stream. Pressure points released. Her breathing deepened, not from arousal but from the systematic unwinding of physical stress.

Soap slicked over skin. She moved easily, each motion serving a function. The heat penetrated deeper, loosening what the run had tightened. Her mind stayed sharp even as her body relaxed. Case details clicked into alignment. Hargrove's positioning, the phone's placement, Ira Malone's connection to the scene. The shower's rhythm matched her thought process. Steady, thorough, purposeful.

She tested the water temperature again. Hotter. The steam thickened around her, creating a controlled environment. Here, she could process without interruption. No phones. No Dawson's excuses. No bureaucratic interference. Just the facts arranging themselves in logical sequence.

The phone in the bush wasn't random. Someone placed it there deliberately. The question was whether Ira knew about it or if someone wanted him implicated. She filed that thought, let the water rinse away the soap and the morning's accumulated grime.

Her hands moved over her body with clinical attention, checking for tension points, ensuring complete cleanliness. Professional standards applied to everything, including personal maintenance. The water pressure remained constant, a reliable variable in an investigation full of unknowns.

She turned off the shower and stood for a moment, letting the last drops trace down her skin. Each one carried away a fragment of the morning's frustration, leaving behind familiar clarity. The case had structure now. Dawson's failures were documented.

She stepped out and wrapped herself in a towel. The crisp fabric of her fresh clothes from the locker room provided a welcome anchor, each movement of dressing a step in rebuilding her professional armor. Blackburn smoothed her shirt, fingertips precise on the crisp fabric. She lifted her chin and met her own gaze in the mirror. The woman who'd slept on a couch was gone, replaced by a detective ready to extract answers from a resistant world.

Chapter 18

Pale sunbeams cut through dusty blinds, laying long bars across empty desks. The HVAC droned its mechanical hymn. Scuffed paint and yesterday's smeared whiteboard held their positions under buzzing LED tubes.

In the pre-dawn gloom, Blackburn's pen scratched against paper. Chair legs creaked when she shifted weight. Paper edges rasped under her nails as she sorted and stacked. Fast, exact. Overhead lights carved hard planes across her cheekbones, fixing the set of her jaw in shadow and bone.

By the time the rest dragged in from traffic and kitchen counters, the day would already be moving. They'd find files turned, red ink bleeding across their work, the shift's shape already defined. They could call her a ghost if it made them feel better. The city kept speaking. She made a habit of listening.

She lounged in her chair, twirling a red pen between fingers that never trembled. The cap tapped a steady beat against her knuckles. Red meant action items, not discussion. Nothing on pause.

Footsteps clicked down the hallway, sharp on tile. Dawson. Slower than usual. Heel then toe, a dragging cadence that betrayed his sleep.

He appeared in the doorway with collar askew, one hand raked through hair that refused to smooth. Stale sweat and old coffee clung to him like guilt.

Blackburn's eyes found the door before he crossed it. Small tells first.

Dawson's steps hitched at the threshold. He clocked her presence, then his own wrinkled shirt, the roughness on his chin. His gaze slid to his desk. Still neat, already marked.

"Good morning, superstar," she drawled, sweetness placed like a blade.

He twitched. Fingers brushed the doorjamb and fell away. He squared his shoulders because there was nothing else to do inside her room.

"Up early again, Detective Blackburn," he managed. "What's the issue? Can't sleep with all those cases piling up?"

Her mouth edged upward. She watched him flinch at her teeth. "Just trying to bump up our clearance rates. Can't afford to sit idle while others slack off."

He moved closer. His gaze snagged on the top page where red ink sat wide under LED glare. He skimmed, stuck on the phrases she'd chosen. 'Sloppy work' and 'missed opportunity.' His shoulders lifted, held. He approached like a man edging live wire.

"What's with the comments?" he asked. "Feels like I'm back in middle school."

Blackburn leaned back, fingers drumming slow, metronomic lines on the armrest. "Consider it constructive criticism," she said, light enough to carry poison. "Those witnesses aren't decoration."

His jaw locked. He stared at the page as if the marks were fresh blood and he owned every drop. Heat bloomed across his cheeks. He did not look up.

"I didn't think it was that bad," he muttered, thinly, defensively, more appeal than stance.

She leaned forward, elbows on desk, fingers steepled where he could see them. "If we want to be taken seriously, how about tracking down that extradition paperwork? Your silence screams 'incompetent,' Dawson."

She let the word hang. Dawson's throat worked. He crossed his arms like a shield he didn't trust, held his ground because movement would read as retreat.

"It's a messy case," he said, pushing steadiness into the words. "Doesn't mean I'm incompetent."

Her eyebrow lifted. "Messy doesn't mean unmanageable." Each word precise. "You know the routine. Put in the legwork, dig out the details. I need you to step up."

He dipped his chin, studied floor tiles. "Yeah, I will." The room's damp heat pressed against his shirt like accusation.

Sinclair entered with chin high, shoulders set. Polished shoes ticked against linoleum, pulling eyes without effort. He looked at Blackburn, couldn't hide the wanting quick in his gaze before smoothing it clean. Blackburn's pen stopped. Dawson's breath cut short, resumed. The room's register shifted.

"Morning," Sinclair said. His voice slid, steadied. He tracked the distance to her desk, read the weather between bodies.

Blackburn let her gaze cut to him and back. A small smile. She marked how his eyes darted between her and Dawson, testing the surface for cracks. "Morning," she said, honey as purposeful as venom. "Glad to see you, Sinclair."

Dawson's shoulders spiked. He answered heat with old anger that lived close. "Yeah, yeah," he snapped. "Why do you tear apart my reports but let him slide? We all know he isn't your type."

She turned hard. The room thinned to wire. She set her eyes on Dawson, kept them there until he shifted. "Explain yourself, Dawson." Clean as a cut.

He rocked on his heels, trapped by the line he'd crossed. Arms tight across his chest, gaze sliding past her as if distance could blur what he'd said. "I don't need to explain anything," he muttered. "You know what I meant."

Sinclair looked between them, searching for purchase. "What's going on? Did I do something?"

Blackburn cut to him. She offered the smallest softness because it bought leverage. "Sit down, Sinclair." She pointed to the chair before her desk. "There's a report for you too. Have a look."

When he sat, she turned back to Dawson, let any trace of warmth burn away. "I treat you all the same, Dawson." Each word placed like weight on scales. "Your insinuations are lewd and unfounded."

Silence carved through the room. Dawson held position with face hot, jaw locked. He kept his eyes on the report as if it were safer ground.

Sinclair settled carefully, flipped pages. His face went to that clean blank they all wore when work demanded it.

The line between Blackburn and Dawson stayed taut until he dropped his gaze, dug into the file. Controlled retreat.

Blackburn settled back, watched Sinclair close the space to her desk in small increments. She turned her chair a fraction, casual on the surface, everything else measuring. "I found myself with some free time," she said, smirk on purpose. "What's your concern, Sinclair?"

The phrasing put him on the back foot. She saw it land. He slid deeper into the chair, flipped pages with fingers too careful. "I'm making progress on the Maxwell case," he said, trying to keep tremor flat. Her stare kept him honest.

She leaned over the file, took in paper and his face simultaneously. Her perfume hung close. It was floral with dry musk, placed to distract as needed. "Just 'making progress'?" Tone quiet, edged. "Look at this. No indication you impounded the vehicle after your search. Did it occur to you that, in a drug-related case, our garage would be perfect to tear that mess apart for evidence?"

He swallowed, came up empty. "I didn't think—"

"Clearly." She cut off the excuse, left it bleeding on the floor. Voice even, all blade. "This is the issue. We're not here just to gather statements, we need to peel back layers. Do you think the killer gives a damn about your thinking?"

He sat caught on hooks she'd placed. Her precision did its work. His eyes dropped back to the report.

Sinclair's fingers twitched when he turned the page. He found the line he could offer. "I can try to get a warrant for the car." The weak ring told her he heard himself too.

She leaned back, gave him a fraction to breathe. "Good idea." Softening the tone by degrees to keep him moving. "They won't expect us to want it back after releasing it at scene."

The room's energy shifted, not gone, just redirected. Sinclair glanced toward the exit, then back, muscles in his feet shifting under the desk. He gathered pages with hands that steadied as he stacked them, ready to move but slow to break the line.

Cooper burst in, foam cup in each hand, grin preceding him. Heat and coffee smell pushed into the cold. "Morning coffee run," he announced. "Ma'am, your latte."

Reeves followed, rolling his eyes. "Suck-up," he said, nudging Cooper.

Cooper grinned, bumped back, offered a cup. "Two sugars, right? Or are you sweet enough already?" Reeves rolled his eyes again, let the smile show.

"It's called being considerate," Cooper said. He cut a look at Dawson, left it there.

Blackburn laughed. Dawson flinched. Sinclair's shoulders pulled tight, released. "Being a suck-up might just be the best thing about you, Cooper." She took the coffee, gave him a wink he'd dine out on.

Her desk phone rang, bright, high, slicing through scattered voices. Chairs scraped. People retreated to stations. She strode to her office, lifted the receiver with no wasted motion, voice shifting to the register she used for the outside world.

"Detective Blackburn." Clipped. "What? Slow down."

Keyboards went still. Cooper's cup hovered. Reeves straightened, stepped closer to hear without being called out. Blackburn's face slid from neutral to strained in controlled increments, one muscle at a time.

"Cindy," she said, letting a hair of softness in because it served the call. "You should speak with Det. Dawson. It's his case."

The name hit the room, settled. Cindy Discart. Mother on the six-month case that slept in Dawson's stack. The ghost he couldn't close a door on.

Dawson drew tight, set his shoulders like for a punch. Blackburn hit the speaker button, set the handset down where they could all see it.

"He doesn't tell me anything!" Cindy's voice filled the room from the plastic grille. Sinclair's shoulders ticked. Cooper and Reeves traded glances, looked away.

Blackburn inhaled once, leveled her tone. Her anger went into the shape of words, not volume. "Cindy, I just read the report. We have a strong suspect. I can't share too much, but there are leads we're actively pursuing."

She kept her voice soft, smooth. Watched the room while working the call, counted tells. Dawson's head came up fast. His eyes widened. Small shock that could be read multiple ways.

"Det. Dawson is an excellent detective, and he's moving forward with the case. But, as you know from television, there's a difference between knowing someone is guilty and being able to prove it. Det. Dawson is trying to prove it," Blackburn said, voice cutting short.

She rode the silence that followed, held the frame tight. Inside the room, edges smoothed. People sat straighter. The lie wasn't a lie if it moved the work and kept the mother above water.

When the call ended, Blackburn set the phone in its cradle with care. She scanned the squad, one face at a time, same even measure for each. Chairs creaked. Eyes went from her to Dawson and back. Fingertips tapped desks. Pens clicked in slow unison while they waited for the next instruction.

Chapter 19

"Dawson." Her voice cut across the bullpen. "Over here."

Chairs squeaked. The room went still. Dawson stood with a stiffness he could not hide. He kept his shoulders tight as he crossed the tile, eyes on the floor, shoes whispering over scuffed grout.

He stopped at Blackburn's desk. The hum of the AC filled the thin space between them. She tapped four slow beats on the polished wood. Then silence.

"Sit."

He sat. Defiance flickered and went dark. His jaw worked once and held.

"Explain why Cindy Discart is calling me for updates on her daughter's case," Blackburn said. Each word even. No hurry.

Dawson shifted. Leather creaked under him. He could feel eyes behind his back. Mugs stopped halfway to mouths. Keyboards froze.

"I've been busy," he said. The answer sounded thin. "The case is complicated and I—"

"Busy." She did not raise her voice. The single word landed hard. "Then be busy doing the right things." She glanced at the phone on his hip. "Your log shows no call to her this week."

He flushed. "I didn't want to give her false hope," he said. His tone edged up. "I don't mislead victims' families."

Blackburn's eyes cooled. She leaned in a fraction, not enough to look dramatic, just enough to make the distance smaller.

"False hope is promising what you cannot deliver," she said. "An update is facts on record. Contacts made. Leads pursued. Timelines. You owe her that."

Dawson started to speak. She lifted a hand. He stopped.

"You will open that file from page one," she said. "Rebuild your timeline. Crosscheck your canvass notes with the latest incident map. Pull traffic cameras within a three-mile radius from the last verified sighting. Call the victim advocate and coordinate your next-of-kin contacts. Then call Ms. Discart and tell her what you have done and what you will do next."

The AC clicked. A chair wheel rolled and settled. No one in the room coughed.

"And the suspect, Dawson," she added, quieter. "Find him. He is either there already in some form or you missed him."

He recoiled. The chair scraped once and steadied. Air left his chest and sat heavy in the space between his ribs.

"So, you want me to fabricate a suspect?" he whispered.

"No." Her answer came flat and fast. "I want you to detect. Look again with fresh eyes. Build leads from facts. Do not invent anything."

Sinclair's pen hung above his pad. Cooper and Reeves exchanged a glance and then looked down, faces blanking out to neutral. In the glass wall's reflection, the hierarchy showed like a faint diagram. No one moved closer, but every back leaned toward the sound.

"And if there's nothing there?" Dawson's voice thinned.

"There is always something there," Blackburn said. She eased back in her chair. Relaxed posture. Sharp gaze. "If you cannot see it, bring in someone who can. Ask Reeves to run the door-to-door against the last three weeks of BOLOs. Have Cooper pull the victim's bank and phone warrants and cross them with ALPR pings. If still nothing, then look elsewhere. Cases get reassigned. Jobs do too."

He swallowed. The message found its mark.

"You put me on this case because you trust me to work it," he said, trying to plant a flag.

"I put you on it because you raised your hand," she said. "So work it. The mother called me because you did not call her. Fix that first. Then fix the rest."

His fingers curled tight on the arms of the chair. Knuckles pale. He nodded once.

"Say it out loud," she said.

"I will call Ms. Discart. I will rebuild the timeline and rework leads." He forced the words through clenched teeth. "And I will ask for help where I need it."

"Good." She did not smile. "Document your steps. Every call. Every door. Enter it in the case management system by end of day. No surprises for me or Chief Hayes when the reporters start circling."

Her mention of the chief dimmed the room another shade. Dawson pushed to his feet. The movement came jerky, not smooth. He kept his eyes on the desk.

"Go," she said. "Start with the mother. Keep it brief. Keep it clean."

He turned. On his way back to his pod, screens lit again. Keys tapped. The bullpen pretended to breathe. Co-workers glanced at him from the corners of their eyes and then away. Slights masked as focus. The sound of his footsteps marked each step to his chair.

Blackburn watched him go. No triumph showed on her face. Only a steady calculation. Her gaze slid to the whiteboard by the glass. Dates. Names. Arrows. A corner note on call frequency. She adjusted a marker half an inch and put it back.

Sinclair let out a breath he had been holding. Relief. Guilt. Something warmer he did not invite. He stared down at his notes until the lines blurred, then refocused on the neat rows. He wrote one word. Updates.

Cooper's jaw tensed. He pulled up the shared folder, already checking his own canvass against Dawson's. Reeves clicked into ALPR logs like a man taking inventory. Neither needed to be told. Both knew a gap when they saw one.

Blackburn's hand returned to the four-count on her desk. Tap. Tap. Tap. Tap. She stopped at four. Always four. She picked up the phone and set it down without dialing. She waited. If Dawson had any sense, he would call her first when he finished with the mother. If he did not, she would call him.

Through the glass, the bullpen settled into a quiet thrum. A muted TV scrolled a news ticker about a city council hearing on police funding. Brynn Cassidy's byline flashed across a lower third in a different segment. Blackburn noted it and dismissed it. That storm would come later.

Sinclair risked a glance. Blackburn's posture did something to him that he did not trust. Calm. In control. Unmoved by the room's churn. He straightened in his chair and fixed his eyes back on the screen. He translated the feeling into work. Safer that way.

Dawson sat and put the phone to his ear. The first call did not connect. He tried again. On the third attempt, he got an answer. He stood as he spoke, head down, voice low. A pause. He nodded. He wrote as she talked. He looked at the board through the glass and then at his notes again. He wrote more.

Blackburn watched the small signs. The jaw unclenching. The shoulder drop. The rhythm of his pen. She looked away before he could look up and catch her watching. Control had a shape you did not break unless you meant to.

At her desk, an email from Chief Hayes waited. A brief note about optics on the Discart case and a reminder about the press conference schedule. She filed it in the folder she kept for pressure she could not use yet.

The room pulled itself back into motion. Someone laughed softly at something on a monitor and stopped when they saw her glance. Reeves stood and rolled out a map, his finger tracing the blocks around the last sighting. Cooper shook his head and got up, walking toward the records tech with a list of pull requests.

Blackburn let the quiet fill in. She was not angry. She had no time for anger. She had time for results, for clean documentation, for a mother who deserved a call. For the hierarchy that kept the machine running.

Dawson's voice carried one sentence through the glass. "Ms. Discart, this is Detective Dawson. I wanted to update you."

It was a start. Not enough. A start.

Blackburn checked the time. She picked up a pen and wrote two new tasks in the margin of her notebook. *Media plan, next-of-kin schedule.* She underlined both once. Then she added a third. *Reassign if needed.*

Sinclair felt the words in his throat before he spoke them. He did not speak them. He wrote a memo draft instead, outlining a supplemental canvass. He kept his gaze on the screen, but his skin prickled with the memory of her attention in the room moments earlier. He let the feeling sit and fade.

The AC kicked again. The lights washed the glass to a pale glare for a moment and then settled. The hum returned to normal.

Blackburn looked back at Dawson. He stood hunched at his desk, nodding, pen moving. He would walk that line for now. She would make sure he stayed on it. Or she would cut him from it.

The room waited, as rooms do, for the next thing.

Chapter 20

Afternoon light sliced through the blinds, dividing her office into thin columns of gold and shadow. Blackburn opened the RMS and scrolled through Hart's property log. Wallet. Phone. Shoes. No shirt. Chain of custody clean. Thomas Greene. Clean lines. She held that picture in her mind and made the call.

Greene answered on the second ring. Trained voice, tight with control. She kept it short. Property from Hart's hospital stay. He agreed to come in within the hour. Fine.

"Reeves, Thomas Greene is coming in. Interview Two when he arrives." He nodded and alerted reception.

Blackburn set the room. The metal table centered under LED glare. Two chairs angled just off square to keep her advantage. The LEDs hummed with a thin electrical whine. A high window laid a wash of pale daylight down the far wall like watercolor on concrete.

Footsteps echoed in the hall. Greene stepped into the doorway. Trim. Groomed. White sneakers without a scuff or mark. Someone who works on his feet and keeps the edges clean.

"Detective," he said. He offered a hand and the problem in his first sentence. "My friend is double-parked out front. How long is this?"

"Not long." Her smile stayed brief as a shutter click. She showed him to the chair.

He sat and folded his hands on the metal surface as if waiting for instructions. She matched him and let the room settle into its institutional quiet.

"We're reconciling what Hart had that night," she said. "His shirt isn't on the property sheet."

His fingers twitched against each other. "I don't handle patient property," he said. "That's not my department."

"Maybe a photo will help." She stood. He half rose, checked himself, and sat again.

In the bullpen, the day moved through its rhythms, slow and methodical. "Reeves," she said, just loud enough to cut through the ambient murmur.

He looked up from his screen. "Yeah?"

"Step outside. If anyone's double-parked, get the plate and write it."

His frown tilted toward the door. She lifted her phone and took a tight shot of his confusion before he could ask.

"What is that about?"

"Go." He went.

The old printer woke with a mechanical groan and dropped a page. She waited a beat for the ink to dry, the chemical smell sharp in the recycled air, and brought it back in.

"This may help." She slid the photo to Greene. A plain men's button-down against a white background. Nothing else to it. "Was this with Hart's effects?"

He barely glanced at it. "No. I don't know it. Mr. Hart was in a T-shirt."

She noted it. Hart had worn a T-shirt at intake. Not when he died. "Walk me through your day, Mr. Greene."

His shoulders loosened a fraction. "Busy. I see a lot of patients."

"In the ER too?"

"Sometimes. When coverage is thin. Nights. Weekends." His cadence smoothed into something rehearsed. A route he knew.

"And Evan Hart." She kept the name steady as a level. "Did he say anything about what happened to him? On or off the record."

He watched the table's scratched edge. "No. Nothing I recall. It was routine."

She let the quiet settle between them like dust. Counted his breaths. Light slid another inch down the wall, marking time. The hum overhead thinned to a metallic edge that set teeth on edge. Under the table, his sneaker tapped once against linoleum. Then stopped.

A soft knock broke the tension. Reeves stood in the frame, face blank in a way that meant more. Blackburn gathered the photo and her notes into a neat stack.

"Need a word, Detective," he said.

"Excuse me," she said to Greene, voice even as glass. "Make yourself comfortable. This won't take long."

Blackburn swept her files together with precision. Autopsy report on top. Scene photos beneath. She left Greene under the steady red dot of the camera. "Don't go anywhere," she said, dry as a blade. The door closed on the neat fold of his hands.

In the recycled air of the corridor, LEDs buzzing overhead, Reeves kept it tight. "Picked up Ash Hepburn. Double-parked on Mercer. No driver's license."

"What's he wearing?"

"Black T-shirt. Jeans. Work boots."

"Good." She didn't ask the brand. "Miranda given?"

He nodded. "Arrested and recorded."

She started walking.

The second interview room was narrower and colder. Lights hummed against acoustic tiles. Scuffed linoleum reflected nothing. A bolted table with a groove worn deep into the laminate from countless hands. A high window let in late light filtered through wired glass, dust motes suspended in the beam. The mirror held a flat version of the room.

Ash Hepburn sat with his elbows spread wide. Big hands. A dusting of drywall powder on his knuckles like chalk. Sweat beaded at his hairline despite the chill. He looked at the mirror, then at her, then away.

"Boots off," Blackburn said, setting her files down with a thud.

He blinked. "Why?"

"Booking inventory. Officer safety. You were arrested." She watched his eyes track the movement. "You understand your rights as they were read to you?"

A beat. Then the scrape of laces against leather. He worked the knots loose with thick fingers. The boots hit the table with a dull weight that echoed.

She turned one sole-up. The heel was chewed at the edge, a diagonal chip through the outer lug. Packed in the channels was gray-brown grit that smelled of damp earth and cold air, like a grave.

She laid the boot down and slid out a glossy eight-by-ten from the folder. A lifted tread from the warehouse floor. Clean and exact. "Look familiar?"

Ash's mouth went flat as pressed paper. "No."

She held the sole to the overhead light and angled it until the chipped lug sat over the same void on the print. The fit clicked into place like a key in a lock. "Looks like a match."

"Lots of people have those boots," he said. The push in his voice caught on exhaustion.

"Not many carry the same soil as the site where Evan Hart was buried." Her tone stayed level as water.

He shifted, shoulders drawing tight against his shirt. "I read the guy got out. Doing fine."

"No. He died at County." She tipped her head, an afterthought. "Detective Blackburn. Homicide."

She looked at the boots again, their worn leather creased with use. "Property clerk will bag these. CSU will test the soil and photograph the tread. Chain of custody will be clean."

He blinked. Then gave a small shrug, as if that might shake loose what she had just said.

"Evan didn't die from the gunshot," she said, sliding the autopsy report across the scarred metal surface and leaving the seal and signature to speak. "He was killed at the hospital."

Ash's eyes found the report and held there. He read, or pretended to read. The words reached him anyway. His face collapsed inward, features drawing tight.

"It must have been Thom," he said.

Blackburn waited. The room settled into quiet except for the steady whisper of the vent. He folded in stages, each piece of truth pulling the next one forward.

"Never meant for anybody to die," he said, his voice catching on rough edges. "It was supposed to be a warning. Keep him quiet about what he saw."

"Tell me about Schuur Construction," Blackburn said. Her pen hovered steady above the pad. "How long have you worked there?"

"Six years. Good company. Steady." The ghost of a smile crossed his face, then vanished. "We're on the Franklin Square job. New offices."

"And Thomas. How does he fit?"

"Met him at Marcel's Jazz on Fifth." Ash released a dry laugh that died in the air between them. "He was looking for spaces off the books. Said he could help my back. Started with a few pills." His fingers found his sternum, pressing there. "Eight milligram Dillies. He said the tracking system was a joke if you knew where to look."

"The hospital connection made it easy," Blackburn said.

He gave one tight nod. "I never asked how. Didn't want to know."

"But Evan recognized him."

"Yeah." The word stuck in his throat before he forced it out. "Previous ER visit, I think. It wasn't supposed to go like it did."

"Walk me through it."

"Thom set up the sale. The guy took one look at him and started laughing. Said Thom better make it free or he'd tell the hospital. Started yelling. Thom lost it." Ash closed his eyes and pressed his thumb hard against his eyelid. "He fired right at his face." The shame surfaced now, raw and visible. "After that, panic. We put him under fast. Thought that was the end."

"But Thomas had other plans," Blackburn said.

"Must have." His gaze dropped to the boot on the table, to the dirt he had tracked across the floor. "I didn't know about the hospital. Swear to God. I read he was okay and figured that was enough to keep him quiet."

Silence stretched between them. Blackburn let it work. Guilt moved through his body, then fear, then the small relief of confession.

"I'm not arresting you for those actions right now," she said at last, each word tempered. "You are under investigative detention based on reasonable suspicion. You cannot leave." She let the words settle. "Another detective will speak with you. Do you need anything?"

His breath escaped in a long stream. "Hungry. Missed lunch."

"I'll get you food." She gathered her notes, squaring the edges with precise movements. "Wait here."

She stood. One evidence bag for each boot, the soles exposed, dirt flaking away in small, damning constellations. Outside the wired glass, harsh LED light washed across institutional paint. Down the hall a door clicked shut on a different story just beginning.

Hepburn's statement gave Schmidt what he needed. Probable cause on Thomas Greene for murder. Clean. Complete. The pieces locked together.

She left Hepburn in the chair. Fear kept him talking. It also kept him cooperative.

Reeves sat at his desk, alert and ready.

"I need uniformed officers on both rooms," she said, her voice low and even. "And get Hepburn a burger and something to drink. He's been helpful."

Reeves nodded, then hesitated. "Why haven't you arrested them? We've got enough."

She glanced toward the interview corridor and selected her words. "This is Schmidt's case. He and his team are buried in the Horseman Murders. I took the interviews because I met the victim."

Understanding crossed Reeves's face. "Jurisdiction protocol."

"Exactly. Get the officers up here. Schmidt will need them."

She watched him move toward the elevators, then returned to the corridor.

Thomas Greene hadn't shifted much. His body betrayed him. One finger tapped a quiet rhythm against the table's surface. His shoulders rolled beneath the thin hospital scrubs. When she appeared in the doorway, he adjusted his posture, mirroring her stance without thought.

"Thank you for waiting," Blackburn said as she settled into the chair. Each movement controlled. "There's been a development. You are now under investigative detention."

The muscles around his eyes tightened. "What does that mean?"

"It means you are not free to leave," she said. Her tone remained level. "Do you want water or coffee?"

"No." His palms pressed flat against the table. "I don't understand. What detention?"

"It is what happens when your friend Ash double-parks and does not have a license. You are held while we sort it out."

A subtle shift. The corners of his eyes drew tighter. His breath hitched, then smoothed.

"I should call my supervisor," he said, reaching for normalcy. "Let them know I'll be late."

His hand went to his phone. He stopped when Blackburn raised her hand between them.

"That won't be necessary. I will notify them." She paused. "Do you need medical attention?"

He shook his head. "I'm fine."

She stood. "An officer will sit with you."

She stepped into the hallway. A uniform brushed past her into the room. The LED fixtures hummed overhead. The floor stretched in hard rectangles beneath her feet. She dialed Schmidt.

Behind one door, Thomas Greene sat rigid in the chair, his eyes fixed on the glass. Behind the next, Ash Hepburn waited for his food, his stocking feet marking time against the linoleum. The hallway clock recorded detention start times. Custody logs awaited signatures. Protocol carried the work forward. Paperwork followed.

Schmidt answered on the third ring. Blackburn drew a disciplined breath and set the next steps in motion.

Chapter 21

The lights cut through the evening dark. Blackburn stepped out of the limo. The flash wash struck first, a white heat that bleached color from the world for half a second. Stilettos bit into the red carpet and steadied her weight. The Roche Building rose in glass and steel, spotlights carving white channels through the darkness overhead. Shutters snapped in bursts as photographers pressed forward, elbowing for angles. Her dress clung to her body, the fabric sleek against her skin, its line engineered to read as elegant, and to be read.

Brynn Cassidy stood inside the press knot, microphone clutched in both hands, jaw slack for a fraction of a second before she caught herself. As Blackburn moved forward, Brynn's grip tightened until her knuckles showed white, the mic head wobbling once on its foam windscreen.

Blackburn kept her face composed, lips curved in a small, controlled smile. She let them take her, pausing in half beats for the cameras. She scanned the crowd in a clean sweep. She saw influencers angling their phones toward the light, entertainment reporters leaning forward with her name already forming on their lips like flowers bending toward a heat lamp.

Hairspray hung thick in the air, mixed with gardenia perfume and the sharp, cold ozone scent from the strobes. The idea of being watched settled across her shoulders like a familiar coat. She took it. Public figure, symbol, instrument. She slowed when the press line surged forward, made them wait for the shot, then gave them the turn they craved.

At the doors, familiar uniforms dressed as donors. Chief Hayes stood near the entrance, his rented tuxedo pinching at the throat. His fingers hovered near the bow tie, almost adjusting it, then dropped. Dawson and Sinclair clocked her approach and went still, their posture shifting to the kind of alert that pretends to be casual.

The carpet ran straight to the threshold. Beyond it lay rooms where money shifted hands and rules bent like light through water, where decisions were made and wrapped in the soft cloth of philanthropy. She could feel the angle of the night ahead, its weight and texture.

Brynn caught her eye. The reporter's shoulders hitched upward. Her mouth opened, then edited itself closed. She swallowed, breath pressed thin before reshaping into a professional smile.

"Detective Blackburn, you look absolutely radiant tonight," Brynn said, her voice bright with admiration that wasn't faked. Her gaze tracked the cut of the dress, cataloging details she would never speak on air.

"Thank you, Ms. Cassidy," Blackburn said, offering a crocodile smile. "It's an important night." The phrase emerged clean and polished, each syllable placed exactly where she wanted it.

She tipped her chin in dismissal and walked through the doors. Inside, she listened to the layers of sound. Crystal touched crystal with delicate chimes. Laughter rose and fell, tuned for proximity. Silk brushed against wool in whispers. Underneath it all ran the low murmur of favors being traded and leverage calculated.

The thousand-dollar-a-plate fundraiser surpassed the most extravagant expectations of New Dresden's elite. Fine linens caught and threw back warm light from the chandeliers. Florals seeded the air with a sweet, expensive green that coated the back of the throat. Servers flowed between tables in quiet lines, champagne and wine balanced on their wrists with the sureness of long habit.

The ballroom held the city's class in one room, conversation woven from politics, money, and carefully crafted small talk. Chandeliers dropped golden warmth that caught in diamonds and cufflinks, turning them to small fires. In a corner, a string quartet stitched sound through the space, creating a polite veil of culture.

As Blackburn threaded through the room, faces lifted to track her progress. A martini tipped in someone's hand until its surface trembled at the edge of spilling, then righted. A knot of socialites shifted, simultaneously opening a path and pressing closer. The coverage of Charles Roche had done its work. Recognition sparked and flared in the eyes that followed her. She mapped the room on reflex, noting where the heads of companies and committees sat like pieces arranged on a board.

Deeper into the crowd, the attention sharpened. Curiosity bloomed on some faces. Admiration on others. A harder edge appeared in the looks that held a second too long. Lust, too, undisguised. She held her spine exactly where it needed to be and let them look. Heat moved under her skin, but not from the lights.

She kept her gait regulated, her eyes working the field, cataloging small frictions between groups and the invisible lines of alliance. The hum of conversation ran on. Glass chimed against glass. A waiter pivoted sharply to avoid a laugh that broke wide and sudden. She nodded at names that mattered and kept her mind moving.

The Roche family sat close together at their table, shoulders drawn in, voices pitched low. Empty chairs surrounded them, creating a soft buffer zone between sympathy and spectacle. Mrs. Roche sat small and rigid at the center, holding herself upright with visible effort, her face composed over something raw and unhealed.

"You look wonderful tonight, Sadie," Blackburn said, letting warmth coat the words. "Charles would be proud."

Sadie Roche met her gaze, gratitude mixing with fresh grief. "Thank you, Morgan. Your help... it means so much to us." The last words thinned and caught, a hairline crack running through her composure.

The murmured thanks from the family came thick with grief pushing through their careful deportment. Blackburn felt the pull at the edges of herself, the tug of responsibility they offered her. She let it touch her briefly, then filed it away, already pivoting to the next angle, the next set of watching eyes.

She moved to her table under the steady prickle of observation. The group assembled there read like a city roster. She knew every name before she sat.

She took her seat between Marcus Holloway, a tech mogul known for his controversial AI projects, and Annie Cabrera, a renowned philanthropist with ties to the city's most influential families. Across from her sat Arthur Blackwood, an aging artist whose provocative works had scandalized and enthralled the art world for decades.

The conversation rose quickly, light on the surface with barbs hidden underneath. Marcus leaned in too close, his wineglass wobbling dangerously, hands carving equations through the air. "The algorithms, they're beautiful," he said, fingers sketching invisible patterns above the table. "We're not just predicting traffic, we're predicting human nature itself."

"It's not just about finding the safest route," he continued. "It's about understanding the dynamic nature of traffic, of humanity. Imagine a world where we can anticipate where traffic jams might occur and then intervene to prevent them from happening. Who wouldn't want their two-hour commute shrunk down to forty-five minutes?"

Annie rotated her glass by its stem, her nails catching the light. "And who controls this oracle of yours? The traffic police?"

"They would be ideal candidates." Blackburn shifted her gaze to Marcus. "Though I imagine certain private interests might have other ideas."

Color crept up from Marcus's collar. "The data would be publicly accessible, of course. But the algorithms..." He dabbed his napkin against his lips. "Well, proprietary technology requires certain protections."

"Speaking of protection," Blackburn said, lifting her glass so the candlelight laid a thin line along the crystal's edge. "Did you know the average American has a one in two hundred chance of being murdered?"

Arthur Blackwood's fork struck his plate with a sharp crack and skittered sideways. "Good God, that's a rather morbid dinner conversation."

"Is it?" Blackburn's lips curved upward. "I'd say it's fascinating. Take gender differences, for instance..."

"Actually," Annie cut in, setting down her glass with a considered clink, "I've read some compelling research about hormonal influences on violent behavior."

"Precisely." Blackburn set her hand flat against the linen, fingers spread wide, her nails reflecting the candlelight. "Though Freud's early work..."

"Freud?" Marcus barked out a laugh. "Surely modern neuroscience offers more insight than Victorian-era psychoanalysis."

Blackburn tapped one nail once against the cloth. "If you'd let me finish, Marcus." He sat back in his chair, properly chastened. "Freud's work, while flawed, opened the door to understanding the role of early childhood experiences in girls. But you're right, modern technology has revolutionized our understanding. And technology will be revolutionizing our reaction."

"My latest exhibition explores violence through an evolutionary lens," Arthur ventured, leaning forward over his plate. "The primal nature of—"

"Fascinating perspective." Blackburn's voice cut clean through his sentence. "Evolution certainly plays its part. Take stepparents, for instance." She lifted her water glass, ice cubes chiming dully against the sides. "The statistics on child homicide in blended families are illuminating."

Annie's shoulders drew up slightly. "As a stepmother myself—"

"Oh, I'm not suggesting anything personal." Blackburn offered her a smile cold as the ice in her glass. "Merely that when we feed all these factors into predictive models—biology, psychology, sociological patterns—we begin to see possibilities."

Marcus brightened, grateful for familiar ground. "Like my traffic algorithms..."

"Exactly." Blackburn fixed him with a level stare. "Though instead of preventing traffic jams, imagine preventing murder."

The table fell silent. Arthur turned his wine glass slowly, watching the burgundy cling to the sides and slide down. Annie stared at her plate and adjusted her fork a precise eighth of an inch to the left. Marcus started to speak, closed his mouth, then reached for water he didn't want.

"The Autonomous Project," Blackburn said into the space she'd carved open, "could revolutionize how we approach crime prevention. Imagine algorithms that don't just predict traffic patterns, Marcus, but human behavior patterns. The same principles, applied to a different sort of flow."

The quartet shifted to a new piece, strings trembling in a way that ran along exposed nerves. Around them, laughter erupted at another table, bright and jarring against the stillness she held at this one. They sat trapped in it while she arranged the frame exactly where she wanted it.

She didn't need to state her control. The proof lay in the way Marcus's next comment died before reaching his lips, the way Annie followed her lead with small, careful nods, the way Arthur watched her mouth as if waiting for permission to speak again. She sipped her water and let the silence stand.

The lights dimmed gradually. A hush rippled through the room as Sadie moved to the podium. Cutlery settled against plates. Chairs turned forward. Sadie's voice emerged thin at first, then warmed with well-worn memory.

"Charles and I met fifty-four years ago," she began, her eyes fixed on something beyond the back wall. "He was the love of my life, my rock."

The room settled into her cadence. Blackburn watched from her seat, her gaze taking in every shift of posture and catch of breath, the way Sadie's hand fluttered up and then anchored itself on the lectern's edge. She couldn't stop analyzing, not even here. It was how she listened.

Handkerchiefs emerged from pockets and dabbed at the corners of eyes. Heads nodded in solemn rhythm. The air carried that sweet floral scent mixed with the salt-sharp undertone of tears barely held back. The metallic smell from the hot lights pressed down. Time stretched and thinned.

Marcus leaned forward slightly, his usual animation dampened by the moment's gravity. Annie held herself perfectly still, her mouth arranged in an expression of sympathy while her eyes remained glossy but clear. Arthur fixed his attention on the stage, his hand resting on his wine glass without lifting it.

As Sadie wove through achievements and domestic memories, Blackburn tracked the tremor in the widow's hands, cataloged each pause that caught on a particular word, each blink that covered a flash of something else. The hitch when she said "love," the smoothing of her dress front when she spoke about time spent apart. Many of the words were lies wrapped in grief.

Blackburn broke eye contact with the podium to sweep the room, logging reactions. Chief Hayes shifted in his seat, his eyes ticking between the stage and the exits as if measuring distances. Dawson sat ramrod straight, his face carefully set while his gaze slid toward the servers, caught himself, then slid again. Sinclair kept his hands folded, maintaining the appearance of attention.

Sadie's voice grew thinner. Her breath caught at the microphone's edge, creating a small pop of sound. Her eyes watered visibly now, mouth trembling. She leaned onto the podium, her weight transferring to her arms. The room's quiet collected into something awkward and sincere. Chairs creaked. Fabric rustled as people shifted without knowing quite what to do.

Blackburn saw the collapse coming before the first tear fell. The tremor in the shoulders, the quiver of the lower lip, the slight sway. She pushed her chair back and rose in one fluid motion, the scrape of wood against carpet muffled but audible. Purpose lit through her limbs. If Sadie's entitled children would do nothing for the widow, Blackburn was happy to take over the show.

Chapter 22

As Blackburn moved for the podium, the room tilted toward her. The slide of fabric was too loud in the hush. She felt the turn of faces, the prickle of attention on the back of her neck, the small ripple of curiosity she had engineered.

Her face carried compassion the way others carried weapons. She reached Sadie and took the old woman's hand, index finger settling on the knuckle with precise pressure, the squeeze controlled. The contrast pleased her. Height, control, poise, set beside a small, brittle frame that bowed toward her.

She clocked the room without turning her head. Hayes edged forward in his chair, the furrow in his brow deepening. From her left, she caught Dawson's nudge to Sinclair, the low mutter, "What the hell is she up to?"

Her palm settled on Sadie's shoulder, weight light, anchoring. A touch that steadied and reminded.

"You're alright, Sadie." Her voice went warm, a softness calibrated to travel. A few faces flicked up, startled by the absence of the steel they had heard over dinner.

Sadie's tears ran unguarded. She looked up at Blackburn with gratitude and fed on the steadiness there. She turned to the audience, voice thin at first, gaining with each breath.

"This is the woman who gave me hope," she said, her voice breaking but filled with sincerity. "Thank you. I..." She paused, overwhelmed by emotion. Then, looking back at Blackburn, she asked, "Can you please say a few words, Morgan?"

The use of her first name landed exactly where it should. Heads tipped forward. Interest sharpened. The room leaned in.

The corner of Blackburn's mouth lifted, the small lines by her eyes softening for effect. She faced them, spine straight. One breath to set the cadence. She let the air fill her chest, then gave it back in a voice built for command and polish.

"Ladies and gentlemen," she started, her tone both commanding and elegant, "Charles Roche was a remarkable man, and his legacy will undoubtedly live on in all of our hearts. But what truly stands out to me is the courage and strength of those left behind, especially Sadie. My solving Charles's murder was not just about bringing him justice, it was about giving hope to Sadie and all those who loved him."

She paused because control lives in silence as much as speech. The quiet held.

"In my line of work, people are more than just case numbers. It's about the lives I touch and the hope I inspire. Charles's case was one of the most significant in my career, not just because of the challenge it presented, but because it allowed me to bring light into the dark night for this incredible woman."

While she spoke, she let her gaze move, not aimlessly but targeted. Reading posture. Counting who nodded, who did not. She squeezed Sadie's hand again when the woman's breath hitched, a tiny cue for the room to look and feel.

"Thank you all for your support, and remember, it's through our collective efforts that we make our community stronger."

Applause hit like heat, rolling up the walls and back again. Each burst slid along her spine and tightened something low in her body. She let her eyes rake the crowd, slow, acquisitive, collecting their worship like precious gems, cataloging faces to polish later in memory. Then she walked Sadie back to her chair and set her into it with care, a napkin straightened, a glass nudged within reach. Only then did she return to her place.

At the table, praise gathered like a tide. Compliments, soft hands, lifted glasses. She gave nods that read as modest. A smile that opened and closed on cue. Inside, she let it soak, cool and clean.

Marcus leaned in, his eyes gleaming with newfound respect. "That was truly remarkable, Morgan. Your words were as powerful as they were touching."

"I must say, I'm impressed. You handled that situation with such grace and compassion," Annie agreed.

Arthur added, "My dear, you've given me inspiration for my next piece. The juxtaposition of strength and tenderness. Simply captivating."

She accepted with the same humility she used in interviews, eyes tipping with satisfaction she did not hide for long. "Thank you all. I did what anyone in my position would have done."

From the back, Brynn scribbled hard enough to tear paper. Blackburn felt the angling of that gaze, the greedy focus. Useful.

The air shifted. She could feel it in the way shoulders dropped and faces smoothed. Even the skeptics softened at the edges. Sincerity was a tool she used well, and the visible change in Sadie paid dividends.

Blackburn lifted her water glass and let the clear surface give her the room in miniature. Reflection clean enough to survey. Even the ones who had avoided her earlier tracked her now. Perfect.

Heat remained under her skin, a live buzz from the applause. She let it run through her, a controlled dose. A drug, but one she measured.

The lights dimmed for the violinist, stage glow thinning into the crowd. Bow on string made a dry, dark rasp. Shadows cut across the tables. In the half-light her profile softened just enough. The smile slid away so her face could rest.

She thought of Sadie's eyes, the unguarded thanks there. The tremor in those veins under paper-thin skin. Her stomach clenched, a sharp flick she smothered with a swallow of wine before it found purchase.

She had taken what she needed. Time to leave. She rose, chair silent against the floor, and dealt polite farewells to the table. One last nod to Sadie, now wrapped in well-wishers. Intoxicating, all of it, and enough.

Near the exit, she caught Brynn again, pen still carving. Their eyes held. A silent exchange that tasted like a negotiation neither had named.

Chief Hayes met her at the door, face flushed, champagne heavy on his breath. "Leaving so soon, Morgan?" he asked, his words slurred. "You were the star of the show tonight."

Her hand slid to his sleeve. Tremor under wool, faint and useful. "Always leave them wanting more, sir," she said, voice honeyed. "Besides, crime doesn't sleep, and neither do I."

He chuckled, admiration threaded with unease. "You're something else, Morgan. Don't know what we'd do without you."

Cool air hit her face, clean after the room's perfume and heat. Satisfaction settled in. The gala, Sadie's speech, her own delivery, all within parameters she set. Untouchable. Invincible. For now.

She walked toward the waiting autonomous limo. The clear night let the city throw light back at itself. A wet gleam on asphalt. A shout from a corner. A horn laid on too long somewhere down the block, the thin buzz of voices hanging above it.

Inside, leather took her weight, the low hum of the car cutting through the street noise as it pulled away. She let herself decompress in inches, inventorying outcomes, filing expressions, tallying leverage. The interior lights cast a pale wash that left half her face in shadow.

As the car slid through traffic, she allowed a small indulgence. Eyes closed. Scent of leather, the faint ghost of her own perfume. She let the night replay beat by beat, timing, entrances, the chosen silences.

Outside, lights strobed across the tinted glass and skated over her features. It matched the churn beneath her composed surface, the tight coil she kept leashed.

Her fingers found the outline of her phone inside the clutch. There was still most of an evening ahead. Anticipation hummed, familiar and clean, a challenge she could sink her teeth into.

She drew the phone out as the limo slid under neon. Blue light broke across her face. A new alert. One tap, and she was in. A dating app notification, a fresh match waiting.

A small, bright spark lit behind her eyes. She opened BDSMessages. The profile loaded, promising on the screen, hints of depth where she preferred compliance.

She swiped right without hesitation, the gesture crisp. A neat punctuation to the evening's script. She leaned back, lips curving. The night still had room in it. New connections offered a different thrill, a clean way to cap the performance.

Chapter 23

Lamplight laid warm bands across Jenna Langston's hardwood floor. Dust floated in the still air. The worn sofa gave under their weight with a soft creak. Red wine caught the light when they moved their wrists.

Jenna let her gaze pass over the room. The leather armchair showed years of use, its surface cracked at the headrest and arms. Books crowded the shelves. Paper edges feathered from handling. The framed photos needed a cloth. Fingerprints blurred a few faces. Nothing matched. Every piece looked earned rather than chosen, a life built one hand-me-down at a time.

Vanilla from the candles mixed with old wood. The flames moved a little and threw long, simple shadows.

Marla Sutton took a sip, set her glass down. "You won't believe what happened today," she said. "One of the guys at work rolled up in a Raider Straight Line. Company lease. Swore it had the latest build. The thing drove straight into a parking bollard."

Jenna leaned in, the sound of it already making her smile. "Please tell me there's video."

"Of course there's video." Marla grinned. "It kept inching forward like the bollard would just accept submission. Sensors chirping. Tires squealing. Smelled like burned rubber for ten minutes. The bollard didn't even scuff. The car has a dent the size of a fist. Stan Raider Group should send a fruit basket."

Jenna laughed. The knot in her shoulders eased. Their talk moved in easy loops, the room settling around them.

A chime cut through the quiet. Clear and small. Jenna reached for her phone. The glass felt cool. Her pulse ticked in her wrist as she woke the screen.

Marla shifted closer. The cushion dipped between them. "Is that what I think it is?"

"Maybe." Jenna unlocked the phone. Blue-white light washed her face. She scanned the notification, then the app. BDSMessages opened on the last thread she had sent. New message. She tapped through the profile first. Location flagged New Dresden. Verification check mark. No social links. Clean photo set. No obvious tells.

"It's from barbwire12," Jenna said. Her voice stayed low. She looked up at Marla, then back to the screen. "A domme I messaged a few hours ago."

Marla lifted an eyebrow. "Barbwire12. Weak. Trying too hard. Or ancient. Sounds like someone who remembers a comic book she shouldn't admit to."

"What comic?"

"Exactly. You're not a fossil."

Jenna let out a short laugh. She took a slow sip and felt the wine climb her throat, dry and neat. "I'm not judging. My handle is kissthiskitty783. I surrendered the moral high ground a long time ago." She bumped Marla's arm with the back of her hand. "There. Balance."

Marla glanced at the phone. "What did she write?"

Jenna did not show the screen yet. She scrolled, watching for pressure points. The message was brief. No pet names. No claims. A question and a time window. She liked that. The profile notes listed hard limits without theatrics and asked for consent checks in plain words. No florid promises. No showy quotes. She breathed out and let herself smile at the restraint.

"She asked if I prefer clear rules up front or a trial scene," she said. "Gave two options. Asked what I want and what I don't."

Marla leaned back. "Not terrible." She picked up her glass again. "But the name still makes me itch."

"You can file a complaint with user support."

"I will. To whom it may concern, this person offends my sense of branding."

Jenna scrolled again. She checked timestamps and saw she had waited before following up. Not pushy. She checked for recycled language in her public posts. Nothing obvious. No copy-paste schemes. She locked the screen and set the phone facedown, next to the coaster.

"Do you ever vet like this for people you date at work?" Marla asked, only half teasing.

Jenna tapped the phone with her fingertips. "I vet like this for pizza delivery."

"Fair." Marla's smile thinned with curiosity she did not fully hide. "So. Are you meeting her or not?"

"Not tonight." Jenna reached for her glass again, then stopped. She glanced at the candles. The flames held steady. "I'll answer with questions. See how she uses silence."

Marla nodded. "Smart."

In the window, the city pushed up its noise and light without intruding. A siren flicked by three blocks away, then cut. The room breathed again.

"What are you going to ask?" Marla said.

"Logistics. Consent habits. What she does when something changes mid-scene." Jenna's tone stayed even. "Whether she listens. Whether she follows up the next day."

"Bureaucrat."

"Alive." Jenna's mouth tilted. She did not soften it with apology.

Marla took that in. "The co-worker with the car is filing an incident report," she said after a pause, returning to safer ground. "IT wants the telemetry. Stan Raider's contact says it was a sensor occlusion. Sun glare off the bollard. They're calling it an edge case."

"Let me know if they call it user error next," Jenna said. "They love that phrase."

"We were all standing there," Marla said. She rubbed the rim of her glass. "At least the bollard has tenure."

Jenna's phone pulsed once. She flipped it, read, and stilled. "She asked for my safe word," she said. "Says she prefers to use plain language safe words instead of colors unless I want otherwise. Suggests a check-in at ten minutes, then five-minute intervals. Clear. Boring. I like boring."

Marla watched her. "It's interesting, seeing you like this."

"Like what?"

"Measured," Marla said. "Counting the beats."

Jenna set her glass down. "Counting keeps people safe." She looked at the photos on the wall and did not reach to straighten them. "And it keeps me honest."

Marla shifted again, nearer by an inch. "She going to get your number?"

"Not yet." Jenna typed with her thumb, unhurried. She outlined a few limits, kept it simple, asked one question she would have to answer with proof of attention. She set the phone down and did not look at it.

Marla's thigh pressed lightly against the seam of the cushion. Heat there. Nothing more than contact. She took another sip of wine and watched the liquid still itself. "If she flakes, we can always mock her later."

Jenna smiled. "Private mockery only. No screenshots."

"Of course. We have standards."

The phone chimed once more, patient as a knock. Jenna did not move for it. The candles hummed. Outside, a delivery truck downshifted, then idled.

Marla's voice dropped a notch. "Do you ever get tired of the vetting?"

"No." Jenna's answer came easy. "Last time I skipped vetting, I got a concussion and a stalker. So yeah, boring is my jam."

Marla nodded. "I get that."

Jenna picked up the phone again and read. Her eyes clicked through each line. She bit her lower lip once, then let it go. "She answered the question I asked. And the one I didn't." She looked up. "That's rare."

Marla lifted her glass in a small salute. "To rare."

Jenna touched hers to it. The sound was quiet and clean. She set the glass down and typed her next reply.

She kept her first message concise. No fluff. Just enough to signal confidence without posturing.

> *Your profile is compelling. I'm a submissive and drawn to power that's thoughtful, and deliberate. I'm interested in light restraint, spanking, and psychological control. What excites me most is structure, boundaries and the moment of being asked to cross them.*

She read it once more before sending. The cadence mattered. Formal, but not stiff. Open, not needy.

Marla leaned in to glimpse the screen, then scoffed. "Jenna, this looks like a cover letter."

Jenna smirked. "Respectfully requesting to be dominated. Please find my kink resume attached."

"Exactly. Like, 'Dear HR, I'm available for emotional surrender and light bruising.'"

"Mock me one more time and you're blocked."

"You wrote it like she's hiring for the Department of Bondage."

"I wrote it like I don't want to attract the kind of person who thinks 'naughty girl' is a complete personality."

Jenna watched the screen. A new message indicator flashed back within a minute. She opened it.

> *You know what you want. That's rare enough.<*
> *I like discipline and I like designing control.<*
> *The way someone moves once they give it up.<*
> *That's beautiful.<*

I have my hands and more if they're earned. I'm interested. Are you?<

Jenna blinked. Not showy. Bold, but clean. No generic chatroom heat, no masks or metaphors. She logged the lines that mattered most. Discipline earned, and designing control. This was someone who at least sounded like she had done this more than once with her eyes open.

"Better," Jenna murmured. "Precise without play-acting."

"Which part are you judging harder," Marla said, "the grammar or the ethics?"

"Both. Words are use-of-force levels here."

She tapped through the photos. She already knew the sequence, had studied them earlier, but she let Marla look again.

The images were willful. No faces in half-light, but no duck-lipped thirst traps either. Leather, yes. Tools, yes. But neat. Arranged. Even framed tight enough to show there was intent behind the shots. One showed electro-stimulation gear in velvet-lined slots. Another, a tangle of silk and jute rope, dyed cool gray. Controlled chaos.

"She's serious," Marla said.

"She's patient. That's different."

Another buzz.

Let's talk limits. Hard lines first. Then soft lines we can press if
earned.<
Safe word or plain speech. I like starting with regular check-ins<
until rhythm builds.<

Jenna felt her breath hitch. Not because of arousal, but because there was nothing in that message to object to. That, in her experience, was unusual.

She replied, careful to keep her tone matched.

> My hard limits are blood, degradation, breath restriction, public scene, and honorifics outside agreed context. I prefer plain speech over colors. I check in early and often until I feel the rhythm too. I'm open to impact and restraint within clean negotiation. Also open to behavioral structure.

Blackburn's typing bubble appeared almost instantly. Then,

Noted. And respected. Structure interests me too.<
Let's say this: if we were to meet,<
I'd want to begin with a simple framework.<
Rules that adjust over time. But only after I earn your trust.<
I'd rather shape you slowly than own anyone fast.<

Jenna let her head fall back against the sofa. She exhaled, not like someone swooning, but like someone who had just cleared a checkpoint.

"Okay," she said. "This one knows how not to fail the first ten minutes."

Marla gave her a sidelong look. "That's your kink? Emotional first-aid kit and leadership qualities?"

"It's progress."

Marla grinned. "Let me know when she shows up with an agenda and a spreadsheet."

Another ping.

What's the last book that made you feel curious? Doesn't have to be kinky. Just honest.<

Jenna blinked. That was unexpected.

She sat with it. Then typed,

> A science memoir. About people who charted extreme environments, looking for places that change your brain chemistry when you stand in them. The author wrote about Antarctica like it was a devotion.

Blackburn's answer came.

I'd like to hear your voice when you describe places like that.<

Jenna re-read the last line. She didn't respond right away. Her pulse was low but steady.

Marla's voice cut through the quiet. "Are we still officially flirting or have we moved into poetic hostage negotiation?"

"I think," Jenna said, "I might actually be interested."

Marla raised her glass again. "How civilized. Shall I alert the rope and discipline division?"

A final message came in.

If I asked you to show me your hands, would that feel exposing? Or safe?<

Jenna's throat tightened. Not because the question was dirty or demanding, but because it was good. Psychological. A precision cut.

She replied,

> *Depends on how you'd be watching. Depends on what you'd look for first.*

There was a long pause. Then,

> *I'd look to see how still you keep them. And whether they belong to someone halfway between obedience and acknowledgement.*

Then,

> *Turn on the camera.*

The screen pulsed. "Incoming Call: barbwire12." Jenna met Marla's eyes, then tapped to connect.

The screen resolved into a frame of soft leather upholstery and moving shadows. Blackburn sat in the back of a sleek black car, the city blurring through tinted windows behind her. Her dress shimmered dark in the dim light. Expensive, sculpted, the neckline cut low. A single lock of blonde hair crossed her collarbone like studied punctuation.

She wore deep lipstick, clean liner. No smudged edges. Her face was symmetrical, camera-ready, but shaped by more than just beauty. She stared through the lens as though looking straight into the room.

Neither woman spoke.

Marla adjusted the frame slightly. Jenna leaned back and waited. The instinct to fidget passed through her quickly and left no trace.

"I'm Morgan."

"Hi. Jenna."

"Jenna," Blackburn said. Her voice was lower than expected. Beautiful, but not soft.

Jenna nodded, resisting the pull to smile. "Yes."

Blackburn's gaze did not drift. The limo moved around a corner. A sharp slant of gold light crossed her shoulder, then vanished.

"You're not what I expected," she said.

"What did you expect?"

"A performance." Blackburn paused. "You didn't dress for one. That tells me something."

Jenna's mouth tilted, just a little. "You're wearing a formal gown. Should I be worried?"

"You should always be thinking," Blackburn said. "This is a transitional moment. I just left an event."

Jenna took her in fully now. The brushed shine of her hair, the cut of the collar, the brightness in her eye line that wasn't quite flirtation.

"You have excellent posture," Blackburn said. "Are you sitting?"

"I am."

"Stand up."

Jenna stood.

"Back straight. Shoulders low. Put your phone on the table. Step back until I can see your full frame."

Jenna angled the phone and complied.

Blackburn watched. Not hungrily. Not like most. More like someone confirming alignment before making the cut.

"You move cleanly," she said.

"I want to make you happy."

"Then kneel."

Jenna lowered herself without speaking. The carpet brushed beneath her knees, familiar and neutral. She straightened again from the base of her spine.

"Hands behind your back."

Jenna handed the phone to Marla and obeyed. Her arms folded behind her, forearms crossed lightly above her waistband. Not rigid, not collapsed.

The city moved past Blackburn's window like soft static. She adjusted slightly where she sat. Her eyes stayed level with the lens.

"Mistress," Jenna said.

The word came easily. Not coy. Not quick.

Blackburn inclined her head slightly.

"The position suits you," she said. "Keep your hands where they are. Don't adjust."

Jenna nodded once. She kept her shoulders back and her mouth quiet.

Blackburn's voice spread through the room like electricity looking for ground.

"Tell me something you'd be afraid to admit in daylight."

Jenna's breath caught only a little. "That I don't know how much to give. Only what it feels like to give wrong."

"And you think I can fix that?"

"I think you notice things. You speak like someone who reads skins instead of signs."

Marla bent forward slightly to adjust the angle. Blackburn's eyes clicked toward the motion.

"Who's holding the lens?"

"My friend," Jenna said. "She's here with consent."

"Good. But she will obey my direction too. Lift the camera. Point it at your face, friend."

Marla hesitated.

"Now," Blackburn said.

Marla turned the phone toward herself, face controlled but cautious. "Hi there."

Blackburn looked into her. Not the lens. Not the room. Her.

"You don't strike me as a voyeur."

"I'm not," Marla said. "Just backup."

"You were listening when she gave her limits?"

"Yes."

"That's useful," Blackburn said. "Back to Jenna."

The camera slid back to Jenna. "Now align the camera with the table. Faced toward Jenna. Angle it low. No drama. Just posture."

Marla did as instructed. The phone rested where the light caught both the frame of Jenna's shoulders and the line of her thighs beneath the hem of her dress.

"You look composed," Blackburn said. "Despite the kneeling. That tells me how much of this pose is familiar to you."

"It's not unfamiliar."

"And the curiosity?"

"That's real."

A silence passed.

Blackburn's voice slid back into the room. Quieter. Composed. "You said you craved structure. That your interest is earned control."

"Yes."

"What happens when control doesn't ask first?"

Jenna looked up. She didn't blink.

"Then it doesn't last."

Blackburn smiled. Not a performance, just a flick that marked certainty.

"You'll kneel longer next time. Bare knees. Back straight. Silence held. You'll wait until I issue the shape I want."

"Yes, mistress."

"Say it again. But slower."

"Yes, mistress."

Jenna tasted the words this time as they passed over her tongue. Nothing about them felt like play.

Blackburn's gaze cooled.

"You'll meet me Thursday. Eight fifteen sharp. No smart fabric. No scent."

Jenna nodded.

"No bright colors. I want to see your restraint before I choose how to unravel it."

"It will be there."

"I believe you."

Blackburn leaned slightly forward. The dark interior of the car blurred behind her. The signal flickered once, then steadied.

"You gave your name tonight," she said. "That means something."

Jenna did not speak.

Blackburn let the silence stretch. When she spoke again, her voice cut cleaner than before.

"Keep your hands behind your back for one more minute after the screen goes dark."

Then, the screen did just that. No goodbye. No nod. No final reassurance.

Only their small apartment and the hiss of latent energy between them.

Jenna stayed on her knees. Her back straightened further in the absence of command. Thirty seconds passed. Then sixty.

Only after that did she rise.

Marla put the phone down, breathing again. Her palms left a faint mark on the table's surface.

"She's different," Marla said after a moment. "That wasn't dirty talk."

"No," Jenna said. "That was architectural."

They sank back onto the sofa. The wine had warmed. The candles burned lower. Marla poured again with a near-silent touch.

Jenna stared into her glass.

"This is going to be something," she said.

Marla didn't call it anything.

Silence returned. The room inhaled around it.

Neither of them moved.

The candlelight pressed soft ellipses against the wall. Outside, a car clicked through a turn four stories down, then faded. The wine in Jenna's glass remained untouched.

She sat upright, spine tall from how she'd held it. Her gaze stayed pinned to the dark screen.

Marla waited.

"You good?" she asked finally.

Jenna blinked once, then turned toward her. Her face had changed, just slightly. Less color. More thought.

"That didn't feel like a video call," she said.

"No. It really didn't."

Marla eased back into the sofa, glass balanced on her thigh. "Do you want to look her up now? Or sit with that a minute longer?"

Jenna breathed out, not quite a sigh. "Let's look."

They brought the phone between them, light washing both faces. Marla typed in the username first, then added modifiers: *New Dresden, blonde, verified.* Jenna leaned forward to read along.

"Start wider," she said. "Strip the handle. Try just the name she gave."

Marla deleted and retyped. *Morgan, New Dresden, gala.* More refined.

They scrolled in silence. Faces passed quickly. Too young. Too filtered. Too wrong. Then a photo appeared. Public, formal, crisp.

"Wait." Jenna pointed. "That's her. Stop. Right there."

Fullscreen now. The same blonde hair, dressed high and sharp under heavy lights. No makeup tricks. People out of focus behind her. Headline: *Charles Roche fundraiser draws hundreds.*

Under the photograph: *Detective Morgan Blackburn solved his murder.*

Jenna sat very still.

Marla said it first. "She's a cop."

"Not just a cop," Jenna said. "Homicide."

They stared.

The article below the photo quoted her on victim empathy, case construction, procedural integrity. Her solve rate was high. She'd spoken at the gala when the widow felt faint.

"She's beautiful," Marla said. "But yeah. Violent job."

"She said it was a fundraiser," Jenna murmured.

Marla nodded. "Black dress, city car, high-profile crowd. Tracks."

"She didn't lie."

"No."

But neither of them moved away from the screen.

Another image somewhere down the article showed her giving a press conference with some cars. Same gaze. Same posture. Wearing power like it fit.

Jenna leaned back and set the wine aside.

"She carries stillness," she said.

"She also carries a 9mm," Marla said.

"Maybe both give her clarity."

Marla didn't answer that. She refreshed the page and scrolled again. Another article. A profile piece from six months back. Quiet commendation. Quiet criticism. Detachment presented as discipline.

"She's cold," Marla said carefully. "In the write-ups, I mean. Clinical. A little off."

Jenna tilted her head. "That scares you?"

"It should scare you."

Jenna looked down at her hands. Her palms rested silently in her lap, fingers perfectly aligned.

"I think," she said, "that's why I'm curious."

Neither spoke for a moment.

Then Marla reached for Jenna's glass and pushed it slightly closer.

"She's not just a Dom. She's law enforcement. That's a bigger trust fall than usual."

"I've done the fall." Jenna looked toward the window. "I got bruised last time. Maybe this time I'll land cleaner."

Marla laughed once without smiling. "That's your pitch?"

"It's not a pitch. It's data. She asked for structure. She returned silence with expectation. She let me speak without interruption."

"And now you want to kneel and be explored by someone who logs chain of custody forms before lunch."

"I want calm hands," Jenna said. "And someone who understands what power does when it's quiet."

The room had cooled, the temperature dropping a half degree with the night. Marla pushed her sleeves higher and rubbed her palms together.

"She looked at you like she was solving you," she said. "That's what unsettled me. Like she already knew the outcome."

Jenna didn't reply.

Marla stood and gathered her bag. She didn't say she wanted to go, but the weight of the evening was already shifting, closing on its own.

"Just be careful," she said finally. "People like that? They're good in emergencies. Doesn't always mean they're good when your hands are handcuffed behind your back."

Jenna walked her to the door.

They hugged.

At the threshold, Marla turned once more. "I'll be here, no matter what. You know that."

Jenna nodded. "Thank you."

She stayed at the door until Marla's silhouette melted into the corridor.

Then she locked up, turned off the living room light, and picked up the phone again. Blackburn's last message glowed faint on the screen. Her number had already been confirmed. *Thursday. Eight sharp. Bar Cline.*

Outside, the street was mostly empty. A transit light blinked yellow on the far avenue. Somewhere, a brake released into the stillness.

Jenna stood barefoot beneath the window, watching nothing in particular. The shape of Blackburn's face curled behind her eyes like an encoded command.

She didn't smile. She didn't fidget. She let the quiet stay where it was.

That, too, was part of the learning.

Chapter 24

The sun pushed through the bedroom curtains and found Jenna awake. She lay still. Listened to the quiet house settling around her. Then swung her feet to the cool hardwood.

No alarm yet.

She showered under water that ran too hot, steam clouding the mirror until her reflection disappeared. Dressed in yesterday's careful choices of a pressed blouse, and a skirt that didn't bind at the waist. Tied her hair back, each strand pulled tight. Coffee steamed bitter in her favorite mug. Toast crunched between her teeth, crumbs scattering across the counter. Keys clinked into her bag with a sound like small bells.

Wednesday. Just one more day.

At her desk, the monitor threw pale blue light across her hands. Each fingertip illuminated. Cells filled with figures demanded attention. Revenue projections that would determine someone's bonus, expense reports that revealed who took cabs home after midnight. She checked a formula. Corrected a header. Sent the file to Audit with a soft click that sealed someone's fate for the quarter.

She kept the workflow moving. The room murmured around her. Phones ringing in precise electronic tones, printers humming their mechanical lullabies, low voices discussing quarterly reports that meant mortgages paid or unpaid. She looked like she belonged inside that rhythm. Another component in the office machinery.

Her thoughts drifted anyway.

Not far. Just enough that the numbers softened at the edges and something warmer slid into the spaces between calculations. Heat pooled low in her stomach, then scattered.

She saw Blackburn in clean white light. Not a halo, not fantasy. A woman stepping from a car, government issue, she guessed, and scanning a sidewalk with alert eyes. Eyes that took a quick read on everything. Potential threats. Escape routes. Witnesses. The cut of a jacket that fit the body that did the work. A wristwatch set three minutes fast because cops arrived early or not at all. No flowers. A zippered portfolio, leather worn smooth at the corners. A detail Jenna kept returning to for no reason she could name.

The keyboard clicked under her fingers. Quiet precision that had taken years to develop. She balanced a budget tab, nudged a pivot table into compliance, clicked Send. The inbox answered with a request from Purchasing. Always Purchasing, always urgent, never actually urgent. She flagged it. She watched the elevator reflection on her screen for the shape of her manager. No shadow yet.

She pictured a small restaurant near the river, where the tables sat close and the servers moved fast and quiet. The kind of place where cops ate late dinners and nobody asked questions about bloodstains on shirt cuffs. She saw herself and Blackburn share a corner booth because it let Blackburn face the door. Always the door. She tasted salt on good bread, clean wine that didn't try too hard. The conversation was light until it wasn't. Blackburn would not waste words. She would listen like it wasn't work but pleasure, head tilted just so, fingers still on the table.

A phone vibrating against wood put a small crack through the image.

In the imagined scene, Blackburn's hand went to the device before the second buzz. She'd read the caller ID already. She would not sigh. Sighing was for civilians. She would tell Jenna the truth with no softeners, voice dropping to the register she used for bad news. A body found. A witness walked in. A warrant signed. She would stand and put on her jacket and nod at the server to close the check. She would touch Jenna's hand once. Two fingertips tracing a slow circle in the center of her palm, callused skin against soft. A promise without ornament.

Jenna would be proud to watch her go.

Her own phone buzzed across her desk, vibration traveling through particleboard and up through her forearms. She glanced for her boss out of habit, a quick sweep of the bullpen. The walk to the copy room was clear. She unlocked the screen and saw Marla's name.

Are you excited for your date tonight?

She smiled. A quick pull at the corner of her mouth that faded just as fast. Heat rose in her cheek, she could feel it, the flush that always betrayed her. She typed.

Yes. I can't wait. I'm going to use lunch to buy a dress.

Marla replied almost at once.

Yellow sundress. Trust me.

Jenna read the suggestion and felt a small lift in her chest, like the moment before a sneeze. She brushed her hand over the fabric of her blouse, feeling the weave beneath her fingertips, cotton blend that would wrinkle by noon. She pictured a dress that would move when she did. Not loud. Not begging. Something that made it easy for Blackburn to see her without having to look too hard.

She closed her messages and returned to the spreadsheet. Checked a reconciliation against last month's close, numbers swimming before her eyes like black insects on white paper. She answered an email with three bullet points, kept it short because nobody read past the first paragraph, anyway. The office air ran cool against her skin, recycled and tasting faintly of toner. The overheads hummed at a frequency that made her molars ache. Time moved with the steady tick of the wall clock.

Her thoughts slipped back to the evening.

Not to an ending. To a start that felt clean. The smell of bread torn open, yeasty and warm, steam rising from the broken crust. The glassware was clear and catching light from candles that had burned low enough to flicker. The scrape of a chair when someone in the next booth stood, wallet hitting the table with the soft thud of folded leather. Blackburn's hand brushing hers on the white tablecloth. Not by accident. Heat sparking, contained, traveling up her arm like electricity finding ground. The kind of touch that asked for attention and got it.

This did not cancel the doubt. It never did.

The doubt came. What if she misread the screen chemistry? What if the timing failed them? What if Blackburn stayed at a scene all night and texted a single sentence at 2 a.m.? *Sorry. Tomorrow.* What if tomorrow never came?

Jenna rested her palms flat on the desk, the wood grain rough under her skin. She breathed in and out once, slowly, tasting coffee and something metallic at the back of her throat. She set the doubts aside like unnecessary memos. Filed them where they couldn't interrupt. She did not need them now.

Noon arrived with the precision of a government operation.

She stood. Slid her chair back. Took her bag. A coworker at the next pod arched an eyebrow. Sandra, who noticed everything and commented on half of it.

"Big meeting?"

"Lunch," Jenna said.

She kept her pace even to the elevator, heels clicking against industrial carpet that swallowed most sounds but not that one. On the street, heat rose off the pavement in visible waves, distorting the air like water. She walked two blocks through air thick enough to taste. The bell over the boutique door chimed when she entered, a bright silver sound that cut through the humid silence.

Color and light assaulted her pupils after the harsh LEDs upstairs. Racks set by size, organized with military precision. A clerk nodded and went back to folding, her movements economical and practiced. The place smelled faintly of sizing and new fabric, sharp chemical sweetness underneath. No florals, no heavy perfume. Clean retail space that didn't apologize for what it was.

Jenna took a slow pass down the first aisle. She touched cotton that would breathe, silk that would cling, a knit with a clean hand that suggested comfort over style. She did not want red. Too obvious. She did not want black. Too safe. She wanted something that told the truth without spelling it out.

She found it in the second aisle.

A blue floral sundress. The print was small and even, scattered like freckles across pale fabric. The straps narrow. The skirt hit just above the knee where it would catch a breeze. It looked simple. It looked like summer without noise.

She lifted the hanger, metal warm from the overhead track lighting. The size read right. She checked the seams and the zipper with fingers her mother had taught to find flaws, an old habit from lean years when returns weren't possible. She brought it to the fitting room.

Inside, she hung her bag on a hook that had seen better decades. Slipped out of her blouse and skirt, fabric releasing the day's heat from her skin. The dress went over her head and settled along her body like cool water. Clean line from shoulder to hem. She smoothed the waist and set the straps on her shoulders, adjusting until everything sat right. She turned.

The mirror answered with a version of herself she recognized. Not transformed. Clarified.

The blue pulled warmth from her eyes, made them less gray and more green. The cut followed her shape without apology, showed her waist where it narrowed, her legs where they deserved attention. The neckline showed what it needed to show and stopped there. Professional enough for dinner, soft enough for what might come after.

She stood still. Then she turned once, slowly, to see how the skirt moved. It moved well, swishing softly around her knees like water finding its level. She let herself like it. More than like it.

A small thought cut in under the rest.

The person Blackburn would see across the table should be the one already here. No costume. No plea dressed up as fashion. The dress joined the plan only if it amplified what was true. If it made the conversation easier, the choices clearer.

She touched the fabric at the bodice and pressed her thumb lightly against her sternum, feeling her heartbeat through cotton and skin. It centered her. She watched the gesture in the mirror and saw something else within it. A different evening that did not need a public table. A room with no eyes but theirs. Her hands held the armrests of a chair while Blackburn's voice found her ear. Clean commands that left no room for misunderstanding. No second chances because first chances were sacred. Consent would be clear and ongoing, a protocol honored like the law itself. Restraint applied like a tool, not a flourish.

Heat rose to Jenna's neck and settled out as resolve. She allowed the image and filed it next to the others, compartmentalized but not forgotten. The timing would be Blackburn's. The choice would be hers. The conversation would set the terms. She knew what she wanted and what she would not allow. That, too, felt like preparation.

She changed back into her work clothes, the familiar weight of professional armor. Carried the dress to the counter like an offering.

"This one," she said.

The clerk rang it up without commentary, fingers moving across keys with the efficiency of someone who'd done this ten thousand times. Jenna tapped her phone against the reader. The receipt printed with a soft whir, thermal paper curling at the edges. Bag in hand, she stepped back out onto the street.

She walked slower on the return. Counted the hours she had left at her desk. Five and a half, minus two fifteen-minute breaks she never took. She thought through the small moves that made a difference later. Fresh polish on chipped nails. Lip color that did not announce itself before she did. No new shoes because new shoes meant blisters, and blisters meant distraction.

Back upstairs, she tucked the bag into the bottom drawer of her desk and locked it with a soft click that felt like a promise kept. She opened a file and entered three lines of notes from a call that had taken place at 10:15, details that would matter to someone, somewhere, eventually. She updated her calendar with a follow-up at 3. She reviewed an invoice and flagged a discrepancy for Accounts Payable because someone had to care about the details.

Work held. She let it. It kept the day honest.

Her phone buzzed again. Marla.

Find anything?

Blue floral. Clean. Not yellow. Sorry.

Marla sent a row of approvals. Thumbs up, smiley face, heart. Jenna smiled and set the phone face down on the desk.

She checked her messages. Nothing from Blackburn. She pictured Blackburn mid-shift. A squad room with cork boards bleeding push-pins and whiteboards marked with crimes that kept the city awake. The sour smell of coffee that had sat too long on a burner, burned down to bitter syrup. Phones ringing in precise tones that meant someone was dead or missing or afraid. A detective at a neighboring desk asking for a case file, voice carrying too many late nights. Blackburn not looking up from the statement she was reading for the third time. A lead entered into a system with a number that would live in databases for years, maybe decades.

She liked knowing that part existed whether she ever saw it or not. It steadied the rest.

Her manager finally drifted past, stopped, and tapped the edge of Jenna's monitor with a knuckle.

"Are we good on the quarter-end report?"

"Almost," Jenna said. "Waiting for a revenue confirmation from Operations. If it hits by two, I can finalize it before I leave."

"Good. Keep me posted." He moved on, trailing the scent of coffee and deadline anxiety.

She exhaled and sent a short note to Operations with the subject line she knew would get a reply. Then she let her eyes fall to the drawer with the dress in it. She did not open it. Did not need to. It was there, waiting, patient as a held breath.

The afternoon stretched in front of her, plain and useful. She took a sip of water, the cool liquid sliding down her throat and settling in her stomach like a small anchor. She straightened a stack of files, edges aligned with geometric precision. She glanced at the clock. The day kept its shape.

She held on to that. The excitement stayed quieter now, more settled. It lived in small things. The zipper she would pull later. The knock on a door. A chair, a table, the space between two hands narrowing until there was no space at all.

Chapter 25

The engine's low hum carried across the lot as Blackburn's black car rolled through torn mist and settled into her slot at 6:55 AM. Gravel clicked under the tires. She checked the mirrors. Nothing unusual. One slow breath. Cool air met her face when she opened the door. Then she stepped out.

At seven on the dot, she moved through the entrance. Heels on polished tile, sharp and hollow. The shift change drifted around her in a tangle of burned coffee, warm fabric, and early-morning breath.

Heads lifted as she passed. Conversations clipped off. Chairs scraped back. Fingers found keyboards. LED light flattened every angle. She did not look left or right. She cut straight through to Homicide.

The chair gave a small complaint when she sat. The Autonomous Project files lay across her desk in dense columns, the paper dry against her fingertips. Diagrams. Acronyms. Lines that knotted and slipped when she tried to pin them. She skimmed once, then twice. The language felt engineered to keep outsiders out.

She kept her face still. Control first. She opened a new email and typed fast. *Willow. Decode this. Show me what it means. Now.* Send.

The reply arrived within a minute. *On my way. Twenty minutes.*

Blackburn's fingers tapped a steady beat on the desk. She typed again. *Make it ten.*

Silence returned with the soft whirr of vents and the faint buzz of lights. The wall clock ate seconds. She read the summary sheets one more time. Predictive deployment. Weighted patrols. Risk flags. If it worked as sold, it would rewire the job. It could put a car in the exact place a homicide was about to happen. It could make her unit look like a relic. She locked that thought where no one could see it.

Her screen lit again. Willow had sent a longer note. *A tool*, she wrote. *QueryQuanta. Free, private, unfiltered.* The words held on Blackburn's eye.

Unfiltered. A promise and a test.

Willow had broken down the use case into clean lines. *It will take complex queries*, she had written. Technical, legal, obscure. *It will not refuse tough questions. Use it to think around the edges.* Then, at the bottom, a dry warning. *Use it wisely.*

Blackburn typed a single word. *Unfiltered?*

Willow answered in a blink.

Most bots hard-stop on anything touching murder. Your project needs the opposite. You may need to ask how offenders adapt. If you start with a system that blocks you, you will miss the pattern. Start with one that will not. That is the point.

Blackburn asked for the link. It arrived. She clicked. A neutral landing page without cheer. She set up a bare-bones account with a personal address. No department tie.

She opened a new chat and tested the range.

What is predictive policing?

The responses stacked up cleanly. Data sources. Models. Hotspots. Individual risk. Anticipate crime with historical data and real-time inputs. Benefits: prevention, allocation, speed. Risks: bias, privacy, overreliance.

She kept going.

How could someone manipulate such models to their advantage?

The answer stayed theoretical. Garbage in, garbage out. Flood a location with false reports to pull resources. Exploit blind spots in features the model weights low. Distort context in public data to tilt the output. Blackburn read without reaction. The exposure window was real. The department would need controls.

Next.

Can the cars prioritize certain areas based on recent activity or officer requests? Also, can they track specific individuals?

Yes, the reply said. A system like this can shift patrol coverage in real time by request or spike. If programmed and authorized, it can follow a person using stored identifiers. Patrol patterns adjust as the subject moves.

She leaned back. A small, contained smile. Fugitive detail, but on wheels. The chair's vinyl warmed under her spine.

She sent Willow a short update. *Your help is not needed at the moment. I have what I need.*

Movement in the bullpen caught her eye. Dawson moved like he had slept in his suit. Tie loose. Eyes at half mast. He kept glancing toward the break room. Stale sugar and old coffee hung there. Sinclair sat upright when he saw her. Color rose in his face.

She crossed the floor.

"Morning, gentlemen." Her voice carried without heat.

Dawson grunted. Sinclair straightened further.

"Good morning, ma'am," he said. "The gala last night. You looked great on the feeds."

She let him have a brief smile. Shoulders back. Chin up. She touched the edge of his desk with one finger and drew it a few inches along the wood. The varnish felt slick. He watched the movement, throat working once. She stopped short of his hand and looked up. His composure slipped, then reset.

Dawson cut in.

"The Autonomous Project," he said. "What does it mean for Homicide?"

"It means the city wants a shortcut," she said. "Whether it works is another matter."

Cooper and Reeves walked in. Chairs pulled. Screens woke with a soft thrum. Blackburn lifted her voice.

"Listen up. You have heard the pitch. Predictive patrol. Data tells the cars where to be. If it performs as designed, patrol arrives before a killing. That changes our work more than anything in the last twenty years."

Sinclair frowned. "Changes how. Exactly."

"You will not get a call for a body and a canvas. You will get a hot spot and a potential actor. You will need to know how to make a case when nothing has happened. You will need legal to detain based on probability. It will change how we justify every move."

A low run of comments moved across the room. Keys ticked. Someone coughed into a sleeve.

Cooper said, "So we all learn a new job description."

Reeves said, "Or we learn to code."

Dawson leaned back, skeptical. "No way an algorithm clean-sweeps murder. People still decide to do things."

"True," Blackburn said. "But if even one killing gets interrupted, that is one scene we never see. Do not joke your way past it. Pay attention."

She held the room a moment longer, then broke off. "Back to work. Cases do not solve themselves."

She returned to her office. The blinds carved the light into narrow bars across the desk. Dust drifted in the beams. She placed the QueryQuanta transcript in a folder and clipped it shut. She wrote a note to herself in steady block print. Audit trails. Data integrity. Access controls. She would need leverage when the project touched her unit.

Her phone buzzed. Atlanta area code. A faint hiss on the line.

"Detective Blackburn."

"Lieutenant Harris, Atlanta PD." The voice carried a slow Georgia weight. "Calling about your boy Malone."

Blackburn stood. The floor felt rigid under her shoes.

"Extradition packet is incomplete," Harris said. "Five hours until we have to release."

"Understood," she said.

"I would need the signed warrant and the cell records you referenced. They are not here."

"Thank you," she said, and ended the call.

"Dawson. In my office. Now."

She watched him through the glass as he rose. Shoulders forward. Jaw set. He shut the door behind him with care. The latch clicked.

"Where are the cell phone records for Malone?"

He looked at the floor. "Misplaced."

"Call the carrier. They will send another copy. The production order is already issued. Five minutes." She pushed the desk phone toward him. The cord tapped once against the blotter.

He did not take it.

"Take the phone," she said.

A beat. He swallowed.

"I never sent the production order."

Silence settled. The room shrank around the word. Blackburn set the phone down and aligned it with the edge of the blotter. The leather under her wrist felt cool.

"Explain."

He spoke fast, then faster. "He did it. He is dirty. I needed enough to get a judge to sign the arrest warrant. I could not get there. So, I drew up a summary of cell hits linking him to the scene. I ran it to Chief Hayes and got the warrant. I knew you would spot it eventually. I was going to backfill. It got away from me."

Her face did not change. The clock resumed its quiet tick.

"Say it." She tapped her finger on the desk. Once.

"Nothing ties him to the scene," he said. "Nothing at all."

She let the statement sit until he shifted on his feet. A faint scuff on the carpet.

"By pulling the chief in, you have contaminated the chain beyond repair," she said.

"I thought I could control it." His voice thinned. "This was supposed to protect the unit. They are measuring us every day now. I was trying to keep one more open homicide off your board."

He lifted his eyes to hers, then dropped them.

"I was trying to help you."

"You helped no one," she said.

He made a fist, then released it. "You cannot tell anyone. This will wreck me. It will drag you and the unit down. We are on the same side."

Her right hand slid to her hip. The leather creaked once under her palm. She did not draw. She closed the snap and stepped back. The air between them cooled.

"Call Harris," she said. "Tell him to release Malone."

He blanched. "What do I tell him?"

"I don't care what story you pick. My name does not appear in it."

She pointed to the door.

He turned.

"And Dawson."

He froze.

"This is not over."

He moved back into the bullpen. Blackburn watched him from the glass. He wiped his forehead with his sleeve and placed the call. His hand shook on the receiver. She noted the details.

Chapter 26

The phone sliced through the hush that lingered after the storm. Sinclair reached for it and paused a beat before lifting the receiver.

"Homicide, Sinclair." He checked the display. Dispatch. He sat straighter.

"Patrol is on scene at 178 Maplewood," the dispatcher said. The voice was clear, unhurried. "Suspicious death. Likely a homicide. The victim is a child."

"A child."

Movement in the bullpen stalled. Chairs stayed half-turned. A cup hovered, then dropped to the desk with a soft click. Pens went still mid-scratch. The room held the stale scent of coffee and damp wool. No one wanted that call.

"Understood," Sinclair said. "We'll send someone." He set the receiver down. His hand stayed there a moment, the plastic cool under his palm.

Blackburn stepped out of her office, heels sharp on the linoleum. Eyes clear and direct. She took in the room in a calculated sweep and chose her target.

"Dawson. You're up."

Color slipped from Dawson's face. His shoulders dipped as if the floor had tilted. "Why me?"

"Because I said so." Her tone stayed flat. "Keep the parents informed at all times. I do not want another Cindy Discart complaint."

A few glances moved across the room. Everyone understood. No one spoke.

Dawson rose. He pulled his coat from his chair and collected a pad and recorder. He looked at Sinclair, then away. Blackburn watched him leave with a stillness that pressed against the air.

The door clicked behind him. The sound felt soft and final.

She addressed the room without raising her voice. "No one assists Dawson unless I ask for it. He runs this one."

Silence reset. People bent to their screens. Keys clicked in uneven runs. Files shifted with a dry rasp. The smell of old coffee sat heavy. No one looked at Dawson's empty desk.

The morning moved because it had to. Calls in. Calls out. Forms signed. Small talk kept low. Sinclair drafted a search request, the cursor blinking like a metronome. Reeves flagged a lab report that needed a follow-up. Cooper typed notes in quick, precise bursts, rhythm steady as breathing. Blackburn stayed in her office, lines of a case file sliding under her thumb as she skimmed and marked.

By the end of the hour, Dawson returned. He moved like he had been out all night. His shirt was creased and dark at the collar. A sour trace of whiskey traveled with him and cut through the coffee smell. He set his pad on Sinclair's desk.

"Want to work it together?" His voice was rough and dry.

Sinclair kept his eyes on his screen. "I can't."

Dawson turned to Cooper. "You free?"

"Not today," Cooper said. Quick. Apologetic.

"Reeves?"

Reeves shook his head. "Tied up on the lab backlog."

Each refusal arrived with the same look. Sorry. Not now. He heard the echo of Blackburn's order in every answer.

His gaze drifted until it landed on her office. She was watching him. A small smile tugged at the corners of her mouth. Nothing big. Enough. His hand pressed against his stomach. He understood the shape of what was coming. He would take the worst work. He would be left alone with it. He could already feel the grind start at the edges.

Blackburn turned a page. Afternoon light cut through the blinds and laid thin bars across her desk. Dust lifted and settled in the beams. Phones rang in uneven waves. Voices rose and dropped beyond the glass like weather moving through.

The tone outside shifted. Cooper appeared in her doorway with a live-wire energy that pulled the room forward.

"Update on Jane Doe CCTR-02399," he said. "The alley."

She gave a short nod. "Go."

"I spoke with the director of parks and forestry. She identified the plant material from the victim's hair and clothes. Common barberry. Jack pine. Box elm. Stinking chamomile."

One corner of Blackburn's mouth lifted. "Stinking chamomile."

"Only one site in the city has all four together." Cooper leaned in as if the news ran hot in his hands. "Poston Park. Western edge."

She set her pen down. "Plan it."

"I'll take two uniforms. Establish a grid. Photograph and bag anything that fits. I'll have them canvass the maintenance staff. We'll map the plant clusters and compare to the plants at the dump site."

"Good." She nodded once. "See if there are cameras on the access roads or private property. Maybe someone kept footage from that long ago."

"On it." Cooper stood. His hands were already moving, the plan settling into muscle.

"Cooper." He stopped. "Log your search pattern. I want it clean."

He gave a tight smile. "Yes, boss."

When he was gone, she opened a new email. Subject line simple. *We need to talk about Dawson.* She sent it and watched the screen clear.

Time thinned. The bullpen returned to its rhythm. The scent of paper and toner sat under the hum of lights. Blackburn leaned back and turned the pen between her fingers. Her eyes swept the room.

An alert on her phone chirped. She glanced at the screen. The tension in her shoulders eased a fraction. She pictured Jenna's mouth tilt and the steady look in her eyes when she waited for instruction.

She wanted a session. Tight rules. Clean edges. Her body remembered what that did to her nerves. She exhaled once and set the phone face down on the desk.

Chapter 27

The sun slipped behind the buildings and left a low wash of light on the street. Blackburn waited outside the Urban Bistro and watched the foot traffic. She kept her back to the wall and her eyes on reflections in the glass. No tails. No lingering faces. The crowd moved on, indifferent. A bus sighed at the curb, and the door breathed out wine and garlic before it sealed again.

She adjusted the line of her blazer and the collar beneath it. A hint of lace. Controlled, not careless. The fabric sat cool against her skin. She checked the time. Three minutes late.

The bistro's windows framed a steady spill of warm light. A clean sign caught the eye without trying. Planter boxes lifted the edge off the brick. Enough polish to pull in a dinner crowd that wanted to feel informed but not studied. Inside, silhouettes moved through amber.

A patrol car rolled past at the end of the block. Tires hissed. She marked the unit number.

A flash of blue. Jenna slipped through the flow of bodies in a sundress that lifted with the breeze. She saw Blackburn and slowed. A hand to her chest. Nerves in the open. The cotton fluttered against her legs as she came to a stop.

"I'm so sorry I'm late," Jenna said, breath light and uneven. A hint of citrus on the air when she spoke.

Blackburn stepped close. Warm breath at Jenna's ear. "You'll answer for that later." A quiet tap to the rear. Not hard. Clear enough. Heat rose through fabric where her hand landed.

Jenna flushed and smiled. They kissed once. Not long. Enough to establish terms. Street noise thinned until it sounded far away.

Inside, the room held its heat low. Amber sconces, brick with age, a piano in the corner. The air smelled of lemon and seared meat. The noise level stayed civilized. Cutlery, glass, voices. No raised tones. Cool air slipped across the back of Blackburn's neck.

Blackburn guided Jenna with a hand at the small of her back. She kept her touch steady, fingers flat, nothing showy. The floor gave a faint grit under her heel. She noted the camera above the bar and the emergency exit past the kitchen swing door. Her seat would face the room.

The host appeared. "Welcome."

"That one," Blackburn said, pointing to a corner table by the window. Good sightlines. A pane of glass for a second angle. No one at their backs. The glass offered a dim reflection of the room and the street beyond.

They sat. Jenna reached for the menu. "Grilled salmon with lemon butter," she said. "Maybe asparagus."

"No." Blackburn kept her voice mild. "Carrots."

Jenna blinked. "Why?"

"The smell. And because I said."

Jenna lowered her eyes. "Yes."

The waiter came. Movies teach servers to see everything. This one saw what he needed and nothing else. He placed water without clatter and waited.

"She'll have the grilled salmon with lemon butter and sautéed carrots," Blackburn said. "Filet mignon for me. Rare. Grilled vegetables. A bottle of Albariño."

Jenna watched her order and let the moment land. "I didn't expect you to order for me," she said. Admiration edged with curiosity. "I like it."

"Good." Blackburn did not look at the waiter when she dismissed him. "That will be all."

He nodded and left. Blackburn turned back to Jenna and brushed a stray hair behind her ear. A small touch. Intentional. The fine strand clung to her finger before falling away.

"I know what I want," she said. "I move toward it."

Jenna's breath shortened. "I don't mind." Truth, not bravado.

"Noted." Blackburn's thumb drew one slow arc over the back of Jenna's hand, then fell away. Warmth lingered in its wake.

The waiter returned with glassware and the bottle. He presented the label. Blackburn glanced at it without breaking focus on Jenna. She lifted the glass for the test pour, inhaled once, and sipped. Stone fruit and salt at the edge. A small nod.

He filled their glasses and set the bottle in ice. No fuss. The bucket creaked softly as it settled.

Blackburn raised her drink. "To a dirty evening."

Jenna touched her glass to Blackburn's. A bead of condensation tracked down her finger. "To a very dirty evening."

Their fingers met as they set the stems down. A brief press. Heat rose through the contact and then ebbed. Blackburn let the quiet hold a beat before speaking again.

"I like details," she said. "Food. People. They tell you what you need if you listen."

Jenna leaned in. "Tell me about your day."

"Paperwork in the morning. More paperwork in the afternoon." Blackburn would never say more than that to a civilian. Ever.

Jenna smiled. "Sounds as boring as my day."

"It is." Confidence without heat. "You work downtown. Financials." Not a question. She had already checked.

Jenna nodded. "Spreadsheets and team meetings all day long."

The food arrived without ceremony. The salmon sat in clean lines with a thin coat of lemon butter that shone under the light. Carrots in a tight row held their color. Steam rose faintly and carried citrus and sea. Blackburn's steak rested under a glossy sear with vegetables answering on the side. The plate radiated heat. The scent of iron and char rose when she cut in.

"Oh my," Jenna said, eyes bright. "This looks divine."

"Eat." Blackburn watched the first bite. Jenna closed her eyes and made a soft sound. Blackburn tracked the pulse at her throat and the way her shoulders loosened as flavor landed.

"It's incredible. The sauce is perfect."

Blackburn cut into her steak. Warm red at the center. She tasted and nodded once. "Exquisite." The juices ran clean and sweet across her tongue.

She held out a piece of steak on her fork. "Taste."

Jenna leaned forward and took it from the tines. Clean. No fuss. Her breath caught. "You're right," she said. "I didn't know I'd enjoy that so much."

"I know." Blackburn kept her tone light. Not teasing. Certain. "I like control. I like consent. I like seeing where they meet."

Jenna's cheeks colored. She laughed softly and let it fade. "I like the way you take the room." Her voice lowered. "It does something to me."

They ate without rushing. Conversation moved around the edges of work and wants. Blackburn offered facts and left out the rest. The rhythm of a precinct that ran on coffee, budget fights, and stubbornness. Jenna offered stories from her office. A contractor's rounding error. A department head who didn't catch it. The picture formed in clean strokes.

Blackburn listened intently to what was not said.

The waiter cleared plates. Porcelain clicked lightly and then disappeared. Blackburn rested her hand on Jenna's again. "I've had a good time," she said. "Are you ready to play?"

Jenna's answer arrived on a breath. "Yes." A tremor she did not try to hide. "It feels like something is pulling me toward you."

"Don't fight it." Blackburn threaded their fingers together. "We follow it. No limits you do not set. No surprises you do not agree to."

Jenna nodded. "I trust you."

"Wise."

They stood. The room kept moving around them as if nothing had changed. Outside, the night had cooled. Streetlights threw soft pools on the sidewalk. A faint breeze lifted napkins on empty tables near the door. Blackburn kept her pace even and her attention wide. A couple argued at the corner. A courier rolled past with a dead rear light. A man in a hoodie watched the traffic and no one in particular. A siren bled through from several blocks away and faded.

Blackburn's keys clicked in her hand. The car waited where she had left it, under a camera and within sight of the hostess stand. She liked that arrangement. She liked the new keys too. The remote gave a soft chirp that echoed off brick.

"Tonight has been..." Jenna searched for her word.

"Perfect," Blackburn said. She stepped in and put Jenna's back against the car door. Bodies aligned. Air charged. Her hand on Jenna's waist. Firm. Certain. The steel at Jenna's spine held a chill that made her shiver.

The kiss was inevitable. Heat and control, no rush. Jenna's fingers found Blackburn's lapel and held on. The scent of her skin rose clean and warm.

"Come home with me," Blackburn said against her mouth. Not a question. Not rough. Final.

"Yes." No hesitation.

Blackburn opened the passenger door and helped Jenna in. She buckled the belt and let her fingers trail once along soft skin. Goosebumps rose. She closed the door and walked around the car without looking back. Her reflection skimmed across the glass as she passed.

The drive moved through thinning traffic. Blackburn kept one hand on the wheel and offered the other. Jenna took it. They sat like that, linked. Held. To be owned. Streetlights cut across Blackburn's profile in clean intervals. Her jawline held steady. Her mouth gave the faintest smile. The engine hummed and the tires whispered over clean asphalt.

"You're staring," Blackburn said.

"I can't help it."

Blackburn lifted their joined hands and pressed a kiss to her knuckles. Tender. Possessive. "Good."

She checked her mirrors. No repeat faces. No car holding her lane too long. She took an extra turn and came back to her route. Habit. Discipline. The city slid by in ordered slices of light and shadow.

"Almost there," she said.

Jenna squeezed her hand. Words were no longer needed.

The night opened ahead of them. Quiet. Certain. Waiting.

Chapter 28

Blackburn killed the engine. Night air slipped in, the block holding its breath. One porch light, a dog two houses over. Jenna caught her sleeve. "Who is that?" Wire-thin. Eyes wide.

Blackburn reached into the car, opened the glovebox, and withdrew the matte pistol. Chamber check, mag seated. In for four, hold, out. "Where?"

"By the bushes. Tall, then gone."

"Stay by the car." She moved low and quietly. Leaves whispering, cooling engine tick, a sprinkler hissing next door. A thin blade of light across the hedge. "Police," level. "Show me your hands."

Silence. No shift of leaves. The hedge gave her nothing back but sap-smell and the small scrape of branch on brick, an absence that could be shadow or a man holding breath.

"Nothing obvious," she said. "Could be shadow. Could be a person. I'm not ruling either out."

"Can we go inside?"

"Of course. Stay close."

Blackburn kept the lights low. Corners first. Hall. Kitchen. Latch firm. The alarm panel was a steady green. Then the counter. Pistol down, pointed safely at nothing. The house answered through its old seams. The fridge hummed, a plank settled. Rain thought about starting. And some of the held breath in her chest unknotted.

"You did right in telling me," Blackburn said.

Jenna stepped into her heat, eyes flicking to the weapon. "You took charge, and something in me went quiet. It was arousing."

"It's my job." A small lift of the shoulder, nothing casual in her gaze. "You knew I was a cop." The truth pleased and pricked at the same time. Want ran fast alongside duty, and Blackburn felt the rub where they met.

"It's deeper," Jenna said, voice dropping. "You protect. You decide. It does something to me."

They held the silence long enough to feel each other's breath. Blackburn traced the line of her throat. Jenna exhaled against her wrist.

"You like control," Blackburn said. "The kind that keeps bad things out."

"The outside thing was nothing. I don't like guns," Jenna murmured. "The way you moved? That was the real thing."

"The gun. The authority." Blackburn glanced at it, then back. "Being with someone who will stand up for you. Who takes the hit if it comes."

"Are you turned on right now?"

"Yes." The flat truth. "Containing a scene does it every time."

Jenna fit herself in, chest to chest. "Say more."

"If I'm responsible for you, I think in outcomes," Blackburn said. "I cut risk. I send my people home. That turns me on."

"I want to give you that control."

Goosebumps rose. Blackburn pressed precise thumbs into Jenna's chest. The small sound that came back was pulled from the root. It landed harder than she allowed herself. She let the flare pass through her and kept the line.

"You liked being scared outside," Blackburn said in her ear.

"I like it when you manage the fear," Jenna whispered under Blackburn's shirt. "With you here, I'm not afraid."

Blackburn reached past her, gaze steady. "I keep what is mine safe."

"I want to be yours."

"You already are." The admission cost a breath. She paid it.

She turned the pistol sideways, dropped the magazine, racked, locked, checked the chamber. She checked it again. A live round jumped free and pinged once, brass kissed the tile, then silence. She stowed everything in the pantry safe, palm plate flashing green at her print. When the door clunked shut, the status light settled to a steady red. Locked.

"I'm glad you did that," Jenna said, relief braided with heat.

"You told me you were scared of it," Blackburn said. "I heard you." Then she turned the deadbolt. The lock steadied her pulse. Keys down. Movement fluid as she slipped back to her guest.

"It does too much damage too easily. It put ice in my stomach. I still want the rest."

"Good," Blackburn said, crowding her against the countertop, close enough to feel the next breath. "I set the terms. You follow them."

"Yes."

Blackburn took Jenna's wrists, placed them behind her back. "Keep them there until I say otherwise."

"I will."

She kissed once, not softly. Compliance held. Heat rose between her legs.

"You like clear orders," Blackburn said.

"I do. You give good ones."

Blackburn tipped her chin. Her other hand drew a path to the sternum. She pressed and released, measuring. She slid Jenna's phone from her pocket and put it into a signal-shield pouch. No leaks.

"You can breathe now," Blackburn said. "We're alone."

Spare living room left, the kitchen island right. Lamps low, one tone. No shadows to distort intent. Jenna stalled at the threshold. Her shoulders were tight, hands flexed into half fists.

"Your hands are shaking," Blackburn said.

"I'm fine."

"I didn't ask if you were fine."

Something eased in Jenna's face.

"You may wait on the sofa," Blackburn said. "Or at the island. Choose."

Rain began, a thin tap that gathered. Streetlights cut diffused bars across the counter. Blackburn let the quiet work. It wasn't a trick, it was a way to let the body arrive in the room and accept what the mind had already said yes to.

"The choice is yours," she repeated. "Once made, it stands."

Jenna looked left, then right. She didn't ask why it mattered. She knew. Her gaze settled on the island. Shoulders unhooked, weight forward. She crossed with purposeful steps. The floor wasn't soft. It was solid. At the island, she planted both palms, fingers spread. Not a pose. A stable plant. Surrender framed by choice.

Blackburn set a glass of water, and a small pear, freshly washed, on the near corner. "Stand where you want," she said. "Hands as you choose. If you need water or a bite to eat, take it. If you need to sit, ask, and I will answer. If you want this to stop, say red. If you can't speak, tap three times on the counter with your right hand."

Jenna drank. Set the glass down without a sound. She nodded. Instruction grounded her more than heat.

"Tonight," Blackburn said, "you'll have clear instructions. You'll speak when asked. You may ask for needs. You will not be punished for asking. Do you understand?"

"Yes."

Blackburn lowered the lights a notch. "Place your hands flat on the counter. Shoulder width. Feet under your hips. Hold until I release you."

Jenna set her hands. Breath found order. Rain drew a perimeter around the house.

"The fear you felt outside was forced on you," Blackburn said again. "What happens in here is what you choose."

"Yes."

"Unbutton your dress," Blackburn said. "Stop at the third button."

Recognition flickered. Jenna's hands trembled, then steadied. One slit opened, then another. At the third she paused, then slipped it free. Warmth bloomed where air met newly revealed skin.

"Good," Blackburn said. A record, not praise. She reached into a drawer.

Blackburn moved to the center of the floor. Neutral ground. The olive-wood spoon lay cool in her hand, satin from long use. A kitchen thing with a different purpose.

"Come here," she said, pointing to a plank scarred by a moved chair. "Stand on this spot."

Leaving the island asked more of her than staying. Jenna lifted her fingers, set them back, then chose. Steps sure and poised. Close now, the pulse at her throat steadied under strain. She stopped where indicated. No anchor. Full exposure. Blackburn felt the thin pull of worry, wanting, and checked the room again in a glance that cost nothing, then let it go.

"Ask me for the first strike," Blackburn said.

Not to receive. To request. Jenna's throat worked. She swallowed once. She found her voice.

"May I have the first strike, please?"

The please was hers.

"Yes," Blackburn said. "You may. Remain still. Breathe normally."

A soft sound in the air. Wood met the curve of Jenna's upper thigh. A clean report and heat bloomed. The sound seemed to hang a beat in the kitchen's hollow, then slide into the rain. Balance wavered, then held. Breath caught, then reset.

"Numbers," Blackburn said.

"Seven at first. Now a four." Jenna's eyes flicked left as if checking herself. Then she came back.

"What kind of four?"

"Defined. Clean." She let a thin breath out, a small correction inside the word.

"Do you want another?"

"Yes." A quick edge of humor tugged at her mouth and disappeared. "Yes."

"Why?"

"It keeps me here."

A second strike, a neighboring track. Same force. Sound cracked and settled. Blackburn watched the swallow she trusted more than language.

"Eight. Then five."

"What kind of five?"

"Solid."

"Close your dress," Blackburn said. A beat. "The top two undone."

Jenna buttoned with care.

"Now, kneel."

She did. The kneeling would do the work now. Controlled descent. The mark showed. An oval blush brightening. Hands on thighs. Spine straight. Dignity inside surrender. The floor bit in a way that clarified time. Blackburn felt the answering weight of the dining chair when she set it down, a twin anchor to the lock's earlier heft.

"How long can you hold this?" Blackburn asked.

"As long as you require."

"Honesty."

"Ten minutes before the floor matters."

"Then it hurts?"

"Yes."

"Keep your eyes on me until I say otherwise."

"Yes," louder the second time.

Blackburn moved away, not closer. A straight-backed dining chair, set for a clean sightline. She sat. Posture exact. The storm tightened the perimeter. On the wall behind Jenna, the alarm panel stayed steadily green. No alerts tripped.

"Be still," she said. "And wait."

Jenna held. Knees to hardwood. Cotton brushing skin. The house amplified small sounds. A pipe's sigh, the fridge's hum sliding to quiet, rain writing the same sentence on glass. The spoon lay where Blackburn had set it. Domestic. Visible. Unneeded.

"Stay with me," Blackburn said.

"I will."

"Good."

They kept the hold they'd chosen. Outside, fear remained what it was. In here, control was a choice kept, the line between them held steady and true.

Chapter 29

Blackburn shifted in the chair, the wood creaking beneath her weight. The sound cut through the stillness. She let her gaze travel the length of Jenna's kneeling form, noting the measured rise and fall of her chest and the slight tremble in her clasped hands that betrayed anticipation. The blue sundress pooled around her knees, the cotton catching the low kitchen light. Cool tile pressed against Jenna's shins. Time to push deeper, past the physical act of kneeling, into the space where real surrender lived.

"Remove your dress," Blackburn said. The words fell into the space between them, simple and absolute.

Jenna's eyes widened slightly, pupils dilating. A flush crept up her neck, warming her cheeks. Her fingers flexed once against her thighs, a small tell Blackburn cataloged without comment.

"Now?" Jenna asked, her voice barely above a whisper.

Blackburn clapped her hands once. The sharp crack rang in the quiet room.

Jenna gasped and reached for the remaining buttons on her dress, fingers working despite their slight tremble. The third button slipped free with a soft click, then the fourth. A triangle of pale skin opened at her chest, visible in the kitchen's austere light. She paused, eyes lifting in a quiet plea for permission or reassurance.

"Continue," Blackburn said.

The final buttons gave way under Jenna's careful touch. She gathered the hem and lifted the dress over her head. The fabric whispered against her skin, leaving a trace of static along her arms that raised a faint line of gooseflesh. Her hair fell loose around her shoulders once freed from the cotton.

Blackburn observed with steady focus. Underneath the dress, Jenna wore simple black lingerie. Functional rather than overtly seductive. The contrast between utilitarian cotton and the ceremony of their actions pleased her. Nothing performed. Nothing false.

"Fold it," Blackburn instructed, indicating a wooden stool near the island with a slight nod. "Neatly."

Jenna smoothed the dress across her lap, aligning seams and edges with careful attention. The cotton held a faint trace of detergent and summer air. She folded it once, then again, each movement deliberate. The task steadied her. Blackburn saw it in the calming of her hands and the even cadence of her breathing. When finished, Jenna stretched forward to place the folded bundle on the stool, then resumed her position. The small task was completed with care.

"Look at me," Blackburn said when Jenna settled back onto her heels.

Their eyes met across the tiled expanse. Connection established and held.

"Touch your breasts," Blackburn said. "Through your bra."

The command hung between them for three heartbeats. Jenna swallowed, throat working. Then her hands lifted, palms sliding from her bare stomach to cup herself through the black cotton. Her touch was tentative at first, almost clinical.

"Not like that," Blackburn corrected, voice level. "Touch them because they belong to you."

Understanding flickered across Jenna's face. Her hands adjusted, fingers curving with intent around the soft weight of her breasts. She applied gentle pressure, thumbs tracing small circles that moved the fabric against her skin.

"That's better," Blackburn said. "Now squeeze. Pinch your nipples through the fabric."

Jenna complied, fingers finding the sensitive peaks beneath the cotton. Her breath caught audibly as she applied pressure. Her eyelids fluttered, threatening to close.

"Eyes open," Blackburn reminded her, sharp and calm. "Look at me. Pinch harder."

Jenna's gaze snapped back and locked with Blackburn's. The effort of maintaining eye contact while touching herself heightened it. Embarrassment, arousal, vulnerability. The combination sat plainly on her face, signals Blackburn read easily.

"Harder," Blackburn instructed. "I want to see it on your face when it hurts."

Jenna's fingers tightened on her nipples, twisting slightly. Her mouth parted, a small involuntary sound escaping. Pain and pleasure crossed her features in quick succession and then settled together.

"Good," Blackburn said. "Keep going."

Jenna continued. Her movements grew more confident under Blackburn's steady gaze. A flush spread from her chest upward, heat brightening her skin. Her breathing quickened, the sound shallow and even. The black cotton did little to conceal the hard points of her nipples, the fabric stretched tight, a faint rasp of material against skin with each motion.

"Your eyes are trying to close again," Blackburn observed.

"It is difficult to keep them open," Jenna admitted, voice tight with effort and arousal.

"Difficult does not mean impossible," Blackburn replied evenly. "Continue."

Jenna nodded once, sharply. Her fingers worked with intent now, alternating slow caresses with sharper pinches that pulled small gasps from her throat. All the while, she kept her gaze on Blackburn's face, though the struggle showed in the minute strain around her eyes.

The dim light skimmed a sheen of sweat along Jenna's hairline and at the hollow of her throat. The flush deepened across her chest, the color pooling at the tops of her breasts where they swelled above the bra.

Blackburn watched every reaction, noting tiny shifts in Jenna's breathing and the micro changes in her expression. Control did not come from touching Jenna herself, but from directing her hands and making her complicit in her own exposure.

"Are you aroused?" Blackburn asked, though the answer was written clearly on Jenna's body.

Jenna nodded, then corrected herself. "Yes," she said, voice low but steady. "Very."

"From touching yourself or from me watching you touch yourself?"

The question landed with precision. Jenna's hands faltered in their rhythm.

"Both," she admitted. "But mostly that you are watching. Telling me how." Her voice broke slightly on the last word, revealing more than she meant to show.

Blackburn nodded once, acknowledging the truth without praise or censure. "Tell me what you feel."

"Heat," Jenna answered immediately. "Pressure. A tightness that spreads from where I am touching down between my legs."

"Be specific."

Jenna swallowed. "My nipples are sensitive. When I pinch them, it sends a direct line of pleasure straight down to my cunt. My skin feels too tight. I can feel my pulse everywhere." She drew a breath. "I am wet."

Rain pattered steadily against the windows, a soft curtain around their exchange. The refrigerator hummed.

"Stop," Blackburn said.

Jenna's hands froze, palms still cupping herself through the cotton.

"Place your hands on your thighs. Palms down."

Compliance came without delay. Jenna lowered her hands to rest on her bare thighs, the change in position straightening her spine further. Without the distraction of movement, her breathing sounded more pronounced in the quiet.

Blackburn assessed her coolly. Dilated pupils. Flushed skin. A slight tremble in her thighs as she maintained her kneeling position on the tile. All clear markers of arousal. More significant was the focus in her eyes, the absolute presence in the moment. No thoughts of before or after. Only now, only this room, only Blackburn's next command.

"Are you aroused?" Blackburn asked again, her tone unchanged from the first time.

"Yes," Jenna answered without hesitation, voice stronger than before. A truth claimed rather than confessed.

Blackburn nodded once, satisfied. "Show me," she said, the two words landing in the quiet kitchen. The clock ticked twice. The command was not vague. They both understood precisely what showing meant in this context. Evidence. Proof. A demonstration of the arousal Jenna claimed to feel, laid bare for verification.

Jenna inhaled sharply, her chest lifting with the breath. Something flashed in her eyes before settling into resolve. Her fingers found the clasp between her breasts and worked it open with an efficient click. The black cotton loosened its hold, warm from her skin.

She drew the straps down her shoulders slowly, not teasing but calculated. Cool air met heated skin. The bra fell away, revealing breasts with nipples already tight from earlier touch. She set the garment aside with the same precision she had shown with the dress. Order remained part of their exchange.

"Like this?" she asked. Her voice stayed steady despite her exposure.

"Yes," Blackburn confirmed. "Now touch them again. Show me how you like to be touched."

Jenna lifted her hands, cupping the undersides of her breasts. Her touch shifted without the barrier of fabric. It grew more direct. She traced circles around her areolae with her thumbs, avoiding the peaks at first. The restraint in her movements suggested experience and control.

Blackburn watched the subtle shifts in Jenna's expression as she touched herself. Lips parted when fingers brushed across nipples. A slight furrow formed between her brows as sensation focused. Each micro expression was noted and stored.

"Use your fingernails," Blackburn instructed. "Lightly across the skin."

Jenna complied. She drew short nails in faint passes across her breasts. Goosebumps rose in their wake, skin tightening visibly. Her breath caught when she traced the tender underside, a small sound escaping before she could silence it.

"And on your nipples."

Jenna circled them with a single fingertip, the touch feathering at the edge of contact. Then she pinched, a quick, sharp pressure that pulled a sound from her throat. She repeated the motion and built a rhythm that balanced anticipation with sensation.

"You've done this before," Blackburn observed. It was not a question.

"Yes," Jenna confirmed, keeping her rhythm.

"For yourself or for someone watching?"

"Both. Different times."

Blackburn nodded once and took it in. "More," she said.

The single word hung between them. Jenna's hands stilled on her breasts. She looked at Blackburn's face and found no ambiguity. She lowered one hand to the waistband of her panties and slid her fingertips just beneath the elastic. The cotton clung to where her skin ran warm and damp.

"May I stand to remove these?" she asked.

"No," Blackburn replied. "Take them off while kneeling."

Jenna shifted her weight, hooked her thumbs into the sides, and worked the fabric down over her hips. The position was awkward and broke the clean line of her posture for a moment. She lifted one knee slightly, then the other, easing the underwear down her thighs and past her calves. The black cotton joined her other clothing, neatly placed beside it.

Fully naked now, she resumed her kneeling position on the hard kitchen floor. The tile pressed cool against her knees. Her right hand returned to her breast, continuing the alternating pattern of gentle caresses and firmer pinches that had proven effective. Her left hand rested on her thigh, held in readiness.

"Between your legs," Blackburn directed. "Show me how wet you are."

Jenna's hand moved with steadiness along the inside of her thigh. When her fingers reached the juncture between her legs, they caught the low light with a glisten that confirmed what she had claimed. She traced the outer lips with a single finger, gathering moisture and spreading it with unhurried care.

Blackburn observed the mechanics of the touch. She studied pressure, rhythm, and location. She also tracked the quickening of Jenna's breath, the deeper flush creeping across her chest, and the faint tremble in her thighs. These were physical responses that did not yield to control.

"Wider," Blackburn instructed.

Jenna shifted and spread her knees further apart on the hard floor. The position opened her more fully to Blackburn's view and threatened her balance. She angled her hips slightly backward to compensate. The adjustment exposed her more completely.

The display was not theatrical. There was no artifice in how Jenna positioned herself. Function and compliance guided her decisions. One hand continued working at her breast while the other traced increasingly focused patterns between her legs. Her breathing grew less controlled. Small catches disrupted the rhythm.

"Both hands," Blackburn said. Her voice stayed unchanged despite the intensity accumulating in the room.

Jenna hesitated only a fraction of a second before releasing her breast. She brought both hands between her legs. With one hand, she spread herself open. With the other, she continued her exploration. Her thumb found her clitoris and circled with precision while a finger traced the entrance below.

Blackburn's focus sharpened without change in her posture. "Tell me what you feel."

"Pressure," Jenna answered. Her voice had tightened. "Heat building. A kind of tightness that wants release." She swallowed and took a breath. "When I touch here." She pressed her thumb more firmly on her clitoris. "It sends waves through my abdomen. When I circle here." She traced the sensitive flesh at her opening. "I feel empty. I want to be filled."

"Don't penetrate yourself," Blackburn said. "Not yet."

"Yes," Jenna acknowledged. She adjusted her touch and kept her fingers shallow.

She held her position with her back slightly arched and her knees spread wide on the cold floor. Her fingers worked with rising urgency and found patterns and pressures that drew a stronger response. Her breathing grew heavier and less controlled. Muscles jumped in her thighs and along her abdomen.

"Faster," Blackburn commanded.

Jenna's movements quickened. Fingers worked with more urgency against slick, exposed flesh. The calculated quality of her earlier touches gave way to something more instinctive. Need drove her hand. Her free hand returned to her breast and squeezed with purpose.

The sounds she made were small but unmistakable. Sharp intakes of breath. A note caught in her throat when a particular touch landed exactly where it should. Her eyes stayed on Blackburn's face. Focus wavered as sensation challenged the discipline of eye contact.

"Are you close?" Blackburn asked. The answer was evident in Jenna's flushed skin and trembling thighs.

"Yes," Jenna managed. The word clipped clean. "Very close."

"Stop."

The command landed. Jenna's hands stilled, her body tightening to stop the motion she had built. A small involuntary sound escaped, not a protest so much as a recognition of the edge she had reached and been pulled back from.

"Remove your hands. Place them on your thighs."

Jenna complied with effort, fingers shaking as she flattened her palms to her thighs. Her breath came fast, shallow. Heat climbed across her skin.

"How close were you?" Blackburn asked.

"Seconds away," Jenna said, voice unsteady. "I could feel it building."

Blackburn nodded once. "You may not climax yet."

Frustration flashed, then smoothed. She shifted. The tile had no give. Despite the discomfort, her posture stayed open, exposed.

"Thank you," she said, the words surprising Blackburn with their sincerity.

"For denying you?"

"For controlling when it happens," Jenna clarified. "For making me wait."

Blackburn studied her face. No insincerity. Not a pose, but an explicit recognition of what control meant to her. The distinction mattered. Blackburn filed it as usable knowledge.

"Do you understand why I stopped you?" Blackburn asked.

"I think so," Jenna said. "Anticipation builds value, delay increases intensity."

"Yes," Blackburn said. "But there is more. When I allow it, you will know it came through permission. That knowledge will shape the sensation."

Jenna nodded, taking it in. Her breathing steadied, though arousal still marked her pupils and skin. The pulse at her throat beat hard.

"Do you want to continue?" Blackburn asked.

"Yes," Jenna answered without hesitation. "Please."

The please was not required, but it revealed her state. Eager. Deferential. Fully inside the role she had chosen.

Blackburn let silence work, a tactical pause that rebuilt anticipation on steadier ground. Rain tapped the windows in a soft, patient rhythm. The kitchen, ordinary and calm, framed what unfolded on its floor.

"We will continue," Blackburn said finally. "But not as before."

Jenna's eyes widened. Curiosity displaced the residue of frustration. She waited, patient despite the need that still thrummed through her body.

"Lie on your back," Blackburn said, her voice as composed as it had been all evening. Not cold, but precise. The command shifted Jenna from active kneeling to something more passive and exposed. It would test different muscles, physical and mental. Surrender stays sharp with variation.

Her palms found the kitchen floor with a faint squeak on tile as she lowered herself backward, vertebra by vertebra, until she lay flat on the cool surface.

The floor pressed into her shoulder blades, her spine, the backs of her thighs. Tile seams met skin with blunt honesty. Blackburn had chosen it on purpose. Comfort was not the point.

"Spread your legs," Blackburn continued. "Wide. Directly in front of me."

Jenna complied, drawing her knees up slightly before letting them fall outward. The position left her fully exposed to Blackburn's view. Vulnerability made plain. Her hands settled at her sides, palms open on the floor, fingers splayed in a neat, intentional surrender.

Blackburn noted the gooseflesh that rose on Jenna's arms, then across her stomach and thighs. Her nipples, already hard, tightened against the cool air. The skin pebbled.

"How does the floor feel against your back?" Blackburn asked.

"Cold," Jenna answered immediately. "Hard. It makes me aware of every part of my body that touches it."

"Good. That awareness is the point."

Jenna adjusted, settling. Her breath came in controlled measures now. The urgency of denied climax eased to something steadier. Patient. The slight discomfort anchored her, kept her present in the moment.

Blackburn leaned forward in her chair, posture shifting for the first time since she had sat down. Wood creaked softly. The movement brought her closer to the junction between Jenna's thighs, her gaze clinical yet intensely focused.

"You are swollen," she said, voice neutral. "Full at the outer lips, more pronounced where you are most sensitive." Her assessment continued, detached yet intimate in its precision. "Wet enough that it is glistening beneath you on the floor."

Jenna's breath caught at the verbal inventory of her most private state. Being seen was one layer, hearing it described added another. Her flush deepened, spreading down her neck to her chest. The faint, clean scent of her skin lifted in the cool air.

"Are you embarrassed by my description?" Blackburn asked.

"Yes," Jenna admitted. "And aroused by it. Both at once."

Blackburn nodded, accepting without comment. "The physical state of your body tells a clearer story than words could. Your arousal is evident in specific, measurable ways. Increased blood flow, lubrication, muscle tension." She gestured toward Jenna's exposed vulva. "I can read your level of excitement as precisely as a thermometer reads temperature."

The clinical framing made it more intimate, not less. Jenna's breath quickened, her skin answered the words as it might a touch. Heat pulsed low, steady and insistent.

"Continue touching yourself," Blackburn directed. "But no penetration. Eyes closed now."

Jenna's hands left the floor, rising to her body with deliberation. Her eyelids lowered, shutting out the visual fact of Blackburn's presence while amplifying the awareness of being watched. One hand returned to her breast, cupping its slight weight before settling on the nipple. The other hand moved between her legs, fingers finding the slick flesh. The soft sound of moisture met the hush of rain as her breath grew thicker in her throat.

The rhythms she established were different from before. Slower, more exploratory. Without the visual input of Blackburn's reactions to guide her, she turned inward and followed sensation alone. Her fingers traced circles without direct contact, heat rising where air moved close, building tension through proximity rather than pressure.

Blackburn watched the changes in Jenna's breathing, in the tension gathering across her abdomen, in the subtle shifts of her hips against the cool floor. She could read the approaching peak in these signs. The control was not in touching Jenna herself, but in directing when and how Jenna touched herself, making her complicit in her own pleasure while simultaneously removing her agency over its culmination.

Jenna's movements grew more focused, the random exploration giving way to patterns that built steadily toward release. Her breathing quickened and grew shallow. The muscles in her thighs tensed, toes curling against the hard tile as if to find purchase. She was approaching the edge again, but with more control than before.

Blackburn stood suddenly. The chair legs scraped across the tile with a rasp that cut through the room's quiet. The sound rang brightly and briefly. She could have risen in silence if she had chosen to.

Jenna whimpered at the noise, a small, involuntary reaction that revealed how the unexpected stimulus intensified her arousal. Her eyes remained closed as instructed, but her head turned toward the source, tracking Blackburn's movement by sound alone. Her fingers did not break rhythm. They worked with steady purpose.

The whimper pleased Blackburn. Not for its need but for its honesty. Unfiltered reaction offered cleaner data in their exchange, more meaningful than anything performed. She remained standing beside the chair, noting how the change in her position altered Jenna's awareness and arousal.

Blackburn stepped closer, her movement deliberately audible on the kitchen floor. Each footfall registered in Jenna's expression. Lips parted, breath caught, then sped. The physical distance between them narrowed while the power distance remained precisely calibrated.

"Continue," Blackburn instructed. "Faster now."

Jenna's fingers accelerated, focusing more directly where sensation gathered. Her back lifted in a slight arch, hips rising to meet her own touch. The careful control of her earlier movements gave way to something more urgent, more instinctive.

Blackburn cataloged the flush deepening across Jenna's chest, the rapid pulse visible at the base of her throat, the tension coiling through her thighs and abdomen. She could read the climax approaching in these signs.

"Not yet," Blackburn said quietly. "Hold it back."

Jenna's rhythm faltered as her body fought the pull of reflex against the command in Blackburn's voice. She managed to dial back the intensity of her touch, drawing herself away from the brink with visible effort. A small sound of frustration rose and was quickly contained. She pressed her teeth to her lower lip until restraint settled again.

"Good," Blackburn acknowledged. "You maintain control even at the edge."

The praise registered in Jenna's expression. The skin around her eyes eased, her mouth softened for a beat, then concentration reclaimed her features. She continued with adjusted pressure, holding herself at a heated plateau without pushing toward completion.

Blackburn moved closer still. Her nearness arrived first as a shift in the air over Jenna's skin, a warmer current that lifted the fine hairs along her arms. Goosebumps rose in reaction. Awareness.

"Keep your eyes closed," Blackburn reminded her. "Focus on sensation alone."

Jenna nodded, lips parting slightly as she concentrated on what her body told her. The motion of her own hand. The hard floor beneath her back and shoulder blades. The awareness of Blackburn standing over her. A trace of citrus cleaner lingered in the room, rain bled a damp mineral scent through the open window. Her pace steadied again, finding the rhythm that maintained arousal without climbing higher.

"How close are you now?" Blackburn asked.

"Close," Jenna answered, voice strained. "But holding back."

"Good girl. Continue exactly as you are. Maintain this level without advancing further."

Jenna's expression shifted as she absorbed the constraint. Determination replaced frustration, and her concentration deepened. Her movements became more precise and more measured, the smallest adjustments sharpened the sensations. She had moved beyond simple compliance into active engagement, balancing her want against Blackburn's requirement with care that showed in the faint tremor of her abdomen.

Blackburn kneeled on the floor near Jenna's hips, her movements precise and unhurried. The change in position was studied, a considered shift from observer to participant that altered the dynamic without disturbing the underlying power structure. The tiles pressed into her knees, cool through fabric, a minor discomfort she registered and dismissed. Her focus remained on the woman before her, flushed and trembling on the edge she had been forbidden to cross.

"Faster now," Blackburn instructed, her voice closer than before, proximity adding weight to each syllable. "Show me how much you want this."

Jenna's fingers quickened, the focus narrowing to where sensation peaked. Her breathing thinned and hitched, small catches spilling when a particular touch landed exactly.

Blackburn observed the physical evidence of Jenna's arousal with professional thoroughness. Color deepened as blood moved to the surface. A fine sheen gathered, proof of the body's preparation for pleasure repeatedly delayed. These physiological responses could not be faked; they were clear communication beyond words or conscious control.

"Your body speaks clearly," Blackburn said, leaning closer. "The color here," she indicated without touching, "tells me exactly how close you are. The warmth shows how long you have been building toward release."

Jenna's rhythm faltered for a heartbeat at the commentary, then resumed with renewed focus. Her lips parted. Air moved faster through her open mouth, each breath a soft, urgent sound.

"I can smell your arousal," Blackburn continued, her voice tempered despite the intimacy of the observation. "Sweet and musky. Distinctive as a fingerprint." She inhaled deliberately, the sound audible in the quiet kitchen. "That scent triggers responses in the brain more primitive than language. Did you know that?"

"No," Jenna managed, the word barely more than breath.

"It is why smell bypasses our conscious filters. Why it affects us so immediately." Blackburn leaned forward until her breath skimmed Jenna's skin like warm silk. "Your scent tells me things you could not hide even if you wanted to."

Jenna shivered at Blackburn's breath on her most sensitive skin. Her fingers kept moving, though her focus had already shifted toward the nearness, the potential contact.

Blackburn extended a single finger and touched the slick heat at Jenna's entrance. The contact was intimate, a composed caress. She withdrew and studied the sheen that clung to her skin.

"Do you want me to taste you?" Blackburn asked, the question a quiet assertion of control.

"Yes," Jenna answered at once, her voice tight with need. "Please."

Blackburn brought the finger to her lips and tasted what she had collected. Her expression remained neutral, thoughtful. "Sweet," she said. "With notes of salt and metal. Complex." She leaned in again and traced a line along Jenna's lips with her tongue.

The contact drew a sharp gasp from Jenna. Her hips rose to meet the touch. Blackburn set a firm hand on her lower abdomen and pressed her back to the floor.

"Remain still," Blackburn instructed. "Continue touching your-self while I taste you."

Jenna's fingers resumed their motion, working with Blackburn's tongue in a counterpoint that sharpened sensation. Her free hand searched the floor beside her, palm skimming tile as if seeking anchor against the building pressure.

Blackburn withdrew after a second taste, her assessment complete. "You taste as your body suggests you would. Intense, honest." She wiped her mouth with the back of her hand, a practical sweep. "Con-tinue what you are doing, but understand this. You may not climax until I am inside you."

The condition registered on Jenna's face. Relief at a promised release mixed with the anticipation of further delay. Her pace shifted naturally, finding the line that maintained her arousal without tip-ping her over it.

"Are you close?" Blackburn asked, though the answer was evident in the tension throughout Jenna's body.

"Very," Jenna said, voice strained. "May I come soon? Please?"

"Not yet," Blackburn replied, tone unchanged despite the plea. "First, tell me what you feel right now. Be precise."

"Terrified," Jenna admitted. "And perfect."

Blackburn nodded once, satisfied. "When I enter you," Blackburn said, "you will feel the difference between touching yourself and being touched. Between what you choose and what is chosen for you." Her voice remained level, instructional rather than coaxing. "That difference matters. It is the space where surrender happens."

Understanding settled behind Jenna's eyes, even as need blurred the edges. Her hips shifted, searching for more direct contact.

"Please," she whispered. "I need—"

"I know exactly what you need," Blackburn said, cutting cleanly across the words. "The question is when you receive it."

With controlling slowness, Blackburn circled a single finger around Jenna's entrance, tracing without entering. The touch remained precise, neither coy nor tentative. It set a clear boundary that would soon be crossed.

Jenna's breathing roughened, control unraveling under Blackburn's dominant circuit. Her own fingers worked faster against her clitoris, building toward the release she had been denied and now stood within reach.

"Ask me," Blackburn said quietly.

"Please enter me," Jenna responded at once, the words spilling together. "Please let me come."

Blackburn slid a single finger inside. The movement was smooth and controlled. She began shallow, then deeper as she read each response. She felt internal muscles tighten around her, felt heat and wet.

Blackburn crooked her finger, pressing. Jenna gasped and froze. Blackburn pressed harder and Jenna trembled.

"You may finish," Blackburn said, her voice steady against the tension that saturated the room.

Permission given, Jenna's control unraveled with speed. Her fingers pressed more firmly against her clitoris, working in counterpoint to Blackburn's careful force. Her back arched from the floor, head tipping back as pleasure rose. A low moan rolled from her throat and crossed her parted lips.

Blackburn felt the orgasm begin from within. Rhythmic contractions seized her finger in pulses, drawing it deeper. She held her position, letting Jenna's body work against the steady presence she provided. The sensation mattered, yet the surrender mattered more. Control was relinquished and perfected in the same breath.

Jenna's sounds were minimal. Short, sharp breaths and a single low moan as the climax peaked. Her entire body locked as pleasure took her. Release came in stages. Shoulders settled to the floor, then her hips, then her legs loosened from their rigid extension.

Blackburn remained, finger still inside, feeling the aftershocks that continued to pulse around her. She watched Jenna's face. Color that had risen during climax receded, the tension around her eyes softened. Only when the internal contractions had fully eased did Blackburn withdraw, the movement as careful as its entry.

"Open your eyes," Blackburn instructed.

Jenna complied. Her pupils, still wide with arousal and release, lifted to meet Blackburn's. The look held directly, unguarded in a new way.

"You did well," Blackburn said. The words were not effusive. They acknowledged an agreement. "Your surrender was complete."

"Thank you," Jenna replied, voice a shade hoarse. The two words carried weight beyond ordinary gratitude.

Blackburn rose from her knees with the same unhurried control that had guided everything else. She extended a hand. "Stand up now."

Jenna took it and let Blackburn help her to her feet. The transition was not entirely steady. Her legs trembled, muscles still fluttering from deep contraction. Blackburn's grip stayed firm, supportive without clutching.

Once Jenna stood, Blackburn guided her to the kitchen island and positioned her with her stomach against the cool countertop. She stepped close behind and wrapped her arms around Jenna's waist in a hold that restrained and supported at once. The embrace pressed Jenna's bare back to Blackburn's clothed chest, a quiet contrast that reinforced their structure.

"Steady?" Blackburn asked, her mouth close to Jenna's ear.

"Yes," Jenna said, leaning into the offered support.

They stood connected for a long moment. Blackburn's arms kept their firm hold while Jenna's breathing slowed toward normal rhythm. The kitchen gathered itself around them. The refrigerator hummed softly. Rain kept its gentle percussion against the windows. The house creaked as it held them within its walls.

Blackburn released her hold gradually and stepped back enough for Jenna to turn and face her.

"Take the water," Blackburn said, indicating the glass at the edge of the counter where she had left it hours earlier. "Off to bed. You obeyed beautifully tonight." She paused, then added, "You are free."

The two final words served as release. Not only from the commands of the evening but from the heightened state they had built. They made clear that what had happened between them lived inside agreed boundaries and that outside those boundaries Jenna's autonomy remained intact.

Jenna reached for the water and drank deeply. When she lowered the glass, something in her posture had shifted. Respect remained, and attention to Blackburn's presence, but everyday self-possession had returned. The change was subtle and unmistakable.

"Thank you," she said again. The words were simple and layered with meaning that needed no elaboration.

Blackburn nodded once, accepting what was offered. "The guest room is prepared. Sleep well."

No unnecessary sentiment colored the exchange. None was needed. What had passed between them required no embellishment, no sweetening with words that would dilute rather than honor the experience.

Jenna gathered her clothing with quiet dignity, neither rushing nor lingering. The blue sundress hung over her arm, undergarments gathered discreetly in one hand. She padded barefoot toward the hallway and paused at the threshold to look back once.

Blackburn remained by the island, posture unchanged. Her gaze stayed steady, neither dismissive nor clinging. A clean line had been drawn between what had been and what would come next.

When Jenna had gone, Blackburn turned to the sink. She washed her hands with methodical care, then the spoon. She returned the wooden spoon to its drawer and straightened the chair to its place. Each action was precise and restoring.

Rain continued outside, marking the line between their contained world and everything beyond it. Inside, the house settled into nighttime quiet and held the evening's truths within its walls.

Chapter 30

Blackburn poured coffee into a mug, steam lifting between her fingers as she checked her watch for the third time in five minutes. Her grey suit held clean lines across her shoulders, not a wrinkle in sight. She sipped and tasted heat and bitterness while morning light stretched across her clean kitchen counters. Behind her, the bedroom door remained closed. The woman inside would need to leave soon. Blackburn had to get to work.

She placed her mug on the counter and adjusted her blue shirt cuffs, the silver links cool and sure between her fingers as she checked them. Last night had been adequate. Nothing exceptional, but sufficient to take the edge off. Jenna had been enthusiastic, if somewhat predictable in her responses. Blackburn preferred it that way. Predictable meant controllable. Controllable meant safe.

Blackburn retrieved the rideshare gift card from her wallet and set it beside Jenna's purse on the shelf near the door. The plastic card made a soft tap against the wood. A clear signal, tasteful and unambiguous.

The bedroom door opened. Jenna stood in the doorway wearing her sundress, her dark hair pulled into a loose bun. Sleep lines marked her cheek, faint ridges that would fade under running water. Her eyes found Blackburn across the room, and something softened in her expression.

"Good morning," Jenna said, her voice carrying a warmth that felt out of place for their level of acquaintance. "Smells good in here."

Blackburn nodded once. "Coffee's fresh. Help yourself if you like."

She watched Jenna cross the kitchen, the rustle of fabric low and unhurried, noting the slight wince as she moved. Their activities had been vigorous, but nothing beyond what had been negotiated and consented to. Blackburn felt no responsibility beyond that point.

"Beautiful morning," Jenna tried again, pouring coffee into the spare mug Blackburn had deliberately left in the cabinet. The scent unfurled with the steam. "Did you sleep well?"

"Yes." Blackburn checked her watch again. "I trust you found everything you needed in the bathroom."

"Yes, thanks." Jenna leaned against the counter, studying Blackburn over the rim of her mug. "How are you feeling this morning?"

The question carried more than the words. Blackburn recognized the probe for what it was, an attempt to initiate the kind of debriefing that some circles considered essential. She had no interest in such indulgences.

"I'm fine. Yourself?" Her response was clipped, professional.

Jenna's brow furrowed. "A bit sore, but in a good way." She paused, waiting for something Blackburn had no intention of offering. "Last night was intense. Would you want to talk about it a little? What worked for you, what might work better next time?"

"Everything was fine," Blackburn said, turning away to rinse her mug in the sink. The water ran scalding hot, steam rising as it hit the porcelain. She could feel the conversation slipping away from her control, and her jaw tightened. "I need to get going."

Jenna set her coffee down, the mug connecting with the counter more forcefully than necessary. "Are you always this clinical the morning after?"

Blackburn turned back, her face carefully blank. The kitchen's quiet hum filled the space between them. Somewhere a water pipe ticked like a countdown. "We agreed this was one night. No strings attached."

"There's a difference between 'no strings' and treating someone like they've overstayed their welcome the minute they wake up." Jenna's voice sharpened, cutting through the quiet kitchen. "Basic aftercare isn't a complication. It's standard protocol."

Blackburn stepped toward the door and lifted Jenna's purse from the shelf. The leather felt cool and structured. She held it out along with a plastic gift card. "For you to get home. Works with a half dozen rideshares in the city."

Jenna stared at the offered items, the muscles in her jaw tight. She made no move to take them.

"Don't worry," Blackburn added. "I've already cleaned the floor."

Something shifted in Jenna's eyes, anger settled into something harder than Blackburn had anticipated.

"Do you think I'm concerned about your floor?" Jenna asked, her voice dropping to something controlled and sharp. "I'm concerned about basic respect."

Blackburn kept her face composed. The faint hum of the refrigerator underlined the silence. "I've shown respect. You seem to expect more."

"Scenes don't end when the ropes come off." Jenna stepped closer. Her anger was contained, the set of her shoulders steady. "Even casual encounters require proper closure. That's not romance. That's human decency."

"I hear what you're saying," Blackburn said, her voice carrying an edge of patience wearing thin. "But it seems we need to clarify what happens after we're together."

Jenna gave a short, humorless laugh. "Do you hear yourself? How about a little humanity?" She shook her head. "The community is smaller than you think. I could make sure everyone knows how you treat people after scenes."

A tightening started beneath Blackburn's ribs. She did not let it touch her expression. "That would be a mistake."

"Would it?" Jenna tilted her head, gaze steady. "I wonder what your colleagues would think about your profile on BDSMessages. Those photos are quite explicit."

The tightness spiraled inward. Blackburn adjusted her breathing and let nothing show. "Are you threatening me, Jenna?"

"I'm pointing out consequences. Maybe your boss would be interested in those photos on your profile." Jenna finally took her purse.

The gift card remained on Blackburn's extended palm. "I don't need your money. What I needed was five minutes of basic human connection after what we shared last night. I didn't want breakfast. I wanted acknowledgment."

Blackburn weighed options as if she were across a table in an interview room. Blackmail threats never went over well. She needed to placate.

"I may have come on too strong this morning," she said, her tone softening just enough to seem reasonable. "Why don't we sit down and talk through what happened between us?"

"Too late," Jenna replied, turning toward the door. "The moment for genuine aftercare has passed. Now it would just be damage control." She paused with her hand on the knob. "You know what the worst part is? You're actually skilled. Technically proficient. But technique without humanity is just mechanics."

Blackburn watched her, keeping her voice level. "What do you want?"

"Nothing from you. Not anymore." Jenna opened the door. Morning light slid over the threshold and across the tile. "Consider this a professional courtesy. Treat your next partner with respect, or find a new community. Word travels fast among people who value consent and care."

The door closed with a soft click that carried farther than a slam might have. Sound thinned in the kitchen until only the refrigerator's low drone and the faint scent of disinfectant remained. Blackburn stood alone with the gift card balanced in her hand. The plastic edge pressed a straight line into her palm.

She set it on the counter and checked her watch. She did not like being threatened. Not at all.

Blackburn rinsed Jenna's cup under hot water and watched steam rise in faint curls. She dried the cup carefully and returned it to its place in the cabinet.

Chapter 31

Jenna moved briskly down the street. Her blue floral sundress, neat and cheerful when she put it on, had become an emblem of expectations gone. Cotton brushed her thighs, cool where shade lingered and where sweat had dried. She folded her arms tight against a shiver and kept walking past the same storefronts that had glowed a few hours ago. Their windows sat dark and indifferent. A faded sign clicked in a stray breeze. The thin gloss of earlier felt stripped away, replaced by grit that caught in her throat.

Her footsteps carried in the quiet morning, steady against the distant hum of traffic and the sharp bark of a horn. Somewhere, a delivery truck sighed as its brakes released. The dress she had chosen with care read as a mockery now, its cheerful pattern at odds with the churn under her ribs.

She checked her phone against the street signs, thumb leaving foggy smudges on the glass as she swiped through the bus schedule. The blue light hit her eyes and made them ache. She needed distance from Blackburn's home, the site of her humiliation and betrayal, the place that had felt private and then turned on her with a twist she could not unsee.

She saw one autonomous cab drive nearby, someone in the rear seat. Unavailable.

The streets ran sparse at this hour. A nurse with a coffee moved past with eyes fixed on the pavement. A pair of cooks laughed quietly, their jackets flung over their shoulders. No one paid attention to the woman in the sundress with red-rimmed eyes and hair that would not settle. Jenna hunched her shoulders and tugged at the hem. Every passing car threw a wash of light across glass and metal that felt like a spotlight. She kept her head down and avoided the bright, alert stares of joggers.

Fragments from the night flared and broke: Blackburn's knowing smirk, the glint in her eye, the sound of wood on flesh, the sting in the air that tasted like electricity. Jenna shook her head hard, as if motion could strip the images loose.

How could I have been so stupid? I thought we had a connection. I thought she cared. But I was just another conquest to her, wasn't I?

Morning air moved cleanly through the street, cool against skin that still held the heat of too little sleep. Birds called from a roofline. She ignored them. She fixed her gaze on the cracks in the sidewalk and counted them. The rhythm steadied her breath.

Her eyes narrowed to hold back the sting of new tears. The small soreness of the spoon. The lingering trace of Blackburn's touch that clung to her skin as if it belonged there. It felt like a violation now, a mark she had not agreed to carry into daylight. What had seemed passionate and charged in the moment felt hollow, the shape of something staged to get her to bend.

"She used me," Jenna said, her voice flat and small in the open morning. "All those commands, all those pained poses. It was just a game to her." The truth steadied and burned at once. She saw how quickly she had leaned in, how thoroughly she had offered herself up. She had wanted something real. She was left empty and set aside.

Her throat tightened. Her mouth tasted metallic. She opened the phone again with unsteady hands and tapped for her contacts. The icon pulsed beneath her thumb as she dialed Marla, reaching for a steadier voice and a way to slow the spin.

The line rang in her ear. Her pulse thudded along with it. "Hello?" Marla's voice came clearly through the speaker. Jenna swallowed and felt a tight pull in the tendons of her neck.

"Hey, it's me," she said, working for an even tone. She lifted her head to read the nearest street sign at the corner. "Can you come pick me up? I'm on Oak Street, near Maple Avenue. I'll meet you at the bus stop there."

Marla's concern came through the line. "Of course, I'm on my way. Are you okay? What happened?"

"I'll tell you when you get here," Jenna said, her voice catching slightly. "Just hurry, please."

Ending the call, Jenna snapped her phone case shut. The click sounded too loud in the quiet stretch of street. She exhaled slowly. Her grip on the phone loosened. She rolled her shoulders and winced at the pull in her muscles, a trace of the night's cost. The click of her heels on concrete tapped in time with her racing thoughts.

As Jenna walked, she reached the bus stop where more people had gathered, moving through their morning routines. Early commuters stood in small clusters, some scrolling through their phones, others sipping coffee from paper cups. The air held a faint bite of morning cool and the bitter scent of brewed coffee. The ordinary scene felt distant to Jenna. It stood in stark contrast to the churn inside her.

She caught a faint whirring behind her. The hair at her nape lifted, and a chill traced her spine. She turned her head, eyes catching an autonomous car easing up the lane. The sleek vehicle moved down the street with electric quiet, its cameras and sensors dim in the low light and no plate on the bumper. It held behind her, matching her pace at a constant distance.

Jenna's pulse thudded in her ears, her breaths coming in short bursts. She pressed a hand to her chest and felt the rapid flutter beneath her palm. Her skin prickled as the car edged closer, its blank windshield catching the morning light like a flat lens. She quickened her pace, scanning for any sign of Marla's familiar car or a police car. The vehicle continued its silent pursuit. Its intentions remained unreadable.

At the bus stop, Jenna kept her gaze fixed on the approaching car. Her shoulders lowered a fraction, and a shaky exhale slipped out. Her fingers curled into fists, nails pressing into her palms, even as the furrow between her brows eased at the sight of the bus turning the corner.

The bus rolled down the street, its diesel engine low in the morning air. Exhaust drifted in a gritty wave. People stirred around her, gathering their belongings under the shelter's camera and shuffling toward the pickup spot.

Jenna's gaze flicked between the bus and her silent phone. She took a half step forward, then back, her grip tightening on the device as if it were a line to Marla. After a brief deliberation, she stepped back and decided to wait. She was rattled thanks to Blackburn. The thought of facing strangers on the bus, their curious glances catching her disheveled state, was too much to bear.

The doors hissed open. The tired nurse in scrubs climbed aboard. An elderly man leaned on a cane and followed. A young student with oversized headphones moved past with a sleepy blink. Each person seemed oblivious to the storm that pressed against Jenna's skin.

She wondered what they would think if they knew the truth about Detective Blackburn. Would they be shocked to learn that the celebrated head of Homicide, the woman whose face graced the evening news, could be capable of such callous manipulation? Would they be disgusted by the way she played with people's emotions, using them for her own sexual amusement? Or would they shrug, another powerful figure abusing her position?

The bus doors shut with another hiss, and it rumbled away. Jenna's jaw clenched. She tasted bile at the back of her throat as the bus shrank down the street. These people went about their lives, unaware of the darkness inside their city's protectors. They saw Detective Blackburn as a hero, a beacon of justice. Jenna now knew the truth. Blackburn was a predator hiding behind a badge and a charming smile.

Jenna shifted and scanned the street for any sign of Marla's sedan, hoping for a quick escape from the morning's grind of fear. The whirring of the autonomous car persisted as it sat at the curb.

The hair on her arms rose. Cold sweat gathered at her hairline as she became hyperaware of the car's presence. A shiver ran through her as it inched closer, its sensors faint in the dim light. She turned on her heel, heart rattling against her ribs, and walked briskly away from the bus stop. Each step felt purposeful, an attempt to slip free of its blank, unblinking gaze.

She glanced over her shoulder, pulse jumping. Its quiet tailing tightened her gut. The thud in her chest kept time, matching the fast pull of her breath. Each heartbeat read as warning, a steady push telling her to pick up speed.

Jenna blinked hard, unsettled by how the lights outshone the morning sun. The glare flattened the familiar block into something alien. Shadows stretched and skewed in ways that made no sense.

Her thoughts staggered. Was this Blackburn's weird revenge? The person outside the house last night? Some freak tailing her in the hopes of a kidnapping? Her stomach clenched, anger and fear working toward panic. Last night's mess shrank beside the immediate threat of this relentless machine. She wanted to call out for help but felt foolish. It was only a car. No driver, no visible threat, just an autonomous ride keeping pace with her. A cab looking for a fare? A car biding time until its owner summoning it?

Jenna's muscles drew tight with each step, her body folding as if to make a smaller target. Sweat tracked her spine. Her sundress stuck to her back. She knew running would feed her fear, yet instinct told her to bolt, and the pressure built.

She gave in and ran. The rhythmic slap of her sandals on concrete kept time with her pulse. She dragged for air, lungs burning with each breath.

The car quickened smoothly, whirring as it held her speed. No matter how hard she pushed, the vehicle kept the same distance, never closer. Its headlights pinned her, two cold lenses on a blank face.

Her breath came in short, panicked pulls. The truth landed hard. There was no escaping this machine. Her legs turned heavy, muscles firing in protest as she forced more speed.

Without warning, the car surged ahead. Jenna's heart kicked as the vehicle swept past, its body a blur. As it went by, she caught the navigation screen. Her own face stared back at her from the display.

"What the hell? Did Marla send a car to pick me up?" She wondered if Blackburn had sent a rideshare to find her. Jenna slowed. That was it. Blackburn felt bad, and sent a car for her.

The car cut to a stop a few yards ahead. Its lights went out and the navigation screen went dark. Silence hit hard, broken by Jenna's ragged breathing and the distant noise of the city.

Jenna slowed to a halt, her legs trembling under her. She watched the dormant vehicle, unsure whether to step in or back away. After a moment's hesitation, she fumbled for her phone with shaking hands. Her fingers, slick with sweat, slid on the glass as she dialed Marla's number.

The phone rang, each tone dragging as Jenna waited, eyes fixed on the shape in front of her.

The car erupted to life with a metallic shriek, its headlights burning white. The engine did not purr. It snarled, a guttural mechanical roar that set Jenna's teeth on edge. Gears gnashed and fluid gurgled as it slammed into reverse, wheels juddering against the curb before climbing the sidewalk with predatory precision. Each movement was wrong, a stuttering, rabid rhythm of pistons and steel that defied everything she knew about how machines should move.

The tires howled, kicking up dust and grit as the vehicle snapped around, the sound ricocheting off buildings like shots in the still air. It reversed past her. Stopped. Accelerated. On the sidewalk.

Run!

It tore past as she cut right, missing her by inches, crushing a garbage can and driving on.

Time narrowed. Each heartbeat stretched long, each breath catching in her throat. The vehicle shuddered and twitched, a machine barely holding together. Steam hissed from the radiator in hot bursts, and the acrid stench of burning rubber and hot oil burned her lungs. This was not just a nightmare. It was violence made real, metal and glass, and it was coming for her. Jenna's heart hammered as she sprinted into the street, fear pushing her forward. The car closed in behind her, its grille cutting the air with steady ease. No matter how fast she ran, it stayed on her, a constant weight at her heels.

A hard screech of metal tore the air as the car surged again, aimed straight at her. Bystanders scattered in alarm, their voices rising through the morning noise. "Look out!" a man shouted, the cry lost to Jenna's raw scream.

The impact struck hard, lifting her off her feet. She hit the asphalt with a dull thud, shock ringing through bone and muscle. She could not breathe. The car reversed over her with cold precision.

Then, as quickly as it had arrived, it dropped into drive and shot away.

Chapter 32

Screams tore from the onlookers, and panic rolled through the crowd.

People surged toward the injured woman, faces blanched with shock and concern. Phones rose with shaking hands as callers punched in numbers. The smell of burned rubber clung to the warm air, threaded with the metallic bite of blood.

"Did you see that?!" a woman shrieked, her voice slicing through the noise.

"Oh my God, call 911!" another yelled, fingers fumbling against her screen.

Three bystanders dropped to Jenna's side, their expressions fixed with purpose. One man kneeled and set his palms on her chest, ribs shifting under his weight. He pressed down, counting to the rhythm in a thin voice that matched the dispatcher's beat. His breath came quickly.

"Stay with us!" he shouted. Sweat ran along his temples and stung his eyes as his hands kept time.

Nearby, a woman steadied her voice as she cried into her phone. "Ambulance! Oak and Maple! Woman hit by a car, not moving! Oh Lord! Hurry!" Her words broke into sobs.

Chaos tightened around them. Orders and pleas tangled in the air. Screams split the street, ragged and raw. The crowd shuffled in tight arcs, shoes scraping grit. Hearts hammered. Breaths hitched. Sirens rose from far off, a thin thread of sound that thickened into a wail. Help was coming, but too slowly.

"Do not stop now!" a man bellowed above the din.

"I feel something. A pulse!" another cried, hope and fear hooking the words.

Seconds dragged. Hands grew sticky and red. They kept working while her life drew down to a thread.

* * *

Jenna's vision swam. Faces bent over her, warped by pain and fear, features sliding at the edges like heat haze. The city's sounds thinned until only the thud of her heart and the rush inside her ears remained.

A bystander dropped to her knees, gravel biting through skin. She took Jenna's limp hand, slick with blood, and held on. "Help is coming. Stay with me," she said, her voice even while her fingers trembled.

Jenna's chest hitched. Each breath rasped in and stuck, air scraping her throat. She tried to fix on something solid. A car door slammed. A shadow crossed the light and drifted away. Sirens cut through the haze and grew louder, insistent. The wail filled her head and drowned the shouts and sobs. She fixed on that sound as the edges of her sight dimmed, a single line to hold in the dark pressing in.

Then nothing.

* * *

The morning had a hard edge as a cyclist rounded the corner, tires hissing on gritty pavement. He braked at the fringe of the commotion, taking in the damage quickly. A woman lay on the asphalt, her blue floral sundress soaked dark. A young woman kneeled beside her and gripped her hand.

"What happened?" the cyclist demanded, his voice cutting through sirens and panicked voices.

The young woman looked up, her face pale and tear-streaked. "One of those weird-looking self-driving cars hit this woman and then drove off," she choked out, disbelief heavy in every word.

The cyclist's focus snapped into place. "I'll get him!" he shouted, voice charged. He pushed off, legs driving hard, chain humming as he gathered speed.

He cut through traffic, eyes fixed on the corridor ahead. His heartbeat matched the spin of his wheels. Cool morning air slid over his face. Exhaust and hot tar stung his nose. He leaned into each turn, compact and steady, handlebars alive beneath his grip.

Metal flashed in the sunlight up the block. He closed the gap and saw the autonomous car limping forward, its front crushed and bumper dragging low. Sparks skittered from the undercarriage with a harsh scrape that set his teeth on edge.

He drove harder, breath tight, drawing even with the listing machine. The windshield was laced with fractures. The roofline had a subtle kink. Panels were bent and torn, edges bright where paint had sheared away.

* * *

A burly man sat in a pickup on the shoulder, hands parked on the wheel. Steam curled from his coffee in the holder, sweet and bitter. A flicker in his side mirror pulled his attention.

In the glass, a cyclist hammered the side of a crippled car, face set, every muscle working. With powerful kicks, he struck the autonomous car. Each blow landed with a hollow thud that vibrated up his leg. The vehicle's skin trembled.

The sleek shell that sold progress now showed ruin. Its nose was crushed and bleeding coolant. The glass was webbed and dull with damage.

The truck driver leaned out his open door to track the chase. The cyclist's voice carried as he kicked the dented panels. "Stop the car! It hit a woman! Stop the car!" His voice cracked as he screamed, each word wobbling with a tremor that betrayed desperation. Fury gave the air a hard edge. Each shout became another strike against the frame.

The driver felt the jolt of a decision. He slid back in, shut the door, and brought the engine up.

He pulled into traffic, matched the car's path, then swung his truck across its lane. Tires barked. He stopped short, full weight planted in the way.

The autonomous car did not react in time. It slammed into the truck's rear with a heavy, chest-thumping impact. Metal tore and folded. Safety glass burst into glittering beads that skittered across the road with a dry hiss. The car's frame groaned as energy bled out of it. Rubber scraped and went still.

Pedestrians froze. Breath caught. A collective sound moved through the bystanders, thin and astonished. Some backed away on instinct, shoes scuffing against curb and concrete. Others stared, held by shock and the wrongness of the scene.

Sound thinned. Steam hissed from the front of the car while sirens swelled closer. The air smelled of hot plastic, antifreeze, and electrical burn.

Then the car spasmed. Lights flashed in a stutter, bright then dark. The horn blared in ragged bursts, each one abrupt and harsh.

The pickup truck driver climbed down, boots firm on the pavement. Heat rolled off the road. He approached with care. The erratic lights and horn faded. The vehicle went quiet, its clean lines now twisted, seams popped open like split fruit.

The cyclist reached him, chest still heaving. Sweat ran into his eyes and stung. He blinked it away and kept his gaze on the side window. His pupils were wide, attention narrow and fixed.

"Where's the driver?" he gasped, words broken by ragged breaths.

The truck driver shook his head, brow pulled tight. "There ain't no driver," he said, disbelief roughening his voice. "It's one of those self-driving cars."

"No driver? Are you telling me that thing just decided to drive itself over a woman?" The cyclist's eyebrows knit together, lips drawn as he inched toward the vehicle, shoulders tense and hands balled into fists. He leaned in and pressed his face to the window, cupping his hands to cut the glare. The interior was empty, the seats pristine, the cabin neat and sterile.

"What did you say happened? It hit a woman?" the truck driver asked, tilting his head in bafflement.

The cyclist stepped back while the trucker dug out his phone. Thick fingers worked the screen and he punched the call through. "Yeah, I need to report a stopped autonomous car. A guy says it hit a lady," he said, gruff but steady. "It's on Oak Street, near Wisteria Road. Looks like it's been in an accident. Before it hit my truck."

The cyclist moved around the wreck, anger settling into alert caution. He checked the rear glass, the seams, the wheel wells. Heat poured off the body and pooled under the hood. He flinched back as it bit his skin. "The car's getting hot!" he shouted, panic scraping his voice raw.

The driver glanced between the cyclist and the phone, palm raised to quiet the noise around him. "Hold on," he said into the receiver, then listened hard. He nodded and lifted his voice. "They say we need to stay back. Keep a safe distance from the car."

A faint hiss rose under the chassis, sharp and steady, like water on a skillet. Onlookers gave ground fast. Arms went up to shield faces, bracing for a blast that did not come. The smell of vaporized coolant turned the air acrid.

"Get back! It's going to blow!" a bystander yelled, waving people away. An older man shuffled his wife gently past the curb and into the shade.

"Goddamn!" the truck driver shouted as he jumped into his pickup. The engine roared, and he pulled his truck a few car lengths forward, eyes on the ruined nose behind him.

The autonomous car shuddered, a final rattle from deep within its body. Lights flickered once and died. Then, silence. The only sounds left were the soft tick of cooling metal and the distant wail of sirens announced rescue.

* * *

The once busy avenue had stalled behind idling traffic and gawkers, creating a quiet pocket around the place where the incident had unfolded. More than two city blocks were sealed off by hastily placed barriers, their reflective tape snapping in the light wind. The familiar street had become a contained strip of flashing lights and low voices. Engine heat wavered above the asphalt while radios murmured at the edges.

Jenna's body lay on the cold, unyielding pavement under a white sheet that could not disguise the stillness beneath it. The fabric lifted and fell with the breeze, a small motion that read as life where none remained. The blue floral sundress she had chosen with care showed at the hem, a quiet marker of a life lost.

Red and blue light pulsed across the facades of nearby buildings, turning storefronts into harsh planes of glare and shadow. The strobe slid over glass and metal, blinking off chrome handles and window displays, a sharp counterpoint to the fixed work at the center. The sweep of color crossed the crowd and glanced off faces. Some people drew back, eyes wide and fixed. Others edged closer to the tape, brows tight and mouths parting as if to speak. A few turned away, hands to their mouths or arms pulled close as the air cooled. Phones rose above heads, tiny screens shaking as they captured pieces of the scene for quick upload.

Uniforms moved through the area with faces set. They worked with drilled efficiency, expanding the cordon with steady hands and clipped directions. Hushed murmurs came from the cluster of officers near the body, their words swallowed by the city's steady hum. Latex creaked as gloved hands placed yellow markers one by one, each plastic triangle a quiet record of what the street now held.

The burned-out husk of the autonomous car sat two blocks away within its own ring of police tape. Sleek lines had folded into twisted, blackened metal, and a faint thread of smoke still rose from the charred shell. The air carried the sour smell of melted wiring and scorched upholstery. Firefighters stood at a distance, helmets dull with ash, watching while investigators combed the wreckage for any clue that might have survived the crash.

Chapter 33

Marla tightened her grip on the wheel, her breath catching as red and blue strobes flared into view. The lights pooled at the bus stop where Jenna should have been waiting. With unsteady fingers, she dug for her phone and tapped the screen to dial the familiar number again. Each unanswered ring pressed into her gut, the silence on the other end was broad and heavy. Her chest drew tight, each breath shorter and more ragged. Cold threaded through her, making her fingers shake as they clutched the phone.

"Come on, pick up," she muttered, her fingers drumming the steering wheel. Silence answered, followed by the tinny, scripted voicemail she had heard too many times already.

She stepped out. The scene hit fast and close. Even from half a block away, sound carried. Camera lights flared white against faces, underscored by the scrape and shuffle of reporters lining up for position. Microphones lifted toward the tape, angled and expectant. Lenses clicked. They pressed in, elbows out, hungry for any line they could air. Voices rose above the din as they fought for a vantage point.

Marla wrinkled her nose and took a step back as the bite of burned rubber hit. The air tasted metallic. She swallowed hard and fought the urge to gag. She moved to the yellow tape, eyes tracking over the street. Uniformed officers moved with purpose, radios hissing on their shoulders, faces set and focused.

Her gaze fixed on a man in cycling gear, reflective strips flashing with each pulse of light. His expression remained shocked and flat. She stepped toward him, her voice unsteady. "Excuse me," Marla said. "What happened?"

The cyclist turned, face drained. "A hit-and-run. An autonomous car." He swallowed, throat working. "Christ. It came out of nowhere." His gaze slid back to the tape, words failing him.

A coldness settled in Marla's stomach. She licked dry lips and pushed out the words. "Who got hit? Do you know?"

He lifted a shoulder, helpless. "No idea. I was too busy chasing after the car. It was surreal, like something out of a nightmare. The way it moved was not natural."

Marla nodded, scanning the crowd for any sign of Jenna. The unanswered calls, the chaos, the bitter smell in the air gathered into a single dread.

Traffic crash technicians moved in lanes of taped-off asphalt, clear on task and sequence. Masks hid their mouths, their eyes stayed flat and unreadable. They documented the scene, taking photos, logging notes, marking points with small, numbered evidence tents. Sweat beaded at their temples, caught every few seconds by the pulse of emergency lights.

One technician crouched, her camera clicking over a bent section of the autonomous car's frame. Another measured a skid mark and logged the length, his pen moving in quick, precise strokes. They kept it quiet, trading small nods and clipped gestures, attention fixed despite the noise pressing in around them.

A few feet away, a third technician bagged shards of glass, each piece noted and recorded. The plastic crinkled as he sealed it, then he set it with the growing line of evidence. Nearby, his colleague kneeled at the pavement and opened a tire tread impression kit. With steady hands, she pressed flexible compound into the marks on the asphalt, coaxing clean detail from the pattern. The compound caught grit and tiny stones. She brushed them away with careful strokes. Her movements stayed slow, keeping every edge intact. Each step remained precise, built to preserve what the street could still tell.

Marla stood at the edge of the tape, her pulse loud and steady with dread. The lights washed over her in regular bursts. She pulled out her phone again, the screen slick under her thumb, and dialed Jenna's number. The call rang, unanswered. She ended it, drew a breath that barely reached her lungs, and dialed again.

This time, as the phone rang in her ear, a flicker of movement drew her eye. A uniformed officer near a covered body lifted a clear plastic evidence bag. Inside lay a phone, the screen lighting with an incoming call. The plastic caught the strobes, blue and red sliding over it. Marla held her breath and watched the officer study the device, waiting for it to go dark as she ended her call.

It did.

She dialed again, hands numb and clumsy with cold. The same ring sounded against her ear. The same screen lit inside the bag. Her eyes stayed on the officer as the glow pulsed and then faded.

With mounting horror, Marla called one last time. The phone in the bag lit again. The truth landed hard, sharp as a blow, and a scream tore through the air.

Marla's knees buckled, and she sagged against the cyclist, her cry turning nearby faces toward her. A police officer a few feet away pivoted at the sound, his eyes widening as he took in her state.

"Ma'am?" he said gently, reaching out to steady her. "Are you alright?"

Marla looked up at him, her vision blurred by tears. She fought to form words, her voice tight with shock. "I think. I think it's my friend. The phone. It's hers. Oh God, it's Jenna, isn't it?"

The officer's expression softened, reading the realization in Marla's eyes. He set a steadying hand on her shoulder, his voice low and controlled. "I'm so sorry, ma'am. We can't confirm anything yet, but if you think you might know the victim, we'll need to ask you some questions. Can you come with me, please?"

* * *

Further down the street, the wrecked autonomous car sat immobile, a stark monument to the aftermath. Its sleek lines had folded into a mangled mass of metal and plastic, the front end crumpled inward. The fractured windshield, the hood, the coolant on the road going tacky under the wash of red and blue lights.

A team of technicians moved around the vehicle with calculated focus. The rustle of Tyvek and the click of tools filtered through the night air. One technician, a woman with graying hair pulled tight, swabbed the smears on the hood, her gloved hands steady. Another, a younger man with yellow-framed glasses, captured photos of the interior, the flash illuminating the empty driver's seat in stark bursts.

"What the hell?" The young technician's voice cracked slightly. He lowered his camera and squinted into the car's interior. "The seat's pushed all the way up to the steering wheel. No way anyone could drive like that."

His colleague nodded, sealing the swab in an evidence bag and marking the label. "We'll need to pull the black box data. This doesn't make any sense. These cars are supposed to be foolproof."

The city kept moving as they worked. Traffic flowed a few blocks away, horns muffled by distance, the drivers unaware of what had unfolded here. A faint tang of electronics hung near the crumpled hood. Glass glittered in the gutter like scattered ice.

Police radios crackled in short bursts, officers trading clipped updates as they locked down the scene and canvassed bystanders. Phrases like "perimeter secure" and "witness statements" carried on the night air, blending with the low murmur of the crowd.

At the tape line, a burly man with a grizzled beard and sunburned skin stood with restless hands. The truck driver who had helped stop the car. A uniformed officer approached, notepad in hand.

"Sir," the officer began, his voice steady and professional, "I understand you were involved in stopping the vehicle. Did you happen to see the driver at any point?"

The truck driver's calloused hands clenched and unclenched at his sides. He shook his head, blinking hard as if to clear a bad image. "That's just it, officer. There was no driver. I saw it clear as day when

I stopped it. The car was empty, moving on its own like some kind of zombie car."

The officer's pen paused over his notepad, his brow tightening. He looked from the truck driver to the wrecked car and back, teeth worrying at his lower lip. "I see. Thank you for that information. Would you mind staying on the scene for a little while longer? We may have some more questions for you."

As the truck driver nodded his agreement, the officer stepped aside and reached for the radio clipped to his shoulder. He pressed the button, his voice low but urgent as he spoke into the device.

"Dispatch, this is 423. Requesting Sgt. Beckett from Traffic Services to attend. We've got a situation here that's, well, it's not like anything I've seen before."

Chapter 34

The sun pressed hard on Oak Street and on the people gathered there, tightening the knots in their stomachs as they took in the scene. The tree-lined block, usually noisy with cars and the smell of exhaust, lay still. Heat lifted off the asphalt in wavering bands. Somewhere, a car alarm screeched a few times and fell silent.

Squalid businesses stood next to sleek new builds. Paint flaked off paint, while the flat panes on the newer builds caught the flash of police lights. Red and blue streaked across the shaded street. Air conditioners droned. Yellow police tape snapped lightly in the breeze and cordoned off a wide stretch of road.

Brynn arrived with Joseph, their van rolling to a stop just beyond the barricade. Hot metal ticked as the engine settled. She stepped out and took in the layout in a quick, trained sweep. A white sheet glared in the sunlight where it covered a body. Emergency vehicles pulsed their lights without sirens, urgency reduced to color and heat.

Her fingers tapped against her phone. She swallowed against the tightness in her throat as the sheet rippled. The air carried a strained hush, broken by the low murmur of a crowd and the thin crackle of police radios. She squared her shoulders and adjusted her press badge. The lanyard rasped against her neck and steadied her the way it always did.

With a nod to Joseph, already unslinging his camera, Brynn approached a traffic cop. Deep lines bracketed his mouth. Shadows pooled beneath bloodshot eyes. A salt ring marked his collar.

"Officer. Brynn Cassidy, New Dresden Today. Can you tell us what happened here?" Her voice held firm against the noise.

He turned, gaze heavy. "Third hit and run this month. At least this driver left their car behind," he said, the words rough with fatigue. "The car is just down the street, about two blocks away."

Brynn followed his gesture. Heat shimmered over the crumpled shape of an autonomous vehicle in the distance. Its hood was buckled, and the windshield spidered. Cones and investigators ringed it while onlookers clustered at the edges.

The crowd near the body held tight to the tape. Faces shone in the high sun, some blanched and others flushed. A few people recoiled, others rose onto their toes, hands covering mouths. A wiry cyclist stood trembling beside a battered bike, the rim ticking as it spun. Near him, a burly truck driver kept still, fingers flexing and relaxing at his sides.

"Joseph," Brynn said, low and even, "let's get some B roll footage. We need to capture the essence of this."

He nodded. She watched him move, grateful for his quiet steadiness.

"Get the car, the skid marks, and the officers," she said, eyes sweeping the taped perimeter. "We need enough visuals to give the viewers a powerful reaction."

The camera whirred alive. Brynn's throat constricted, a reflex as automatic as the press of a record button. She cleared it twice. The lens gathered what there was to see. Emergency lights pulsed in time, washing the street in hard reds and blues that flattened edges. Onlookers with set jaws and wide eyes, phones raised in a small forest of glass. The reek of hot rubber hung above faint traces of coolant. Debris glinted on the pavement beside a somber sheet that marked the end of a life.

The camera panned across the block, holding on the white sheet, then slid to the damaged vehicle down the street. Sunlight flashed off bits of shattered glass. Brynn watched the feed on the small monitor and mapped the shape of the story they would have to tell.

After a few minutes, Joseph lowered the camera. "I'm ready," he said. "Where do you want to start?"

Brynn breathed in slowly, bracing for the live shot. She smoothed her hair and straightened her jacket. The fabric tugged at her forearms. The gesture helped line up her thoughts.

"Let's begin here," she said, choosing a spot that would frame the accident scene behind her. "We'll start with what we know so far. Sgt. Khamal, can we talk to you?"

"Yes, of course. Where would you like me?" Sgt. Khamal asked. As the media liaison for the force, he was the official source for the bare facts.

"Right here. Is that right, Joseph?" She positioned him just out of the frame. Joseph lifted the camera to his shoulder and gave a short nod. The red light blinked on to show they were recording. Brynn faced the lens. She squared her shoulders and softened her gaze, the same look she had perfected across countless tragedy reports.

Brynn stepped to the liaison with the camera rolling. "This is Sgt. Khamal, media liaison with New Dresden Police. Sgt. Khamal, can you tell us what happened here?" Her tone stayed professional and warm. She held the microphone steady. The foam smelled faintly of dust.

Sgt. Khamal drew a slow breath and scanned the scene. A radio hissed at his shoulder. "A woman was struck by an autonomous vehicle," he said, voice dry, each word careful as he massaged his throat. "The car continued for several blocks before being stopped by a pickup truck driver." He ran a hand over his face and looked past her at the crowd. "It was a tragic incident. We are still gathering details."

"Some people say that autonomous cars are unsafe and should not be on the road. Sgt. Khamal, what is your understanding of the safety protocols for these cars?" she asked. Her voice carried over the throb of distant sirens and the hum of idling cruisers. She watched him shift his weight, boots scuffing grit.

"Independent reviews show autonomous cars reduce risk compared to human drivers," he began, keeping his tone even.

"There were 1,175 traffic fatalities in New Dresden last year, the highest number since 2010. Nationwide, traffic related deaths grew by nearly 17 percent, while New Dresden's fatalities rose by almost 30 percent in the last three years. Do you think autonomous cars are part of this increase?" Brynn asked, already pressing the advantage.

"I am not aware of the statistics on traffic fatalities involving autonomous cars, so I cannot answer that," Sgt. Khamal said with a small shake of his head. Radio chatter crackled at his shoulder. He knew the game as well as Brynn did.

"Is the time of day a factor? We know these cars are not great in low light."

"Once again, we are still gathering facts. I am sure it will come out."

Brynn nodded, her expression solemn under the strobe of blue and red. "Thank you for your time, Sgt. Khamal." She turned to the cyclist waiting just outside the taped line. The tape snapped lightly in the breeze. The cyclist's fingers drummed against his handlebars in an uneven rhythm. Chain oil and warm rubber scented the air. Brynn lowered her microphone slightly, giving him a little more space.

"Can you tell us what you saw?" Brynn asked quietly.

The cyclist swallowed before speaking. "It was like something I will never forget," he said, voice unsteady. "I saw her go down, and the car kept moving. I tried to keep up on my bike, but I could not catch it until the truck driver blocked it." The words came fast, as if they had been held in too long.

As Joseph captured close-ups, the red tally light steady on the camera, Brynn confirmed the spelling of the witness's name and his route. She then approached the truck driver. His eyes were distant, still working through the sequence in his head.

"Twenty years on these streets, and I ain't never." He drew a breath. "The damn thing moved with no one in command. No lights, no response, just an empty metal box pushing straight at everything in its path." He punctuated each word with a sharp gesture, calloused hands cutting the air. A muscle twitched in his jaw. He raked a hand through his hair and stared at the empty road. He blinked hard, as if to clear the vision. "No one inside was responding. I had to pull in front of it to make it stop."

Joseph's camera dipped an inch as he glanced left and right. "No. No way. These systems have failsafes on top of failsafes."

Brynn stepped into frame, the accident scene a hard line behind her. Joseph adjusted the shot until the police tape, shattered glass, and pulsing lights sat in balance.

"I am here at the site of a tragic and unusual accident involving an autonomous vehicle that took the life of a pedestrian," she began. She dropped her pitch half an octave and let each word strike clean. "The circumstances are still under investigation, but what we know is that the vehicle did not respond as designed. Autonomous vehicles are built to prevent collisions, which raises serious questions about system failure and oversight."

She paused and tipped her hand for Joseph to pan wide. The lens found the white sheet, its edges lifting slightly in the breeze, stark against asphalt. Farther on, the crumpled autonomous vehicle sat skewed to the curb, metal twisted and glass blown out across the gutter. The smell of coolant and hot wiring hung low. Onlookers pressed forward on tiptoe, then rocked back again, stuck between the urge to flee and the need to see. Whispers passed through the crowd. "How could it just keep going?" "But these cars are supposed to prevent this." Each unfinished thought carried a thin edge of fear. A low, uneasy pull held the crowd at the tape.

Brynn faced the camera again, her voice steady and cool. "Given the complexity of this case, and the fact that an autonomous car was involved, it is likely that specialists in crash reconstruction and vehicle data will be needed to unravel the events that led to this fatal accident. One name that comes to mind is the renowned Detective Blackburn from the New Dresden Police Homicide Division. Detective Blackburn is known for solving intricate cases, her involvement could shed light on this incident. The police will get to the bottom of this tragedy, and we will be following this story every step of the way. This is Brynn Cassidy for New Dresden Today."

The camera light clicked off. Brynn held her smile a beat longer, then let the real one surface. The air felt cool against her skin. "Time to make a call."

Chapter 35

While Joseph packed their gear, Brynn called New Dresden Today. Her words came fast, each possibility stacking on the last. "Hey, Carl, listen to this. I've got an incredible story that could easily expand into a few more segments. An accident with an autonomous car. No driver. A pedestrian dead. Might be a homicide. We can dive into the issue of self-driving cars in the city. This accident has raised serious questions about their safety and reliability. We could explore the ethical and legal implications of autonomous vehicles in urban environments. This could engage our audience and spark a broader conversation. It will have play. What do you think?"

"Get your ideas together. Present them to me after you've finished your piece. Way to go, Brynn. I knew I could count on you." A grin touched her mouth as she ended the call. She pumped her fist once, twice, then checked herself and reset to professional neutral.

The paramedics shifted from urgent to methodical, boots scraping asphalt in a steady rhythm. Sirens receded to a steady hum. The crowd's whispers thinned. Paramedics lifted the body onto a stretcher, their movements respectful and precise. The white sheet gave way to a black body bag, the zipper's rasp carrying down the street with a finality that pressed on the air.

Joseph, sensing the change, powered the camera back on. He panned across the scene, capturing the paramedics as they wheeled the stretcher toward the waiting ambulance. Red and blue lights strobed across windshields and slicked the black bag in cold color.

Brynn faced the camera, posture professional despite the circumstances. She wrapped her final lines, voice steady as she summarized the day's events. "As we conclude our coverage, we're left with more questions than answers about the safety of autonomous vehicles in our city."

Her words fell away as something caught her eye. On Evergreen Drive, just a block away, a sleek, dark autonomous car glided along the street. Brynn's hand shot out, grabbing Joseph's arm. The familiar tingle rose at the base of her skull. The same sensation that had led her to three breaking stories last month. The car. Same obsidian paint. Same tinted windows mirroring the emergency lights. Even the chrome trim matched.

"Joseph. Look." Her voice cut sharp with urgency and excitement. She pointed toward Evergreen Drive. "Over there, it's another one of those self-driving cars."

Joseph's elbow jerked, sending the camera swinging before his trained hands steadied it. He twisted the focus ring and tightened the zoom to catch the vehicle in the distance. The car moved with precision, quiet and watchful, as if aware of the attention it was drawing.

Brynn leaned forward, captivated, her breath catching. Her press badge swung against her chest as she tracked the vehicle's movement.

Self-driving cars were still uncommon on the streets of New Dresden, and seeing one so soon after the crash was too coincidental to ignore. "That is so weird," she said to Joseph.

Just as Joseph managed to get a clear shot, the vehicle's lights flashed. Without warning, the car surged. Tires screamed against the pavement, a harsh peel that drowned the murmur of police radios and sent pigeons beating into the afternoon sky. The smell of burned rubber rolled over the block.

"Damn it, it's getting away." Joseph fought to keep the rapidly moving vehicle in frame. The camera wobbled as he traced its path, but the car vanished into the maze of side streets, shadows swallowing the shine of its paint.

Brynn jerked her chin toward the retreating blur, already stepping forward. "Let's go check out the smashed vehicle," she said, her voice low but firm. She shouldered past a cluster of onlookers, the press of bodies sticky with heat and nerves. Joseph fell in close behind. The camera bag slapped against his hip as they moved toward the second scene, gear clattering lightly, almost forgotten in the pull of the chase.

The two moved at a briskly, threading through knots of onlookers and emergency crews. Heat pressed up from the pavement, the air carried the sting of burned rubber. Responders worked with quiet efficiency, faces drawn, eyes down, radios murmuring. Ahead, the autonomous vehicle sat inside the tape, its sleek shell scuffed and still. Brynn took it in, filing questions as she walked.

"Joseph," she began, her tone curious, "do you know much about these self-driving cars? I mean, beyond the basics we have reported on before?"

Joseph's brow tightened. "I have been keeping up with the trend. I was thinking of buying one if I ever won the lottery," he replied. He forced a weak chuckle that died against the wash of flashing lights and yellow tape. "From what I have read, autonomous vehicles are generally considered safer than human-driven cars. The National Highway Traffic Safety Administration reported that over ninety-four percent of serious crashes are due to human error."

They paused at a crosswalk for the light. Brynn nodded for him to continue.

Joseph warmed to the familiar topic. "You know what is wild? These things could save nine out of ten people who die in crashes. At least, that is what they are saying in the studies I have been reading." He shifted the camera higher on his shoulder. "Another report showed that in over ten million miles of testing, autonomous vehicles were involved in fewer accidents per mile driven compared to human drivers."

"So, you like them, eh?" As they crossed, Brynn kept her eyes on the damaged car. "That is what makes this so strange," she murmured. "If they are supposed to be so safe, how did this happen?"

Joseph's mouth thinned as he adjusted the strap, attention split between the wreck and Brynn. "That is the thing. Statistically, they are safer. But no technology is perfect. Human error, almost every time."

"And some of the witnesses said there was no human driver," Brynn said.

Heat gathered beneath Brynn's collar. The pavement pushed warmth through her soles, sweat beaded under her hairline. Beyond the tape, the vehicle wavered in the glare.

Joseph swiped at his brow, camera solid against his shoulder. "You know," he said, his voice strained, "our news van has driver assistance, like adaptive cruise control. But that is the lowest level of automation."

Brynn leaned into her pace, focus narrowing on the wreck. "And from there?" she prompted.

"It goes up. Some cars manage most safety-critical driving functions like automatic lane changes and navigating highway interchanges. At the top end, the cars are fully automated," Joseph explained. "The highest level is capable of being completely driverless. Full-time automated driving in all conditions without need for a human driver."

The scent of hot oil grew sharper as they neared the tape. Brynn squinted against sun off torn metal. She stepped to the edge of the line and read the manufacturer's name along the panel.

She traced the manufacturer's plate with her eyes, mouthing each word before speaking. "This is a Raider Straight Line. Jesus. It says here it has partial automation," she called out to Joseph.

Joseph frowned, adjusting his grip on the camera. "That means it needs a driver," he said firmly. "There is no way it could operate without one."

Brynn turned back, studying him. "But witnesses said there was no driver," she countered.

Joseph shook his head emphatically. "That is just not possible," he insisted. "A car with partial automation absolutely requires a human driver. There must be some mistake in the witness accounts."

Brynn examined the scarred surface. Sensor housings were empty and charred, wiring exposed. Cracks webbed the hood, breaking the afternoon light into hard fragments. Her shoulders tightened. She rubbed the back of her neck, skin salt-slick against her palm.

A faint hiss rose from under the chassis and sharpened into a crackle. "Get this!" she snapped at Joseph. He lifted the camera and rolled. A thin line of smoke pushed out from beneath the car, then another, then a third. The acrid bite of burning electronics hit before the volume of it built. Plastic on the tongue, metal in the nose. Smoke surged from the seams, black and heavy, until the car disappeared inside it. The scene was swallowed by a cloud of dense, black smoke.

The few police officers and firefighters near the vehicle pulled back fast. The officers, hands up, ordered the growing crowd to move back, widening the perimeter around the smoking vehicle. Radios crackled. Acrid smoke curled in gusts that made eyes sting and throats rough.

"Come on, Brynn," Joseph said as he gripped her shoulder and walked backward, camera up and recording.

Firefighters uncoiled their hoses with quick motions. Canvas slapped the pavement. Valves clanked open. Water hammered in hard streams at the base of the thick smoke.

"Those idiots," Joseph said, zooming in on the battery compart-
ment. He knew what was coming. "We need to get back now," he
urged. His words came faster, pitched higher, as he edged away from
the vehicle. Sweat beaded on his forehead. "Lithium battery fires can
get hot. Fast. And water is useless against a thermal runaway. This
could explode any minute. It is not safe here. Move." Brynn stumbled
backward, Joseph's hand firm on her shoulder as he pulled her away
from the scene.

Bright orange flames burst from the car's underside without warning. The lithium battery ignited. Cells fed the blaze with a hard,
unnatural heat that roared under the frame. A wave of heat rolled
outward, forcing people to shield their faces and step back.

"Get back. Get back!" a firefighter shouted, swinging his arm to
push the crowd farther from the danger.

The fire climbed the sides of the car with relentless speed. Tires
softened and sagged, then melted, releasing heavy, toxic fumes that
coated the air. The smell of burned rubber and a sweet chemical
bite settled on the tongue. Sparks jumped as the flames reached the
electrical systems, and blue white flashes snapped beneath the hood.

Behind glass, onlookers pressed their palms to the windows.
Mouths hung open. No one turned away from the inferno below.
Phones rose in a glittering field to capture every second. The roar
of the burn deepened to a steady thunder. Popping and crackling
layered over it as plastic and metal gave way.

As the fire raged, the car's frame buckled. Metal warped and pinged
in the heat. The hood sagged. Windows fractured, then blew out

one by one, sending glass skittering across the pavement in bright, dangerous arcs. The sleek lines vanished under blister and char. What remained was a twisted, blackened husk.

Firefighters held their line. Hoses hurled water and foam across the blaze. Steam boiled up and drifted in veils. The air stank of solvents and scorched wiring. Joseph's shoulders tightened as he adjusted the zoom and tracked each violent flare. His feet kept a tight pattern, three steps back, pivot, crouch, the lens steady on the destruction while grit pressed through the knees of his jeans.

Brynn watched from a safer distance. She craned her neck, keeping Joseph in her line. Ash freckled her coat and settled on her tongue with a bitter taste. Her fingers twitched toward her notebook, but her eyes fixed on Joseph's viewfinder. When he moved, she moved to stay behind him. It gave her the best and safest angle on what he was filming.

"God, this is good," she murmured, voice roughened by smoke. "Keep filming, Joseph." She raised her voice. "We are staying until the fire is out."

Over the next thirty minutes, reinforcements arrived, and Brynn took note of everything.

Does the fire department have specialized training for lithium batteries?

Water is not effective; do they carry dedicated equipment?

What safety is in place for the crowd against smoke? Is there a health risk and environmental impact?

Any link to the Raider Group or the police project? Is this a coincidence?

When the fire was finally extinguished, the autonomous car was scarcely recognizable. Its sleek shape was gone, replaced by a misshapen shell that steamed in the cold air. The crowd, kept at a safe distance, watched in stunned silence while firefighters moved in to probe for lingering hotspots and dull them with short, controlled bursts.

Then it was over. The flames were out, the scene cleared.

The only sign of death was a thickening pool of blood, diluted and pushed along in red swirls toward the sewer drain by a firefighter's spray.

Joseph loaded his camera gear into the van and climbed into the driver's seat, Brynn stood with the passenger door open and looked back at the wreck, sorting what she had seen.

Joseph clambered in and turned the key. The van rumbled to life. Brynn kept her gaze on the scarred asphalt and the thin streamers of steam still rising from the carcass. She drew a slow breath, then climbed in and closed the door.

As they pulled away, she watched the rearview mirror. The scene shrank. Sodium lights washed over smoldering metal that sank into darkness at the edge of the block. "Something does not add up." The words left in a whisper. Her breath fogged the passenger window as she leaned closer to the glass.

Joseph glanced over, brow furrowed. "You mean the fire?"

Brynn shook her head, still watching the receding chaos. "No," she said softly. "The timing. The police sign a contract with the Stan Raider Group, and bam! Their car kills someone and melts down."

Chapter 36

Blackburn stepped into the precinct, the LED hum settling over her like a thin film. Coffee hung stale in the air. Phones chirped from distant desks. A copier clicked and whirred. The encounter with Brynn lingered, contained behind a steady face.

Cooper lurched up from his desk as she approached and nearly toppled his chair in his rush to meet her. Wide-eyed and grinning, he bounced on the balls of his feet.

"Ma'am," he said, falling into step beside her, "we have got a potential breakthrough on the Jane Doe CCTR-02399 case."

Blackburn stopped, one brow lifting as she turned to him. She leaned in a fraction, reading his expression, then opened her office door and stepped inside. "Go on."

Cooper followed, close but careful. "We found evidence at Poston Park that might be connected to our victim. Women's clothing, shoved into a hole in a tree. It looks like they were deliberately hidden. Maybe with the killer's DNA."

Blackburn sat, the leather creaking under her, and leaned forward. "And the size?"

"Fantastic," Cooper said, eyes bright. "They look about right for a small woman, just like our Jane Doe."

Her shoulders loosened, irritation ebbed. "Excellent work, Cooper. This could be the lead we have been waiting for."

She ran the checklist in clean order, keeping her voice even. "Secure the scene. Call CSU. Photograph, bag, and tag. Gloves only. Prints and DNA off the clothes if we are lucky. Trace from the cavity and soil. Pull park cameras. Notify Parks to hold the trail. Log the find with the case number and time."

She looked up with the decision already formed. "I want you to get the sketch and the clothing description out to the press immediately. Include the location where the clothing was found. We need the public's eyes on this."

Cooper nodded, reaching for his notepad. "Right away, ma'am. I will draft a press release. Media Relations will have it out within the hour."

She lifted a hand. "Wait, Cooper." Urgency tightened her tone. "Before you draft anything, call New Dresden 24/7. They are the quickest to move."

Cooper's eyes widened. "Of course, boss. I will get right on it."

"Good man." Blackburn nodded. "Follow up with the other outlets once New Dresden 24/7 airs the information. We want maximum coverage."

The office air felt cool against her skin. She allowed herself a brief private smile as she pictured Brynn Cassidy when the segment hit. The pen in her fingers tapped once on the desk, a dry, precise click. She kept the surge down. Brynn had pushed too far when she called Willow. She could scramble for crumbs now.

Blackburn imagined Brynn's frustration when she realized a rival had scooped her. Her pulse ticked up. She flexed her fingers and focused on the advantage. The smile threatened again as she pictured Brynn missing a major story.

"That is what you get for digging where you should not," Blackburn murmured, satisfaction curling her lips as she turned to the case file. She steadied her breathing and mapped the next steps, marking each action with a neat underline. The taste of victory, over the case and over Brynn, was a clean sweetness at the back of her tongue. It sharpened her focus and stoked the need for the next move.

"Hey, boss," Reeves called through the glass wall that separated her office from the bullpen, voice cutting through the steady room noise, "the chief was looking for you."

Blackburn rolled her eyes. *When was he not?*

Chief Hayes' office held its quiet. The hum from a vent threaded through it, thin and steady, sending a faint coolness over Blackburn's hands. She watched his face while he studied Dawson's warrant request, noting the slow grind of his jaw. He turned each page with heavy care that rasped like dry paper dragging against skin. The administrative assistant who had delivered the paperwork had retreated, closing the door with a soft click that lingered in the hush. The room smelled of old coffee and lemon polish.

Hayes' reading slowed when he reached the cell phone records. His fingers drummed against the desk once, twice. Then he set the papers down and removed his reading glasses. The motion was controlled, yet Blackburn caught a slight tremor in his hands. The lenses left faint half-moons on the wood. He blinked as if the air stung.

"You've reviewed these?" His voice came out carefully neutral.

"Dawson made sure I did not." Blackburn's smile had the warmth of a December morning. "But even a first year rookie could spot these discrepancies." She reached across the desk and tapped the page with one manicured nail. The crisp tick of nail on paper marked her point. "The suspect's phone apparently pinged these three towers simultaneously. Unless we are talking about quantum mechanics instead of a murder case, it never happened."

Hayes watched the spot where her finger rested. The leather of his chair groaned as he shifted. "So he faked it."

"Yes."

"He played me." The words sat between them. "Used my trust to get his arrest. The bastard is done."

"Firing him would raise questions." Blackburn settled back and crossed her legs. The fabric of her slacks whispered, neat and con-tained. "Questions about oversight. About who signed what, and when." She paused and let the implications settle. "The kind of questions that travel to the commissioner's office. Gets chiefs fired."

Hayes' reflection bent across his brass nameplate as he lifted it, studying the dull shine. A thumbprint smeared and cleared beneath his sleeve. He turned the metal in his palm and felt its weight. "Not me. I'm smarter than that. This will not touch me."

"Sir, it already has. It is your signature."

"But the paperwork went nowhere."

Blackburn leaned back in her chair and shook her head, her blonde hair shimmering in the overhead light. "As far as I know. But I cannot be sure, sir. Maybe he has copies."

Hayes sighed a smile onto his face. "You are a very honest cop," he said. "This is your first time dealing with falsified records, isn't it?"

Blackburn tilted her head. "Yes, of course." She gently picked up Hayes's nameplate. Brass. Solid. Cold. The metal cooled her fingers as she tested its edge.

Hayes grinned and looked at the wall. News articles of big arrests, commendations, photos with politicians. The frames caught the light in hard rectangles. A corner of one print had begun to curl beneath the glass. "No harm has been done. No one jailed. No lives lost. Dawson made a mistake. He never should have gone past you. And he never should have come to me." The corner of his mouth curved. "No paperwork, no formal reprimand. Handle it my way."

"Just an adjustment of priorities?" Blackburn set the nameplate down with precise care.

"Sometimes keeping it in house is more effective."

Silence stretched between them. Outside the door, a phone rang and stopped. Hayes reached for the warrant request. Each movement looked deliberate, a man choosing the next step. He fed the pages into the shredder at the edge of his desk. The motor rose to a thin whine, and the bin filled with warm confetti that smelled faintly of hot paper and motor oil. Static made strips cling to his wrist.

"I trust your judgment, Detective." Hayes' words carried both permission and a warning. "Just make sure there is nothing left to trace back here."

Blackburn stood and smoothed her slacks with flattening palms. "Consider it handled." She moved toward the door. Her heels clicked in a steady rhythm that marked time more than it made sound.

"And Blackburn?" Hayes called after her. "Make it hurt."

She did not turn. Her smile sharpened, clean as a cut. "That is a guarantee."

Chapter 37

Blackburn sat at her desk, the flat light of her monitor carving hard lines across her face. Phones rang and keyboards clacked beyond her door, but her gaze stayed on the screen, fingers held still over the mouse. The muscles around her eyes tightened, shallow creases forming as she took in the details in front of her. She picked up the phone and called Dawson into her office. She could have yelled for him, but she had already done that this week. A phone call, she thought, was the sharper move. Stealth scares.

"Dawson, I would like an update on your case," she said as she watched him through the glass. He turned at the sound of her voice.

"Which one?" he asked, flatly.

"How about the one you just got? The child who died?"

"Yeah," he said as the receiver clicked back into its cradle.

Through the glass, Blackburn saw his shoulders slump as he glanced her way. His lips pressed into a thin line, and his nostrils flared as he snatched up a loose pile of papers. With each step toward her office, his shoes scuffed the worn carpet. The door creaked open, and he stepped in. The faint hum of the vents filled the pause.

"You wanted an update?" Dawson asked. His voice held an edge, the words clipped as if forced out, then softening at the end as though giving in.

Blackburn leaned back in her chair, eyes fixed on his face. The air felt tight in the room, pressing against her skin. She could almost taste the salt of his anxiety. She let the silence stretch and watched the discomfort settle over him.

"Sit down," she said, her voice cool and commanding.

Dawson complied, sinking into the chair across from her desk. He set the file on his lap. His fingers tapped the manila as if testing its weight.

Blackburn watched him squirm under her gaze. The tension held.

"Give me an update," she said, her voice cutting clean through the air.

Dawson shifted. "I will type up the report right away," he said, eyes sliding off hers.

Blackburn's teeth met hard, a muscle ticking in her cheek. Her fingernails bit into her palms, leaving faint crescents. "No," she snapped, the word echoing off the walls. "You will give it now."

She leaned forward, attention narrowed to a point. Then she raised her voice toward the bullpen. "All of you. Get in here." The three detectives hurried into her office, footsteps loud against the floor. The room felt crowded, the air carried Blackburn's displeasure. They traded quick glances, reading the warning in their superior's eyes.

"Dawson is going to give us an update," she said, locking her gaze on him and daring refusal.

Dawson cleared his throat, glanced at the others, and began. "The victim was found lying down."

Blackburn lifted a hand, stopping him. "Does the child have a name?" Frustration edged her voice.

"Deonte Mills," Dawson said with a brief shake of his head.

"See, that was not hard to treat a victim like a person, was it, Dawson?" Blackburn's voice stayed flat with disdain, her eyes unblinking on him.

The other detectives' gazes skittered, never settling. Their bodies shifted in a tight pattern. A foot slid back, a torso turned away, arms crossed over chests. Sinclair took a small step backward as if distance could save him from what was coming. He felt a twinge of fear draw tight in his groin, his balls pulling up to safety.

Dawson's throat constricted, his Adam's apple jerking upward. Sweat gathered on his forehead. One droplet slid down his temple. His hand twitched toward his face, then clenched into a fist at his side. "Deonte Mills," he began again, his voice steadier this time, "was found in his living room at approximately 7:30 AM."

Blackburn leaned back in her chair, fingers steepled under her chin. The leather gave a quiet sigh beneath her. Her gaze never wavered from Dawson's face, and he felt it as a steady weight he could not ignore. The room held its breath. The air conditioner hummed above them. From beyond the office door came the low murmur of phones ringing and footsteps moving down the hall.

Dawson cleared his throat, glanced at the others, and began. "The victim," he said.

"Deonte Mills!" Blackburn shouted, cutting him off. Her voice came sharp enough to sting. Everyone in the room flinched. "Use his name!"

The office seemed to shrink. Her words clung to the walls.

Sinclair's heartbeat pounded in his ears, each thump heavy and unhelpful. Sweat slicked his palms. He kept his eyes on Blackburn's fierce expression and her pointing finger. He studied her face, her hands, the clean line of her blazer, the rise and fall of her chest. His gaze drifted to the shape of her breasts. He imagined the pull of a nipple against his mouth.

Heat crept up his neck and spread across his cheeks. He shifted in his chair and crossed his legs to hide the pressure building in his trousers. The blush on his face betrayed him.

He glanced at Sinclair and raised an eyebrow, a small signal that threatened to break the moment, then looked back to Blackburn. She held him with the same implacable focus. The other detectives exchanged quick, uneasy looks. Their breathing sounded shallow in the close air. No one spoke.

Blackburn's voice, purposeful and cold, cut through the quiet again. "Deonte Mills was a child. A child whose life was brutally taken from him. I want his name used when we discuss this case. I want everyone in this room to remember we are not dealing with a faceless victim but a little boy who deserved better than what he got." She let her eyes pass over each of them until they stopped moving.

Dawson's tongue stuck to the roof of his mouth. He nodded.

Sinclair stared at the floor. Shame tightened his gut while Blackburn's words settled in. He pulled his jacket closer as if it could contain his body's betrayal. He knew Blackburn's power. Her passion. He had also heard the rumors. Women. Threesomes. Toys and an appetite that did not quit. Leather. He could not help himself sometimes.

Blackburn's gaze found him. She gave the slightest nod, almost private. It felt like a recognition of what had been running through his mind and a warning that she knew.

Chairs shifted. Fabric whispered. The others waited to see what would follow.

A bead of sweat slid from Dawson's hairline down his flushed cheek. He drew in a breath and held it for a second. The sound of it marked the silence. He found his voice.

"Deonte Mills appears to have suffered blunt force trauma. His father claims he was out at the time of the incident. The father is a known drug user with five convictions. We have not located the mother yet."

Blackburn did not blink. Her gaze weighed each word and the flickers around them.

"Who was with Deonte?"

"Dad, Caleb, said he left the kid alone." Dawson flipped through his thin notepad without looking up.

"For how long?"

"I did not ask."

The LED lights gave a faint electrical buzz. Blackburn leaned back and laced her fingers. The pose looked casual, but the room felt less forgiving.

"Walk me through the scene. What was the boy wearing?"

Dawson shifted again. "Kid's clothes. You know."

"No, Detective Dawson, I do not know. Was he in pajamas, play clothes, or a school uniform?"

"PJs."

"Temperature of the body?"

"The ME is handling that."

"Who found him?"

"The dad."

"And you verified that with what?"

"The dad told me."

Blackburn tapped her pen against the desk. The sound was soft, exact, relentless. "Neighbors? Security cameras? Any independent verification?"

The other detectives in the room went still, their attention fixed on the exchange unfolding before them. The LED lights hummed overhead.

"What's your theory?" she asked, her voice dangerously soft.

Dawson hesitated, the silence narrowing to a fine edge. "I think the father is lying," he said, barely above a whisper. "I believe he killed his son."

"Why?"

Dawson straightened his shoulders, a flicker of confidence returning to his eyes. "Because the father is a druggie scumbag," he declared, his voice gaining strength. "And I just do not think his girlfriend did it."

"Girlfriend? Jesus, Dawson. There was a girlfriend? Are they both here?"

"Uh, no. There was no reason to arrest them," Dawson mumbled.

"As witnesses?" Blackburn growled.

Dawson shook his head. "Refused to come in."

"Drug tests?"

"Waiting."

"State of living. What about the kitchen?" Blackburn cut in. "Any food on the stove? Dishes in the sink? Signs of recent meals?"

Dawson's confidence drained away.

Blackburn's stare sharpened, her anger narrowing the room around him. "Evidence of neglect? Have you ruled out the possibility that the mother killed her son and then fled?"

Dawson opened and closed his mouth, struggling to form words under Blackburn's unrelenting stare. The sound of a copier whirred in the distance, too loud in the quiet.

"Do you have any proof the mother is alive?" Blackburn continued, each word precise. "Or is it possible the father killed her and her son, but only managed to hide her body?"

"I did not. It was the mother. The mother..." Dawson blinked sweat from his brow and lost his thought. "I mean."

"Did you ask about her?"

"No."

"The boy's room. Did you check it? Clothing missing? Signs of packing?"

Dawson's silence was answer enough.

"Photos on the walls?" Blackburn pressed. "Recent ones? Old ones? Any showing the mother?"

"I can go back."

"You are damn right you will go back." Blackburn's voice dropped lower. "But first, tell me about the scene. Position of the body. Blood spatter? Signs of struggle? Items out of place?"

"The kid—"

"DEONTE!" Blackburn shouted as her palm hit the desk. Wood screamed under the blow. Everyone jumped.

"Deonte was taken to the hospital. The place was a stinking mess. Crime scene techs took control of the scene. Uniform will call me when they are done," Dawson snapped. "I am not a fucking moron."

Color climbed his neck and spread across his cheeks. He searched for something else to say, mind racing, but found nothing. The ticking wall clock sounded loud, each second marked by his shallow, uneven breaths. The other detectives shifted, chair legs scraped. Fabric rustled.

Sinclair cleared his throat, the sound startling in the tense silence. "I have a theory. Is it possible there was a babysitter involved? And the father is protecting her? Like his girlfriend or her mother?" he asked, eager to impress Blackburn. His eyes flicked between her and Dawson, hoping for a sign of approval from the woman he admired.

Dawson's fist slammed onto the desk, and the pens rattled. His voice cracked as he spat, "Whose side are you on?" He glared at Sinclair.

Blackburn's gaze moved from Dawson to Sinclair. Sinclair felt his skin prickle as she slid her eyes back to her prey. Her words cut through the heavy air. "Do not hit my desk again. Ever. And do not get angry," she said, voice dangerously calm. "Sinclair has a good theory. Dads may kill their kids, but sometimes they have friends who kill their kids." She let the words settle. "Press the father for more information, talk to the girlfriend, and find the damned mother."

Blackburn watched them all, her eyes assessing each one in turn. The air held, ready to ignite at the slightest spark. She drew a breath, let it out, and composed herself.

"Thank you, Dawson," she said, voice devoid of emotion. "You are dismissed. You all are."

Dawson nodded tightly, unable to meet her gaze, and hurried out. Sinclair stayed leaning, legs crossed, willing his arousal to ebb. Cooper and Reeves filed out. Blackburn turned to Sinclair.

"Sinclair," she said, low and seductive. "Not you." She paused, a glint lighting her eyes. "Stay."

Sinclair's throat went dry. "Yes, ma'am," he managed. He shut the door.

"Sit there," Blackburn said, pointing at the chair Dawson had used. The green leather chair waited, the cushion showing the last sitter's shape.

He crossed over and sat. The leather creaked under his weight. His heart thudded in his chest.

"Sinclair," Blackburn began, her voice sweet and dripping with honey. "I noticed you were staring at me just now." She leaned back, hands behind her head, blouse pulling tight across her chest. She smiled. "You were, were you not?" Her eyes were hooded.

Sinclair nodded, unable to speak. Heat rose under her gaze. Heat tightened low again.

"That is okay, Sinclair," Blackburn purred. "I like it when people pay attention to me." She leaned forward, and her white blouse opened just enough to deepen the view of her cleavage. "Now, go into the bathroom and get rid of that thing," she said, flicking her fingers toward his bulge. In a low, sultry voice she added, "Do not tell anyone if you think of me while you do."

Goosebumps lifted along Sinclair's skin, a shiver passing through him. His pulse pounded. Fear and thrill threaded through his veins.

"Ma'am?" he whispered.

"Yes, Sinclair?" Blackburn asked, one eyebrow arched.

"Are we okay?" he asked, voice cracking.

Blackburn smiled, mischief glinting in her eyes. "Get out of my office."

Her phone rang, its shrill tone cutting through the charged atmosphere. She waved a hand, dismissing him. Sinclair walked out stiffly, face flushed, gait awkward. Blackburn watched him angle toward the washroom and smiled, a predator's glint in her eye.

As the phone kept ringing, Blackburn smoothed her features into a mask of professional detachment. She picked up the receiver, voice crisp and authoritative. "Detective Blackburn."

Chapter 38

Brynn sounded keyed up. "Detective, it's Brynn Cassidy from New Dresden Today. Got a minute?"

Blackburn exhaled and eased back in her chair. The woman was getting under her skin. She wanted to like Brynn. The reporter's tenacity and wit felt familiar. And she was attractive in a television kind of way. But lately she was crossing lines. And the way she talked to Willow? Well, Blackburn would not have it.

"For you? Always," Blackburn said, her tone warm but guarded. "What can I do for you, Ms. Cassidy?"

"I'm calling about the tragic hit and run in the city's east end," Brynn said, her voice flattening into something more serious. "I was hoping you could give me some details."

Blackburn's brow tightened. "Hit and run? That's not my department. You should be calling Traffic Services or Major Crimes."

Blackburn could hear the faint hiss of the line and the low thrum of the squad room outside her door. When Brynn spoke again, her voice dropped, focused and intent. "I think it might have been a homicide."

Blackburn straightened. "A homicide?" Her interest sharpened. "What makes you say that? Other than the desire to sell television ads."

She leaned back, fingers tapping a steady rhythm on the polished desk. The varnish felt cool under her knuckles. Her toes pressed inside her shoes, a small, familiar current running through her. She cleared her throat and kept her voice level.

"There was no driver. None. These autonomous cars don't do that," Brynn said. Blackburn knew better. Some models could run without a human at the wheel.

"How do you know that?"

"No one saw anyone in the car."

"Just because no one saw a driver doesn't mean there wasn't one," Blackburn said, measured and even. She picked up a pen and rolled it between her fingers. "People often miss crucial details in the chaos of an accident."

"I thought of that too," Brynn said, gaining confidence. "But I spoke to the truck driver who stopped the car. He swears no one got out before the police arrived."

Blackburn leaned in. Her chair gave a soft creak. "And how do you know this truck driver was being truthful?" The pen stilled in her hand. She eased forward, fully engaged, her voice dropping to a low, controlled register.

Brynn's voice tightened. "There was also a cyclist who said the same thing. Both of them swear it was an autonomous car with no driver."

Blackburn's eyes cooled. Her grip firmed on the receiver. "I am sure Traffic Services can handle it," she said, cool and dismissive.

Brynn did not back off. "That's not all," she said, words gathering speed. "The car bricked itself."

Blackburn's forehead creased. She set her mouth and tapped the pen against the desk. A quick rhythm. "Bricked itself?" she repeated, the term unfamiliar. "What does that mean?"

"It went dark," Brynn said in a near whisper, conspiratorial at the edges. "It turned off completely after being stopped. And then it went up in flames."

"So what? Cars burn," Blackburn said, tone sharp.

"That would make data recovery difficult. Maybe impossible."

Blackburn pinched the bridge of her nose and let out a slow breath. "It is still something for Traffic Services."

Her gaze drifted to the squad room beyond her door. The overhead lights hummed. Sinclair stepped out of the washroom, face flushed, gait a touch unsteady. Their eyes met for a beat. Blackburn gave him a slight wink. Color rose in his cheeks as he turned to his desk and bent over his files.

She brought the phone back to her ear. Brynn pushed on, urgency rising. "Traffic Services can't get the event data recorder because the car went up in flames. It burned too long and hot for the recorder to have survived," Brynn said. "And my cameraman thinks there's more to it."

Blackburn settled against the chair back and watched dust float in the narrow beam of light across her office. "Why do you think that is suspicious, Ms. Cassidy? I hear those things catch fire all the time," she said, voice low.

Brynn's voice came tight and bright through the line. "Not that often. And it's not just the bricking and the fire, Detective. The witnesses say the car reversed after initially hitting the victim. It's like it deliberately ran her over, then ran her over again."

"Now that is unusual," Blackburn said. "Do you have any information about the victim?"

A thin hiss filled the pause. "No, I don't," Brynn said, frustration pulling at the edges of her words.

"Were you expecting me to provide that information?" Blackburn asked, a trace of dry humor in her tone.

"No, not at all," Brynn said, and the lie skimmed the surface. "I was hoping you might investigate and uncover those details yourself."

Blackburn let a small laugh slip. "Yes. Finding out who the victim is, in fact, is something detectives do." Her fingertips tapped a steady rhythm on the lacquered desk. The sound steadied her thoughts. "Let me summarize what you are telling me. An autonomous car, which rarely causes accidents, not only hit someone but then reversed to run them over again. Then it bricked itself and caught fire, destroying any evidence. Is that correct?"

"Exactly," Brynn said. "Autonomous cars are programmed to avoid accidents. It doesn't make sense."

Blackburn watched sunlight break into pale stripes across the office floor through the blinds. Her breath evened. She rose and walked the room, the quiet hum of the air system and distant bullpen chatter setting a cool backdrop. Each step helped her sort the pieces. This was not a routine hit and run. A driverless car reversed over a downed pedestrian. That pointed to intent.

"Thank you for bringing this to my attention, Ms. Cassidy," she said, her voice level. "This is certainly intriguing."

"Does this mean you're going to investigate?" Brynn asked. Hope threaded the question.

Blackburn allowed herself a controlled smile. "If I do decide to look into this, I am sure you will be the first to find out," she said, giving nothing away.

She leaned back. The chair gave a quiet creak. The phone remained warm against her ear. Brynn's account settled into order. An autonomous car designed to prioritize safety, struck a pedestrian, then appeared to reverse and strike again. Fire followed, systems and shell reduced to scrap. Start with the VIN and EDR. Pull backend telemetry. Lock down the OTA logs and the update schedule. Canvas for cameras and scrape traffic sensors. Secure the tow yard. Put a hold on the wreck. Interview witnesses before they settle on a single story.

She disliked the way Brynn tried to maneuver her, to set terms. But now she wanted the case.

She ended the call. The bullpen beyond her glass wall carried its usual soundtrack. Phones rang. Keyboards snapped. A copier clicked and released a faint ozone tang that cut through the stale coffee in her own mug. The noise dimmed as she mapped what came next. Who was the victim, and what had she done to trigger a response this calculated and cold? Who would choose to weaponize a vehicle meant to keep people safe, then scrub the trail by fire?

If she took it, this case would not be like the others. She would have to move through vendor ecosystems and control stacks with care, leverage access and policy, and force cooperation where it did not exist. Motive and opportunity would bend in unfamiliar ways when machines carried out human intent. It would show her what kind of threat this technology posed to her murder team. To her.

She stood at the window. The glass held a faint warmth from the late light. Sirens stitched a thin line somewhere far below, swallowed by the city's larger hum. Gleaming towers reflected a sky going colorless as the afternoon thinned. Somewhere in that spread of streets and traffic sat the reason a car hunted a body twice and then burned its memory clean.

She turned back to the desk. Files lay open in layered stacks, pages marked with notes from other lives and other endings. Familiar weight. Familiar disorder. Yet one set of facts had pushed to the front, edges hard and insistent in her mind.

She glanced at Sinclair. His head was down over a report, a pen balanced between his fingers. He would follow her lead. They all would.

Blackburn reached for her suit jacket. Decision settled cool and precise in her chest. She would take the investigation from Traffic Services. The case would sit with her where it belonged. Whatever she found would be hers to control.

She slid her phone into her pocket and rolled her shoulders once to reset her focus. She would not stop until she understood exactly what had happened. The game, as they say, was afoot. And Blackburn was ready to play.

Chapter 39

Duty shoes squeaked on the linoleum of the Traffic Services corridors. Blackburn threaded past harried uniforms clutching coffee and radios, her stride unhurried. She gathered fragments of talk about speeding tickets, fender benders, and patrol schedules. The low buzz turned into white noise that kept her purpose hidden. The air smelled faintly of disinfectant and stale coffee, with a thin undercurrent of toner and warm plastic from overworked machines.

In the women's washroom, LED lights hummed as she studied her reflection. Cool tile pressed through the soles of her shoes. Her fingers traced the angles of her face, then pressed at the corners of her mouth, smoothing stern lines into something softer. She widened her eyes a fraction and let them catch the light. A blink and the predator receded behind a warmer mask. The door swung open on a gust of hallway air, and another officer entered. Blackburn adjusted her blazer, settled her collar, and slipped out.

The shift moved through her with each step toward Sgt. Hal Beckett's office. Her usual knife edge posture eased into something looser, almost musical. She let her shoulders relax and allowed a pleasant brightness to settle over her features while the corridor's hum steadied her breathing.

Beckett's office door stood open, light filtering through dusty blinds that striped the carpet. The room was cramped and smelled faintly of feet and old coffee. He hunched behind his desk, a newspaper spread before him like a shield. His reading glasses had slid to the tip of his nose, one sudden movement away from falling.

At her footsteps, he glanced up. The newspaper crinkled as he tossed it aside, and his chair groaned as he pushed to his feet. "Well, if it isn't my favorite detective!" His arms opened wide and pulled her into a bear hug.

"It's been too long, old friend." Blackburn patted his back, three gentle taps just as she had rehearsed. Heat bled through his uniform. Her fingers registered the weight he had gained since their last meeting and the slight tremor in his grip.

"Have a seat, sweetie." He gestured to the leather chair across from his desk. The cushion was worn slick, and a spring nudged up beneath the surface. Blackburn shifted to avoid it and let herself wince, a small concession to the room. The leather creaked under her.

"How's the family, Hal?" She tilted her head just so, inviting confidence.

Beckett's weathered face creased deeper. "Oh, you know, the wife's a pain and the kids are asses!" His belly laugh bounced off the walls and rattled the blinds.

Blackburn matched his rhythm, her laugh a careful echo of his. She counted the seconds, one, two, three, then let her mirth soften into a warm smile. Her fingers curled around the cracked armrest, and she noted where it yielded and where it held firm.

"Ah, but seriously." His voice lowered as he spoke of his wife's travel plans, his son's restaurant job, his daughter's academic achievements. Each detail settled into Blackburn's mental archive, neat and ready, ammunition for later use.

"Your kids are all grown up, eh?" A note of wistfulness colored her words.

"And you?" He angled himself toward her, elbows on the desk. "How's life treating you?"

She let out a small, self-deprecating chuckle. "Oh, you know me." Her shoulders lifted in a delicate shrug. "Still single, still working Homicide, still do not have a Ph.D." She paused and watched his chest swell with paternal pride. "Your daughter must be smart."

"Takes after her mother," he said, pleased.

"Oh, come now." Blackburn kept her tone warm. "I would say she got plenty of smarts from her father too."

His laughter filled the room again. Between chuckles, he wiped his eyes. "What brings you to my neck of the woods, Morgan?"

"My feet." The old joke landed cleanly. As his guffaws ebbed, Blackburn leaned closer and lowered her voice. "Hey, I wanted to give you a heads up. A reporter from New Dresden Today called earlier about a car accident."

Beckett's laugh lines vanished. His chair creaked as he straightened. "Called you?"

"Something about a hit and run with a weird car. A woman died." Blackburn kept her eyes on his face and cataloged each small shift.

His shoulders drooped by millimeters. "Ah, yes." His fingers drummed once on the desk. "That would be the anonymous car case. I went on scene. Terrible accident. Hit and run."

Blackburn could not believe he did not know the word autonomous. She tilted her head, softened her gaze at the corners, and leaned closer to the desk. "I know you hate talking to reporters, so I wanted to let you know they are sniffing around and trying to make a big story out of it."

The LED lights caught every crease in his face and deepened the shadows under his eyes. His shoulders sagged beneath his wrinkled uniform shirt. "It is a weird case, no doubt about that. But why did the reporter call you?"

She kept her face still, a skill honed through countless interrogations, while her mind moved three steps ahead. The stale scent of coffee hung in the air. "Well, it seems Brynn Cassidy thinks the hit and run might be a homicide. She was trying to get information from me. But it isn't a homicide, so I had nothing to give her."

Color climbed Beckett's neck, spreading across his cheeks. He rubbed a thumb against the edge of his desk as if smoothing a rough patch only he could feel. "A homicide? Good God, that's the last thing we need. I don't want that kind of case on my hands."

"I understand," Blackburn said quietly. Her voice carried no edge.

"I'm not up to speed on these anonymous cars," Beckett said as he shook his head. The LED light caught the sheen on his skin. "I'm hoping some of my younger guys might be able to handle it. This new technology is beyond me."

"That's great," Blackburn said. Her tone was warm. Practiced. "I just wanted to give you a heads up. Ms. Cassidy seems determined to turn this into a big story. One way or another."

Beckett's brow folded again. "Why's that?"

Blackburn leaned in slightly, her voice low. The chair leather creaked under her weight. "Well, according to her, there was no driver. That means the conspiracy nuts will say it came alive and killed someone. You know, sentient technology."

He squinted, mouth working before he spoke. Doubt settled into the usual lines. "Oh Christ. I don't understand those guys. We just need to find the driver. That's all there is to it."

Blackburn eased forward, patient and steady. "Hal, Ms. Cassidy claims she has two witnesses who say there was no driver. The car was self driving. Autonomous."

Silence took the room while he processed. The wall clock ticked with soft clicks in the pause. His eyes met Blackburn's, uncertain. "What do you think about all this?"

Blackburn shrugged, her face neutral. "I haven't seen the file, so I don't know what happened. But I'm sure you can handle it."

She rose as if to leave. Beckett waved her back down with a quick flick of his fingers. The chair legs whispered against the floor as she sat again and watched him think. He scratched his chin, the rasp of stubble faint in the quiet.

"You know," he began, "I might approach Chief Hayes and transfer the file over to Homicide. Would that be okay with you?"

Blackburn's eyebrows lifted a fraction, but she stayed silent and let him talk.

"Your division has that dedicated IT specialist," he reasoned. "And if it does turn out to be a homicide, you'll already be one step ahead."

"We are awfully busy," Blackburn said. "Dawson just picked up a child homicide." Blackburn set her features to reluctance, though inwardly she was thrilled.

"But he's working the case by himself. I might have time." Heat pricked the back of her neck at the neatness of it. She kept her hands loose in her lap, her face a mask of professional concern. "I guess," she said, her voice hesitant, "if Chief Hayes says it's okay, I suppose I could take the case off your hands."

Beckett nodded, relieved. He held up a finger to keep her there and reached for his phone. Blackburn allowed herself a small, contained smile that vanished as he looked up again.

Beckett's fingers trembled as he dialed. The phone was slick in his palm. Blackburn watched him, steady and intent. The line rang twice before Chief Hayes's gruff voice answered.

"Chief, it's Sgt. Beckett, Traffic," he began, his voice wavering slightly. "I've got a situation I'd like to discuss."

As he explained the hit and run involving the anonymous car, Blackburn stayed with him, her gaze fixed on his face. She nodded at each pause, an easy rhythm that kept him moving.

"Sir, I think it might be best if we transfer this case to Homicide," Beckett concluded, his voice steadier now.

There was a pause on the other end, a faint hiss of air in place of speech. "Is Detective Blackburn with you?" Chief Hayes asked, his tone curious.

Beckett's eyes darted to Blackburn, seeking guidance. She shook her head hard, mouth forming the words came by earlier. A flicker of confusion passed over his features, but he recovered.

"No, sir," he replied. "But she did come by earlier to pass on some news about a reporter." He glanced at Blackburn, who gave a single nod. Approval sat plainly in her eyes. "I've reviewed the case since then, and I think Homicide should take it. They have the IT resources, and honestly, you know I'm not good at talking to reporters."

Chief Hayes grunted. "Fine. Transfer the file to the Homicide Division. Tell Blackburn I said so."

As Beckett hung up the phone, the click sounded loud in the stale air. Relief spread across his face. He turned to Blackburn, unaware of the quiet satisfaction under her skin. She had steered him into a lie, though the case did not require it. A small lever of control, and enough.

A hint of a smile touched Blackburn's mouth, a small light in her eyes. Her fingertips traced the desk edge, each tap a methodical count while Beckett did his part. Perfect timing, clean execution. It was like striking a key and hearing the exact note.

Beckett sank into his chair. The cushion hissed, and the frame creaked as his shoulders dropped. A tired sigh escaped. "Well, it's all yours now," he said, his hand drifting toward files on his desk, as though the reach cost more energy than he had left.

Blackburn's lips curved into a small smile, her eyes steady. "Oh, I see how it is," she teased. She pitched her voice higher, putting warmth in each word. "Just looking to make your life easier before retirement, aren't you?"

Beckett threw his head back, his laugh loud in the tired room. The sound bounced off metal cabinets and old glass. "Hell yes, that's the way to do it!" he exclaimed, slapping his knee. "No shame in passing the buck when you're on your way out."

As his laughter subsided, he rummaged through the clutter on his desk. Papers rasped. A few pens rolled off and tapped across the floor before coming to rest against a chair leg. Sticky notes curled at the edges in the dry air. Finally, he located the file in question.

"Ah, here we go," he said, holding up a manila folder with a small grunt of triumph. He handed it to Blackburn with a flourish. "Good luck, and don't let all that tech stuff win, you hear?"

Blackburn accepted the file. The manila felt rough against her fingertips, the paper weight firm. She chuckled, her voice warm with affection. "I promise not to become a robot," she said, her tone mock-serious. "Though I cannot make any guarantees about my colleagues."

Beckett snorted, shaking his head.

"I will be in touch with your staff about the rest of the paperwork and digital files," Blackburn added, her voice turning professional. "Thanks, Hal. Say hi to Betsy and the kids for me."

As she turned to leave, controlled satisfaction moved beneath her calm. She had set the transfer in motion cleanly. Beckett requested it, and Hayes demanded it. Now the case was hers to run.

She wondered if it would be as interesting as the walking dead man.

Blackburn took the paper file and walked out of Traffic Services, her steps measured. The folder in her hands read like a clean handoff, proof that she could move pieces when needed.

Blackburn strode down the hallway. The click of her heels carried along the polished floors, sharp against the constant hum of LED lights. The waxed air smelled faintly of disinfectant and paper dust. She had set the transfer in motion. The case was hers to run.

As she approached the Homicide Division, she flipped open the file. Traffic fatalities were usually straightforward. A few witness statements, some tire marks, maybe an insurance issue.

The photograph stared back at her.

Jenna Langston's driver's license photo. The same face that had looked up at her from the floor less than twelve hours ago. The same mouth that had whispered threats when Blackburn suggested the rideshare instead of driving her home.

The file slipped. Pages skated across linoleum with a dry slap. Her breath caught, a sharp intake that sounded loud in the quiet hallway. The lights buzzed overhead, too bright, casting hard shadows that wavered at the edges of her vision.

Jenna Langston. Age 28. Time of death: 6:48 AM. In front of 472 Oak Street.

Less than an hour after she left Blackburn's home with that parting threat.

Blackburn crouched and gathered the scattered pages. The paper edges bit at her skin, but her hands held steady. Not here. Not where anyone could see. Her mind ran the numbers. The timing, the threat, the figure Jenna thought she saw outside.

Had someone followed the car? Had someone been watching the house?

Had someone been watching her?

How did Brynn Cassidy know?

A detective emerged from the break room with coffee in hand. Steam rose from porcelain, carrying the scorched smell of the pot. "You okay there, Blackburn?"

"Fine." The word came out steady, professional. She straightened, papers reassembled. "Just a little slip."

As she pushed through the door to Homicide, her reflection caught in the glass. Pale, pupils dilated. She looked like prey.

For the first time in years, Detective Morgan Blackburn did not feel in control of anything.